G000126301

THE CRAZY ONE

Rebecca Markus

b
joy

PUBLISHING

Markus, Rebecca J

The Crazy One/ Rebecca Markus

ISBN: 978-0-692-14263-9

Printed in the United States of America

Cover design by Robin Ludwig Design Inc.

www.gobookcoverdesign.com

for Christine, Julie, Michelle and Natalie

CHAPTER ONE
Denver, Colorado – Present

Her demeanor seemed to be in contrast to the violent acts that put her in this prison. She didn't appear to be unhinged but seemed like a sweet lady. Not much to look at. She was short, plump, and had dark, frizzy hair. But her smile was pleasant. She sat with her hands clasped on the table between them.

Elijah Rhee, a mildly successful true crime author, sat across the table from Lucy at the Denver Women's Correctional Facility. Two guards were stationed in the noisy room to make sure the inmates and their guests behaved themselves. Elijah had requested this meeting with the hope that Lucy's story would bring him the literary achievement that had so far eluded him.

"True crime is a hot seller," he told her. "People want to know the dirty details. They want to hear it from your point of view."

"I don't know if I have anything interesting to tell." She spoke in a calm and steady voice, loud enough to be heard over the other people in the room. "I told the court and I told the media. What else do they want to know?"

"They want to know why. They want to see it through your eyes. I can help you tell your side of it. Can you tell me what lead to your obsession with Joel Ruskin in the first place?"

"My obsession with Joel? That's a weird way to put

it."

Elijah noticed an almost imperceptible rocking motion between her arms. One elbow pressed into the table. Then the other. This happened a few times on each side until she was still again. He dismissed it and continued his careful questioning.

"How did it all start, Lucy? Why Joel? Were there others?"

Her eyes fluttered, and she shook her head.

"Other what?"

He sucked in a breath and let it out audibly. It would not help to let her get to him. This wasn't the first guilty party he'd interviewed for a book. Most of the people he'd talked to in places like this would at least tell him their twisted version of their story. But this lady was giving him nothing. Why?

Maybe it was the way he looked. People had told him before that he had a serious face. It was because he was constantly analyzing things. Since he was a boy he'd wanted to know more about things. Whatever he learned in history class was incomplete. He needed to know what happened next. That's how he'd ended up as a crime writer. Nothing satisfied him more than finding the truth under the madness.

He tried to soften his expression to gain her trust. First, he relaxed his forehead, and then his mouth. When he spoke again, he kept his voice level.

"Were there other celebrities you had your eye on?"

Lucy shook her head again. She looked away from him and began to watch a table across the room. He thought for sure he had lost her. For a long time she was quiet, thinking, until her silence was interrupted by another inmate who had entered the room.

"Hey, Crazy Laura," the woman shouted as she approached. She stopped behind Lucy with her hands on her hips. "You finally got a friend, huh?"

Lucy didn't acknowledge the other inmate. She tucked her lips between her teeth and bowed her head to the table. Within seconds a guard had crossed the room and put her hand on the woman's shoulder.

"Keep moving, Brown," she commanded.

Brown smirked in Elijah's direction and then took her seat opposite a man and two young children. Elijah looked back at Lucy who still had her head down and was tugging forcefully on her earlobes until they were fire red.

"Lucy?" He ducked his head in an attempt to make eye contact. If he couldn't get her back, he couldn't get her story.

"I don't know why they keep me here." It wasn't clear if she was mumbling to him or to the table. "The women here are always yelling. They call me Crazy Laura all the time." She finally looked at him. Her eyes were glossy with emerging tears. "My name's not even Laura."

"Does anyone visit you?"

"My mom and dad." She smiled. "And sometimes Joel."

"Joel?" He tried to keep the shock out of his voice. There was no way this was true.

Lucy caught his skepticism. She cocked her head and pursed her lips.

"Sometimes we go out." She took interest in the scuff marks on the table in front of her, tracing them with her stubby index finger.

"You go out of the prison?" He had to be careful with his questioning. If she felt he was mocking her she would shut down and he'd never learn the truth. But he didn't appreciate being made a fool.

"He takes me away from here." She looked toward the high windows at the far end of the room. "He's trying to find a way that we can be together."

Elijah scowled. He let out a frustrated breath again. Visitation was almost over and he didn't have time for games.

"I'm here to learn the truth," he reminded her.

She looked back at him, her face softening in the process. He wouldn't have been surprised if her head spun around like the girl in *The Exorcist*.

Sitting up straight, she spoke slowly.

"You want to know how I met Joel?"

Yes. For Pete's sake, yes.

"Well, how you met him, how all this happened," he prompted.

She didn't answer. Instead she seemed to shut down. It was as if an invisible wall went up between them and she wasn't seeing him anymore.

He conceded to the fact that she wasn't going to tell him anything in this setting. Luckily, he'd planned for that. He pulled a notebook from his bag. No spiral. Prison-approved.

"Here." He placed the notebook between them. "You can write it down for me. " *It's not like you don't have time.* "Tell me everything from the beginning. What got you interested in him? Why was he so special that you would do all this? You can write it like a memoir. I'll polish up your words and we'll make a bestseller. When you get out of here you'll be a rich woman. And famous."

"I'm already famous." She didn't blink. It wasn't a joke.

Elijah wondered if she'd been reaching for notoriety all along. Had she done all of this for attention? Was she actively trying to be the next John Hinckley, the next Dawnette Knight? Maybe so. Maybe she'd gotten exactly what she'd been after. It was obvious the best way to win her over was to feed her delusion.

Elijah grinned. He patted the notebook and leaned closer to her.

"Yes, you are."

CHAPTER TWO
Omaha, Nebraska – 2015

Lucy opened her laptop on the store counter. She was aware of the stream of people passing in the mall hallway. They were a blur of moving bodies. She was alone in the store.

She pulled up a Beau Castle video on YouTube. The music began and she stepped into a fantasy world in which she was dating the international rock star.

They were dancing in a bar. All eyes were watching them. Beau's hand slipped under her shirt and pressed against the small of her back. The roughness of it rested there against her skin. It sent fire through her body. If only he would lean down and kiss her. If only he would hold her tighter.

The swaying and the drinks and the music—they were all clouding Lucy's mind. She shouldn't be letting herself feel this way. If she could think straight she would realize this was an impossible relationship.

He was funny and caring and, of course, incredibly sexy. There wasn't a street he could walk down where he wouldn't be recognized. Women everywhere wanted to sleep with him. Plenty of them had. But right now, in this moment, he belonged only to her.

He leaned down and planted a kiss on the tip of her nose.

"You're so good for me, baby."

He put his other arm around her and looked into her eyes. His were blue. She gazed into them as her hands roamed over his tattooed biceps.

"I'll be good to you, honey."

His smile melted her knees. She punched a button and stepped back from the counter. She stared at his frozen features. He was paused with that beckoning expression. She knew every shadow and line on his face from months of study.

"I know you will." She said it out loud. Nobody was around to hear.

There was little chance of any passerby disturbing her fantasy. Even casual browsers rarely stepped into Gobo's, a small store that sold framed prints of varying sizes. She'd been working in her Uncle Gordon's store since she was in high school. It was the only job she'd ever had, and she was coming up on her eighth anniversary. Eight years of watching mall walkers and teenagers who rarely gave her even a side glance.

She hit the play button on the laptop again.

"So stop me guessing now and, baby, please come here." Beau delivered this line with intense emotion, his hands clenched in fists. She paused the screen again. This was her favorite part of his new video; the part that cut away from the music and showed Beau standing alone on a lighted stage, speaking the chorus. She dragged the line on the video and pushed play again.

"Baby, please come here."

His eyes called to her, making her heart race. She ached for him. He should be saying these things to her and only her. Someday he would. They had a connection through space and time.

She closed her eyes and listened to his words. He kissed her again, deeper this time. She tilted her head and lifted her chin.

"Baby, please come here."

Her hands grasped the air in front of her, feeling for his invisible arms. He was almost there with her. It was almost real. With her eyes closed maybe she could conjure the actual Beau Castle and he would materialize there in her waiting arms.

"What are you doing?"

A female voice shattered her concentration. Lucy's eyes popped open and she stared at her coworker standing in the doorway. Her chest heaved with the panic of being caught. She reached for the keyboard to stop the music.

"That was the weirdest thing I've ever seen you do." Joni removed her leather jacket as she approached the counter. She flung it into the corner and then took a seat on the stool. "Honestly, you do some weird shit sometimes. I thought you were having some kind of standing seizure."

Lucy packed the laptop back into her bag. Her face was flaming. Joni was younger and prettier. She wasn't awkward. She had friends and went on dates. She probably never had to create a fantasy life to make up for a sad real one.

"Do you ever listen to anything other than Beau Castle?" Joni asked.

"I like it."

The credit card reader had been bumped and the top

was no longer flush with the counter's edge. Lucy adjusted it, running her finger along the back of the plastic base to make sure it was even.

Joni shifted on the stool and adjusted her tight shirt. She clicked her tongue. "I should have got coffee on my way in. I'm so tired. There's a freaking street light across from my bedroom window. It's literally like the sun and I can't sleep. I need some dark curtains or something."

"You should get a sleep mask." Lucy was glad for the change of subject. She liked the opportunity to give advice. As the older friend, wasn't that her job? "Victoria's Secret has pink satin ones."

Joni waved her hand above her head. "I don't do sleep masks. I used to have one. It had Velcro on the back. I kept it next to my bed. Then a spider crawled onto the Velcro and got its legs stuck in the loops and it died there and crusted up like they do. Now I can never ever, ever..." She froze in place a full three seconds, then continued, "...ever have a sleep mask ever again."

Lucy laughed. "Seriously?"

"For real. Just seeing a sleep mask makes me think of dead spiders. Literally."

Joni had a story for every situation. Because her life was full of action. Lucy's was made up of daydreams.

Lucy began counting the cash in the drawer even though she knew it hadn't changed in the six hours she'd been there. Even if she'd made a sale, nobody paid with cash anymore. But if she didn't count she would be haunted by the thought of it for the rest of the day. She printed the register report and slipped it into the slot in the drawer.

Her left index finger pressed into the corner of the drawer, leaving a slight indentation for mere seconds. The feeling lingered and before she could step away she needed to press her right index finger against the opposite corner to even out the sensation. "The Evens", as she called it, was a nervous habit she'd developed in middle school. She'd gotten it under control for the most part, but when she was uneasy The Evens came creeping back.

This time was because of Joni. She was the kind of girl Lucy wished she could be. Her long, black hair was so shiny it appeared to reflect the overhead lights of the store. Her perpetually tan skin was flawless, and she had a natural talent with makeup, something Lucy had never gotten the hang of.

In school, Lucy never could have been friends with someone like Joni. The pretty girls only ever saw her as someone to avoid and to pity. Not even her parents' money could elevate her from untouchable status. But here in the store there was no one else around to judge Joni for being nice to her.

What was it like to be pretty, someone who grabbed people's attention without even trying? What would it feel like to walk down the street and have everyone's eyes on her? These thoughts nagged at her. And so, she was often flustered when Joni was around, which made her feel the need to keep everything under control; to keep everything even.

After a few presses on the drawer corner with alternating index fingers, both sides finally felt even, and she could go. On her way out, she waved to Leron at the baseball hat store next to Gobo's. He saluted her halfheartedly and went back to staring at his smartphone.

She exited through the hallway behind some stores and out to the parking lot. Her step quickened as she neared her car at the back of the lot. Tonight had been on her mind for days. It was date night and she was giddy with anticipation. As she drove her mind was only on Beau. He would be there waiting for her when she got home.

CHAPTER THREE

Within fifteen minutes she was in her apartment. It was a third floor studio accessed by an elevator and a long hallway straight out of *The Shining*. The walls and carpet were beige. There was one window and a sliding glass door out to the balcony. She'd wanted something with more character, but her parents had refused to pay more than eight-hundred a month. Not when she could live at home with them for free.

Lucy could imagine it was more. She pictured herself arriving at a high-rise building downtown. The doorman greeted her as he did every day. She rode the elevator to the luxury apartment on the top floor.

Beau had bought the apartment for her at the beginning of their imaginary relationship. She'd been too embarrassed to let him visit her little place, so he'd come up with his own money-flaunting solution. He had a key and could visit any time his heart desired.

In reality, she'd found the apartment online, saved pictures from the real estate website to her computer, and looked at them every once in a while to jog her memory.

Pretending her takeout order had just arrived, she set microwaved mac and cheese on the coffee table in front of the TV. Most Saturday nights were this way. Although, sometimes she would join Joni and Leron and some other mall employees at a bar and grill nearby. She never fit in, though, and would sit awkwardly silent for most of the night.

Tonight there would be no distractions. She was ready to devote all her attention to Beau and she wanted zero interruptions. He'd been on the *Late Show* the night before, and she'd recorded it on her DVR but hadn't had time to watch it. Now she was ready. It was finally time for their date.

She was settled on the couch and hugging a throw pillow when Beau walked onto the set, waving and smiling that million dollar smile. She waved back at him from across a restaurant in her imagination. He kissed her cheek and they sat down.

The first subject of the interview was Hollywood parties. Beau admitted he'd been to many.

"It's all necessary, you know," he said. *"Hollywood networking and all that. But it's fun. I like hanging out with that crowd a little bit. Like-minded people, you know. But not too much."*

His fifteen-minute interview was stretched to almost an hour as she paused to study his expression, backtracked to hear his words again and again, and imagined he was saying some of those things directly to her. She pressed play again. Now he was discussing his romantic life. This was good for her. This was what she wanted to hear.

"I want to tell you something," Beau said. She leaned forward and clasped her hands over the coffee table as if he held them in his own. He had her undivided attention.

"I said to her, 'You are lovely.'"

"You're amazing, Beau," she whispered, overcome

with emotion. The way he appreciated her in that moment made all the time apart worthwhile.

"I wanted to say it. It's not something I can just Tweet about, you know?"

"Of course. I know. I feel the same way."

She paused the DVR at the right fraction of a second. Beau faced the camera, mid-sentence, with his mouth slightly open. He was speaking to her. On the other side of that screen, he was waiting for her.

She could imagine him there with her so strongly she thought she smelled his mixture of cologne and perspiration. Although she'd never met him in person, she knew what he smelled like. She'd once read an interview in a teen magazine where he'd been asked what kind of cologne he likes to wear. *Eros* by Versace. The next day she'd bought a bottle. The throw pillow she was now clutching had been sprayed with it. All she had to do was squeeze it tight and watch every move Beau made on TV.

Beau's segment was over and she was ready to put in his concert DVD. She let *the Late Show* run while she retrieved the disc. The next guest was now sitting on the couch making the host and the audience laugh. Lucy recognized him but didn't know his name.

Normally he wore a suit and held a microphone while he hosted various TV specials with a larger-than-life personality. Now he was the one being hosted. He was funny and humble and a little self-deprecating. And he was cute. He wasn't hot like Beau Castle–he didn't have tattooed biceps or an edgy haircut–but he had a sweet face and an infectious smile. He looked like the stereotypical guy you'd like to take home to your mother.

14

She rewound back to the beginning of his interview.

"Ladies and Gentlemen, please welcome Joel Ruskin." Applause. He walked out–big, colorful tennis shoes under black dress pants–and his smile seemed to beam even brighter than Beau's. He sat and was questioned as per the formula.

"So, you're single, Joel." Cheers and hollers from the ladies in the audience.

"Yes, yes." Shakes his head. Bashful smile.

"I hear you're quite popular with the moms." More whoops from the crowd.

"I am. They try to fix me up with their daughters."

"Is that right?"

"I get several messages a day from moms who think I'd be the perfect son-in-law."

"Well, you're very non-threatening. Do they just get you online, or does it happen in person, too?"

"Sometimes they stop me on the street and try to push their daughters onto me, like literally."

"Are the daughters on board?"

"Not always." Roars of laughter.

She paused the show to study Joel's face. He was mid-laugh and looking toward the camera. She imagined he was laughing at something she'd said. They'd just met and he thought she was fascinating. But, he'd better be careful. She was here with Beau Castle. And Beau could be possessive.

The interview resumed at the push of the button.

"Beau was telling us he enjoys all those Hollywood parties. Are you the same way?"

Joel scrunched up his nose and gave an awkward

smile to the audience.

"I'm not so sure," he said. *"I usually feel awkward around all those famous people. I don't feel like I'm one of them."*

Her heart leapt. He was saying he was socially awkward, just like her.

"You are. Of course you are."

"I know." He shifted on his seat. *"But I feel like an imposter. I never know how to act. I'm faking it most of the time."*

The crowd laughed and applauded.

"I've heard you have a few favorite charities."

"I do," Joel replied and nodded. *"I'm active with the ASPCA."*

"Ah, you love the animals."

"I love the animals, yes. I care very much about their treatment."

"And you support cancer research."

Joel nodded. He looked toward the camera. Lucy's hand pressed to her heart. Could this man be real? He was funny and smart and loved animals. The next bit of information pushed her from mere interest to infatuation.

"It says here you recently visited a young fan at St. Jude's hospital."

Joel nodded again and grinned modestly. The crowd cheered and whistled.

"I did. His teacher had contacted someone who got in touch with me and we made it happen."

"But you didn't stop there."

A picture of Joel surrounded by children in a hospital flashed onto the screen. They were smiling at the photo

16

opportunity. It was all overwhelming. Suddenly he was like some kind of knight that had swooped into her life and saved the day.

"That's right. I saw a lot of kids that day. I didn't know that many would know me, but they did. We ended up spending all day at St. Jude's. It was a really great..." he stuttered, *"...great experience."*

By the time she crawled into bed it was ten after one in the morning. She stared at the red digits on her bedside clock, feeling them burn into her retinas, waiting for the final zero to turn to a one. When it finally read 1:11, she squeezed her eyes shut tight, turned her head, and opened them only when she knew the red glow wouldn't invade her peripheral vision and make her start all over again.

As tired as she was, her mind raced too much for sleep. She'd spent the evening researching Joel Ruskin online. His face was scorched into her mind. It appeared in the darkness in front of her.

Was she a terrible person? She'd started the night with Beau and now here she was mooning over another man. What would Beau think if he found out he was being upstaged by someone down-to-earth like Joel? All of these new feelings nagged at her as she drifted to sleep.

Joel Ruskin invaded her dream. He was talking to her on her mom and dad's living room couch. His words didn't make much sense, but it didn't matter. She was focusing on his smile. His teeth were slowly growing in brightness and she had to look away. She suggested they go upstairs to her old bedroom for a bite to eat.

They walked separately to the wide staircase. But

17

when she started to ascend the stairs Joel slipped his arm around her waist. They climbed the stairs side by side, arms clutching each other possessively. Joel's hand groped her hip as they kept climbing. Climbing. The stairs seemed to have no end. He turned his head and kissed the top of hers.

Lucy was startled awake by thunder outside her bedroom window. She was back in her apartment. The room was pitch black except for the light of her alarm clock. Her heart was racing as if it might jump out of her chest and she was breathing heavily. It was easy to recognize this physical reaction. She was in love with Joel Ruskin and she knew there was no way she could shake it. She knew she didn't want to.

CHAPTER FOUR
Lucy's Notebook

Elijah,

Thank you for letting me tell my side of the story. Below is a full account of my relationship with Joel Ruskin from beginning to end. I hope this gives you what you need for your book. I hope to see you soon.

Lucy

I met Joel Ruskin at a party. I was there with my rock star boyfriend Beau Castle. I wore a black, sequined dress that was short enough to show off my legs but not so short that a wrong move could show off everything. I still wasn't comfortable around all of these rich Hollywood people, being a nobody from Nebraska. My first drink hadn't taken the edge off enough for me to relax, so I was on the prowl for another.

Beau was off somewhere talking to important people and I was standing alone, casually scanning the room for that next drink. I hadn't noticed Joel standing near me because, frankly, I didn't know who he was. To me, he was just another guy at the party not talking to anybody.

A waiter walked between us carrying a tray with one martini. When I reached my hand up to grab it, so did Joel. He graciously offered it to me and we squabbled over it for a second while the poor waiter stood there, helpless. Finally, Joel took it from the tray and handed it to me.

"You have to take it," he insisted. "Martinis make me uncomfortable."

"Really? How so?" I chuckled at him and tilted my head in anticipation of his surely witty answer. His eyes were bright and his smile was infectious. He looked familiar, but I still couldn't place him.

"I never know what to do with the olive." He tapped the end of the black stick that rested in my glass. "Is it just for decoration or is it cretinous for me to eat it?"

I laughed out loud this time. Then I drew the stick from my drink and removed the olive with my teeth. I told him, "I guess you feel as out of place at these fancy parties as I do then."

"Are you out of place?"

"Just a little bit."

"Then you must be here with someone." His face still looked hopeful but dropped slightly when I nodded my head.

"My boyfriend, Beau Castle." I motioned in the direction I thought Beau might have gone. I couldn't see him anywhere. Joel grinned and nervously shoved his hands into his pockets.

"That Beau's always been a lucky man," Joel mused.

"Do you know him?"

"I've worked with him before." He clearly saw no recognition on my face because he said, "I'm sorry. I didn't introduce myself before I mischievously tried to steal your martini. I'm Joel Ruskin. I hosted a charity concert that Beau was involved in last year."

I gasped and Joel's eyes lit up. I swear he smirked a little. Maybe I imagined it.

"I know who you are," I said. Then I touched his arm. "I'm so sorry I didn't recognize you."

"Were you there?"

"No, but I watched on TV. You were great."

That was the moment Beau decided to make his reentry. He slipped his arm around my waist and pulled me to his side as if claiming me as his own. He stretched out his other arm to shake Joel's hand.

"Good to see you, Ruskin," he said. "What are you up to these days?"

"A little of this, a little of that."

Beau and Joel had a short conversation. I didn't listen. Instead, I stood back and watched the two men, amused by how unalike they were. Joel was a relaxed-looking guy with unruly hair. He wore a button-down shirt with black pants and beat-up tennis shoes.

Beau, on the other hand, wore short sleeves that showed off his mean tattoos and he had tons of gel in his bleached hair. They were as different as they could be. In fact, the whole room was full of an odd mixture of people who seemed very different from each other but were tied together by one common interest.

After only a few minutes Joel excused himself to go find a drink, "since your girlfriend took the last martini." He winked at me and then hurried away.

"What were you two talking about?" Beau put his arm around my waist again and gave me a squeeze.

"Nothing. He introduced himself. He said he'd worked with you."

"Ruskin is trying to move in on my girl," he teased. I rolled my eyes. His possessiveness got to me sometimes. I knew he fooled around when he was on tour, but I chose to pretend to ignore it. The fact that he ever got jealous was hardly fair.

The rest of the party was loud and jumbled. Beau kept his arm around me the remainder of the time, as if he'd realized I might get away. He had nothing to say about leaving me standing alone for so long. I wasn't sure how long it had been. When Joel had shown up I'd stopped keeping track.

There was another moment when we were about to leave that Beau left me standing on my own again. Someone had swept him away for one last thing. I waited impatiently by the door, trying not to let my face show how badly I wanted to get out of there. Then Joel appeared and I suddenly didn't want to leave anymore.

"I was just leaving," he said nervously. "I'm not stalking you."

This made me laugh.

"Beau ran off again," I explained. Then I whispered loudly, "I really am ready to get out of here."

"I feel like a schmuck," Joel said. "I didn't get your name."

"Lucy," I answered. I was smiling. I realized I'd been smiling most of the time when Joel had been around. A knot of guilt formed in my midsection and then dissipated. We were just talking, after all. There was no reason for Beau to worry.

"Pretty name. Are you on Twitter, Lucy?" He pulled his smartphone from his breast pocket and swiped the screen. I told him how to find me there and I quickly heard the notification from my phone in my ridiculously tiny purse.

"There," Joel said. "Now you can follow me and we're friends, as they say."

I nodded and then laughed. We were friends. Just friends.

CHAPTER FIVE
Omaha − 2015

Lucy discovered that Joel Ruskin was highly active on Twitter, so she set up an account for herself. She could get to know him in his own words. Most of his posts were funny, some were informative, some poignant, but all of them made her smile as if she were reading personal messages from a good friend.

She was at work and Joni was going on about her crazy Saturday night while absently flipping through a Victoria's Secret catalog. Lucy put down her phone and listened intently so she could picture herself as part of Joni's story. She imagined herself cracking witty jokes and being the life of the party. Maybe Joni would be jealous of all the attention she was getting. Maybe she would finally see how cool and interesting Lucy was. Her emotions during these regular recaps swung between excitement and envy.

One time she had gone to meet Joni at a club but had lost her less than an hour later when Joni slipped out the front door with a strange guy. She'd been left standing in the middle of the noisy and crowded club with a drink in each hand. It was as uncomfortable for her to be surrounded by scantily clad, self-assured people as it was to have the bass thumping in her ears and rocking her chest. She'd never fully forgiven Joni for that.

When Joni finished her tale, she stared at Lucy who

was lost again in her own thoughts. She'd let her mind go off on a tangent that involved her ditching Joni at the club instead of the other way around.

Joni rolled her eyes.

"So, what did you do Saturday night?"

The worst thing in the world would be to let her think she didn't have a life of her own. She couldn't let on she had no social life outside the walls of the shopping mall. So she lied, kind of.

"I went to a party."

"Oh?" Joni leaned one hand on the counter and eyed her skeptically. Or maybe it was interest. Lucy was never good at reading people.

"It was cool." She acted casual as if going to parties was like eating lunch or getting a haircut. "I met a guy. He's really funny."

"Really?" She drew out the word to accentuate her interest. "What's his name?"

"Joel." Lucy scratched her left arm which left a white streak on the skin. It tingled. She had to scratch the right one to even it out.

"Is he hot?"

"He's cute. He's not super hot, but he's nice and he's funny."

"Hmm." Joni went back to her catalog. She wasn't the type who liked to hear tales of kind-of-cute guys who are funny. She liked the hot and suave types, preferably with muscles and cars with loud stereos.

"We're just friends. It's no big deal." She wanted to backtrack. She should have said he was hot. But would Joni believe that? What hot guy would ever go for Lucy

Bonneville? In fact, so far no guys had gone for her. There was her cousin's friend who'd gotten her virginity right after high school, but she'd never heard from him again so it didn't count for much. In her whole life, the only boyfriends she'd ever had were imaginary. Joni didn't need to know that.

"Did you invite this guy to that Beau Castle concert tomorrow night?"

"No. You want to go?" It was an empty invitation. She had only bought one ticket. She'd bought it the minute the pre-sale opened. She'd been waiting months to see him in the flesh. That was before she'd met Joel. Guilt began to gnaw at her, but Beau didn't need to know her mind was on someone else. Still, she had to get to him. Maybe meeting Beau for real could cure her newest infatuation.

Joni laughed. "Are you kidding? Two hours in the car with you singing Beau Castle songs? Pass."

Lucy rolled her eyes, mimicking Joni's attitude. It was a relief. She had plans beyond seeing him in concert. Joni would try to stop her.

CHAPTER SIX
Kansas City, Missouri – 2015

Beau Castle and his band finished their final song and walked off stage, leaving their instruments behind. The lights didn't dim and the crowd didn't budge. Instead, they shouted a deafening roar for their mega-star hero because they knew the show wasn't over. Rock concerts never end without at least one encore anymore.

While the crowd raged around her, Lucy commenced her mission. She squeezed down the row of cheering fans and out of the large arena. Around the back of the building, she found a crowd of people who'd apparently had the same idea. Two large security guards were blocking the back doors. A few women in tight clothes were talking to them, but everyone else stood in an orderly group. Most of them were holding something they wanted the celebrity to sign. She silently joined them.

A high fence surrounded the rear parking lot where four buses and a semi were parked. There was a gate directly behind the two guards. It was standing slightly open. Here was her opportunity. She crept closer to the edge of the group. One of the women was showing the guards her somewhat intimately placed tattoo. One slow step at a time positioned her behind one of the guards. No one in the group was paying any attention to her. It was a skill she'd been cursed with her whole life; she was a forgettable person and could go unnoticed because few people seemed to care.

When she knew no one was watching, she slipped through the gate and casually walked toward the three buses. A couple of guys wearing lanyards passed her but must have assumed she belonged there since the guards hadn't stopped her. It was a crazy miracle, really. She'd tried this stunt many times before with many bands and had never been successful. Now that she was here what was she supposed to do next?

All three buses were black. They were numbered on the front, but there were no markings to indicate which one Beau would be using. Fate decided which one she would go to. The doors of all the buses were open. The three drivers were standing together in front of the middle bus smoking. They were absorbed in a conversation. Lucy walked with purpose as if she belonged there. When the drivers could no longer see her, she sprinted to the door of the first bus and climbed inside.

The interior was immaculate and shiny with blue lights around the ceiling. There were brown leather couches on both sides and a booth for eating. The tiny kitchen area was crammed with bottles of water and soda and booze. She touched everything. She wanted to feel what Beau felt. For months she'd been imagining he was her boyfriend and now she was actually standing in his world.

At the back of the bus was a narrow hallway with two sleeping bunks on either side. Beyond that was a bathroom which was much nicer than what she'd expected to find. There was even a full-sized shower.

But there was no private room for Beau. He was an international rock sensation. She knew there was no way he would be sleeping in one of these little bunks. So this couldn't be his bus. She needed to find a way to get into the other ones.

As she made her way to the front of the oversized vehicle she heard voices outside the door. The driver had returned. She looked around for the emergency exit. That wouldn't do her any good. She couldn't bust out the window of a tour bus even if she had the strength to do it. She would surely be caught then.

When the driver's boot hit the first step she knew she was trapped. She spotted a narrow closet behind the driver's seat and ducked inside, pulling the door closed behind her. It was a cramped space filled with hanging jackets and a few pair of shoes on the floor. She stood in the dark with her head between hangers and prayed silently that the driver would soon go away.

Eventually, she heard another ruckus outside the bus. Her legs were tired by then and she squatted down with her knees pressing painfully into the side of the closet. When the riders boarded the bus, she let out a quiet sob. There seemed to be no way out of her situation that didn't involve the police.

"Beau," she imagined one of them saying while dragging her by the back of her shirt. *"We found this woman hiding in the closet on our bus."*

"Call the cops," said another one.

"Wait." Beau held his hand up. That hand was on the end of a muscled and tattooed arm that she yearned to feel around her. And she did. Beau approached her and

put that arm around her waist.

"I feel like I know you," he said, looking down into her eyes. Of course, he did. She'd been watching him for months. She'd seen every recorded image of him she could get her hands on. She'd thought about him so obsessively that there was no way he hadn't been affected by it in some cosmic way.

"You want me to call?" the man said again.

"No," Beau replied. *"It's fine. She's supposed to be here."* Then he kissed her.

She snapped out of her daydream when a person stumbled and fell against the closet door. Another laughed. She could hear female voices. They could have been the backup singers, but the conversation that ensued made it clear they weren't. They were fans who were getting a tour of the bus. Most likely all parties involved were hoping for much more, although their goals probably weren't in sync.

All she could do was wait them out. The pressure on her feet was uneven. The ball of one foot was stinging from her position, but the other wasn't. She needed to make them even, so she shifted her weight as best she could. Now it was too much. She shifted back. There didn't seem to be a way to make it right without falling over and out of her hiding spot. But she tried.

An hour or so later the female visitors finally left. She hoped everyone on the bus would find a reason to disembark, but they didn't. To her horror, the bus lurched forward and was on the move.

She began to cry silently again. She was stuck on a tour bus. It wasn't even the right bus. Her knees throbbed and her back ached. She desperately needed to use the bathroom. Would it be possible to hold it until she got out of here?

Every bump of the ride made her bladder ache a little more. Her compact position didn't help. Soon her tears were more for her struggling bladder than her impossible situation. Another bump did her in. Her bladder released and a warm stream trailed down her jeans, where it soaked into her sock and trickled onto the floor. She heard a tap-tap dripping onto a shoe over which she crouched. Holy crap. Her dream meeting with Beau had become a nightmare.

Hours seemed to pass. Lucy had no idea how long she'd been in that tiny space. She thought she might lose consciousness in the unvented closet which now reeked of her own piss. She knew it was late. The guys inside the bus had quieted down. Was she going to have to ride like this all night? What hell.

Then she felt the bus make a curve to the right. The driver announced over the loudspeaker that Beau wanted to pull over at a truck stop. This was her chance. She somehow worked her way up to a standing position, although her knees protested the whole way.

The bus rumbled to a stop and the doors hissed open. She listened to the voices retreat. How long should she wait before she made her escape? Taking shallow breathes, she listened for any other signs of life on the bus. The only sound she heard was the pulsing of her blood in her ears.

Suddenly, she heard the clomp of a shoe on the step. She let out a yelp and covered her mouth with her hand.

"It's too cold out there," said a man's southern accent. "I need my jacket."

Jacket? Lucy was surrounded by jackets.

The man yanked the closet door open and blue light flooded in. His head jerked back when he saw her. She stared at him wide-eyed and wordless.

"Who the fuck are you?" It was Beau's bass player James. "You guys," he shouted over his shoulder. "There's a chick hiding in the fucking closet."

She panicked and lunged toward James, her shoulder making contact with his stomach. He actually laughed as she pushed past him and stumbled down the steps of the bus. The others had already come back to check out the commotion.

When her feet hit concrete she thought she was free. But she was caught by the driver himself who had her wrist in a vice-like hold.

"Where'd you come from?" She couldn't tell if he was angry or amused. He held onto her anyway as he reached into his pocket and tugged at his phone. She tried to wriggle from his grip, but he was freakishly strong.

The occupants of the other buses joined the small crowd of onlookers. She scanned their faces but didn't see Beau. He was probably waiting on his bus for the crazy one to be taken care of. Why didn't he come out and help her? Why wasn't their cosmic connection working?

The driver had managed to get his phone out of his pocket and tried using one hand to call someone. It might have been the cops. She couldn't tell. She wasn't going to stay to find out. She tried twisting her arm around to release his grip, but he held strong. She leaned over, grabbed his thumb with her teeth, and pulled. The driver's phone flew from his hand and he yelled the F-word at the top of his lungs. Everyone else watched in shock and amusement as she was freed and fell to the ground.

"Oh, my god," said a feminine voice of unknown origin. "She pissed herself."

The other voices in the crowd laughed and murmured. Lucy didn't dare look up at their faces. She got up quickly and ran as fast as she could into the dark and away from the lights of the truck stop.

The day had been sunny and slightly above seventy degrees. Now that the sun was down the wind had picked up and Lucy felt frigid. She crouched in the weeds of an open field next to the trucker haven. The wet denim clung to her left leg like a vile icicle. How insane that she was hiding in the dark, watching the buses she'd run from.

One of those busses contained the man she'd pined after for months. She could do nothing more than wait for his caravan to leave so she could go back and figure out a way to get home. They were taking their sweet time. She might freeze to death in that field before they were gone.

As she watched from far away, she imagined she'd been invited onto that bus instead of being a castaway. She saw herself taking Beau's hand as he helped her down the stairs of his bus and into the cool night air. The music from the speakers overhead was just loud enough to be heard over the hum of the bus engines. A country song came on.

"Oh, my god," she squealed. "This is my song."

Beau grinned, lifted their hands to the sky, and twirled her around. They danced close under the florescent lights of the truck stop. She lay her head on his strong chest where his t-shirt stretched tight against his firm pecs. His hands rested on her hips. They forgot about the others in their group, about the concert, about the fans. It was just the two of them; wrapped up in each other.

She continued this scenario in her head until the buses eventually pulled out of the lot. Whoever was in charge had apparently decided not to call the police on her and make a thing out of it. She figured it was something they were used to dealing with. It would be another crazy story they would tell about the road.

She trekked against the wind, back to the contrasting brightness of the truck stop. She was basically stranded. She refused to hitch a ride because she knew what happened to women who did. She had only one option. She had to call her dad. She had to ask him to drive all the way from Omaha to somewhere outside Kansas City and pick her up. Then she would have to explain why. At least she had a couple hours to think of a good excuse.

Humiliation filled her mind while she waited. She'd come close to meeting Beau. She'd been right there. Instead, she'd pissed inside a camper and scuffled with one of his guys. A cold, spiked ball of regret grew in her belly. A thousand shards of ice ripped at her insides. The more she replayed her actions in her head, the more she convinced herself Beau had seen her and that he'd been laughing at her. It was almost as if he'd thrown her off of that bus with his own hands. She was sure she could never face him again.

CHAPTER SEVEN
Omaha – 2015

After the concert fiasco, Lucy returned home to her drab life. The days went back to the same routine as every other day leading up to that moment. What was the point of trying to make it different? She had missed her opportunity to better herself and become the actual girlfriend of a touring musician as opposed to play-acting alone in her room.

In the car on her way home from work one day, a Beau Castle song came on the radio. It was a sad ballad about a lost love. Her stomach twisted in knots as she imagined telling Beau she couldn't handle their long-distance relationship anymore. This time she wouldn't be swayed. He pleaded with her to reconsider. He begged her to move to Nashville. But as she had told him time and time again, she wasn't cut out for the life of a rock star's girl. She wiped the tears from her cheeks as she pulled into a parking spot in front of her apartment building.

Once inside, she escaped to her private island. The sound of the waves. The call of the gulls. She closed her eyes and let the song of the ocean transport her to paradise. She could be everything she wanted to be. When loneliness clawed at her, she crept inside her mind and thrived in her fantasy. She could feel the joy and heartache of love she would never know. She faded into a life she had always wanted, absorbed into her make-believe.

Lying on a beach towel on her apartment floor, she imagined the tropical sun sizzling on her skin and turning it brown. An app on her phone looped the sound effects. The bikini she wore had never seen the light of day.

This ritual had begun when she was ten years old. She'd lamented to her babysitter with a broken heart that she wished she could visit the ocean. Her parents were there, in the Bahamas, and it was New Year's Eve.

It was normal for them to be gone somewhere exciting without her. They took a two-week vacation every year "to get away from the stress of every day." She assumed she was part of that stress they were always escaping.

It wasn't normal for them to be gone over a holiday. They'd left two days after Christmas. As always, she was dropped off at her Grandma Edna's townhouse in a gated community of seniors. And, as always, her Grandma Edna had plans of her own.

That's how she'd come to be in the company of a college freshman named Ginny on the most important night of the year. They'd watched three romantic comedies in a row. The clock was ticking closer to midnight.

The loneliness had come on before school dismissed for winter break. She was used to waving goodbye as her parents went off without her. She figured that was the way all families did things. When she grew up she could go on trips, too.

Then she started to hear stories from her private

school classmates. Stories about exotic places. France. Mexico. New York City. One girl's family spent every Christmas at Disneyland. They called these "family vacations." Family. As in, all of them.

That was the first time Lucy recognized that she was lonely. Her life was boring. She never went anywhere. Her parents bought her anything she wanted. They never expected anything of her. But they never took her with them.

When Lucy began to cry, Ginny rushed to her side. She squeezed her shoulders and stroked her hair.

"Shh. We can go to the ocean," Ginny said with cheer in her voice.

Lucy looked up at her like she was crazy. Why would she say that? There's no ocean in Nebraska.

Ginny laughed. She went through the kitchen to the patio door and slid it open. What was she doing? There was a scraping sound and then she emerged dragging a plastic lawn lounger onto the tiled floor. Lucy hugged her arms around herself to shield her from the cold December air that blew in. She watched as the babysitter pulled the chair into the living room and positioned it to face the TV. Grandma would be mortified.

"Welcome to the Bahamas." She waved her arms in the air, then sprinted up the narrow staircase. Moments later she appeared again with her arms full. She spread a colorful beach towel over the chair and patted the seat.

Lucy approached, giving Ginny a suspicious side-eye. When she sat, the chill of the plastic seeped through the towel, through her Christmas pajamas, and into her skin. She pressed her legs down so both sides felt the same, then bent her knees quickly to relieve the sting. She lay back and let Ginny continue with her tropical charade.

Grandma Edna's sunglasses were placed over her eyes. A margarita glass of soda was brought to her hand. Ginny fanned her with a magazine and spoke in a terrible accent Lucy guessed to be possibly Bahaman, if there were such a thing.

"Now, Miss. Is there anything else I can get you while you watch the ball drop?"

"No." Lucy giggled. The pantomime was working. It didn't make her forget her parents were gone, but she did miss them a tiny bit less. They couldn't stop her from enjoying her own vacation. It wasn't even close to what the ocean would really be like. But if she closed her eyes and dreamed really hard, she could almost hear the waves crashing.

From that day on, whenever Lucy needed to escape the stresses of the world, she spread herself out on a lawn chair or beach towel and teleported. She became skilled in the art of pretending.

Tonight, the artificial oasis didn't satisfy her for long. Her mind drifted back to Joel. Soon she gave up the beach towel and moved to the couch. She replayed Joel's interview from the *Late Show*. She knew Beau was there in that same studio, waiting in the green room, unsuspecting that the man talking was about to steal his girlfriend. Her heart beat faster. What a shameful thing she was going to do.

She checked Joel's Twitter account on her phone. He had posted a photo twelve minutes ago. It was a picture of a lamp on a table in front of a framed painting on a brick wall. The caption read, *"Bought a lamp for my living room. In case anyone cares."* Then there were twenty-one responses from female fans who assured him they cared about his lamp purchase. To her, they sounded like lame and desperate attention-seekers.

She saved the photo to her memory card and made a mental note of his living room wall. She scrolled down through his previous posts.

"Coffee shop across the street is out of Ethiopian blend. Going back to bed."

There was another photo. This one showed a view of a park. The caption read, *"Out for my mid-morning jog in Central Park. Not an early riser."*

She saved the picture. He lived close to Central Park. This was good information, although she knew little about the city. Still, she had a bit of information about where Joel lived: a New York apartment, probably an old building, with a coffee shop across the street. She could imagine herself inside his apartment, admiring that new lamp and telling him she thought it was a great accent for his décor. She was dying to see the rest of his place.

She did a search for "Joel Ruskin home." An old article came up with the headline, *"Joel Ruskin sells Los Angeles home after Fiona Sterling breakup."* This sent her down a rabbit hole of pictures of the actress. She was blonde and incredibly beautiful. Her cheeks burned with envy at the pictures of the two of them arm-in-arm on the red carpet. Fiona's smile never faltered. She seemed to have no flaws. Joel looked happy beside her in every shot. But that was in the past. How happy could they have been? Joel was single now.

It was almost nine and she had neglected to eat dinner. Her stomach rumbled. She retrieved a bag of chips from the kitchenette and continued her search. This time she stumbled onto a Map of the Stars which showed names of celebrities living in New York and pointed to the approximate locations of their homes. She spotted Joel's name just blocks from Central Park. Her heart skipped. She was getting closer to him.

She pulled up a satellite map of the area and zoomed in to get a better view. The Map of the Stars only gave an approximate location. She'd have to guess which building was his. She didn't even know what street he lived on, so she zoomed into the map until she was virtually standing on the streets of New York. She maneuvered around. Except for the frozen people with blurred faces, she had the sensation of actually being there. Her pulse quickened at the thought of being on the street where Joel lived. Her hands trembled when she realized how close she could be to standing right in front of his home. If he looked out his window right now, would he see a ghost of her standing there?

Finally, after an hour of wandering the streets of New York, she gave up her search. She would need more information to pin down his exact address. It was nearly midnight. She had to sleep.

When her head touched her pillow, she had the very real sensation that she had been walking in New York City. It had been a satisfying trip. Her heart still beat wildly from her imaginary time with Joel.

There was an ache in her heart when she thought of how perfect they were for each other and how he might never know it. If only she could have a few minutes alone with him for real. He was a nice guy. Surely he would see past her dowdy exterior and recognize the value of the person inside. She only needed to get near him.

Before letting herself drift into sleep, she picked up her phone and opened his Twitter account again. With one swipe, she set it to alert her every time Joel posted. She didn't want to miss anything he had to say.

Moments later her phone chimed. When she looked at it she saw that Joel had replied to one of his fans who had commented on his photo. He said simply, *"You know it."* Then there were a dozen congratulatory tweets from other fans to the woman who'd gotten the reply.

There was a flutter in Lucy's belly. She imagined he'd been replying to something she'd sent him. It was as if he was actually communicating with her. She stared at his message on her screen and willed it to be true.

"I have to go now, Joel," she said to his picture on the phone. "Goodnight."

CHAPTER EIGHT

For the next few weeks, Joel and I exchanged witty remarks on Twitter every now and then. It was a little flirtatious, but again, we were just friends. He was funny and often self-effacing. I didn't think much of it. Of course, I didn't mention it to Beau. Not that we talked about that kind of thing much.

During this time, Beau and I had grown apart. His schedule had gotten so crazy that we weren't getting much time together at all. I wasn't ready to quit my job and move to Nashville. What if it didn't work out? And being the full-time girlfriend of a hot rock star was a life in the fast lane. It was a life I didn't think I was cut out for.

Finally, I came to a painful decision. I couldn't keep seeing Beau.

The last straw was a Skype conversation we had the afternoon before his show in Cleveland. He often called me when he was feeling alone or bored on the road. I loved seeing his face on my computer screen, especially knowing he'd been thinking of me enough to call.

But this time our call was interrupted. Beau asked me to hold on when there was a knock on the door of his bus. He stepped out of view and left me looking at the top of the leather couch and the tinted window opposite the desk where his laptop sat. I heard a range of voices. A couple of them I recognized as band members. Then his manager came into view. He sat down on the couch, followed by a young woman in shiny clothing. There were so many people talking I could barely make out what they were saying. Another woman came in and sat on the couch. Then another. The scene in front of me quickly turned into a tour bus party.

Beau sat down in front of the laptop again.

"I'm sorry babe," he said. "It looks like I have company. I'll have to get back to you."

"Okay," I said, aware that he probably couldn't hear me over the noisy guests. "Will you call me later? Tomorrow?"

Beau nodded but I knew he didn't know what he was nodding for. He was distracted by one of the women who had put her hand on his shoulder and offered him a drink.

"Miss you," he said to me. "Bye." And then he disconnected. I had the same old sick feeling in my gut I always had when things like this happened. Inadequate. Self-conscious. Plain.

I knew Beau wasn't going to call me later, and probably not tomorrow. He'd call when it was convenient for him. I was well aware he never tried hard to make time for me when there were better options at hand.

I decided to end it.

We broke up amicably a week later when I was finally able to talk to him again. He let me keep the two-bedroom downtown apartment he'd bought for me when I was too ashamed to bring him home to my crappy studio. Although there were no hard feelings between us, I knew I'd miss his infectious smile and the whirlwind of excitement that happened every time he unexpectedly blew into town. Every lonely night I found myself wondering if I'd made the wrong decision. I had to use all my willpower to keep myself from texting him. I wondered if he was feeling the same.

Even though my relationship with Beau had never been public – we were photographed together a few times, but I was only ever billed as "mystery girl" – Joel somehow got news of our breakup. He sent his sympathies for my romantic loss via a private Twitter message, waited a respectable forty-eight hours, and then sent me a quick email stating he'd like to take me out sometime. This caught me off guard. Despite the flirting, I'd had no idea he was interested.

I called him to discuss it. Joel told me he had some time off in his schedule and offered to come to Omaha for our date. He'd love to take me to dinner. I was nervous, to say the least. Beau and I rarely went out for dinner in Omaha. He was too recognizable, and his fans were never subtle. Joel was a laid back, casual kind of guy. He wasn't the same type of celebrity Beau was. I had no good reason to turn him down. Beau and I were officially over. And Joel made me laugh. So, why not?

Joel requested "someplace with a good steak." This was different, too. Beau followed a strict diet: unseasoned, antibiotic-free chicken, organic vegetables, and a special blend of freshly-juiced organic fruits. Every time he came to town I had to hide my junk food, and he'd send his guy to Whole Foods for more appropriate provisions.

I made a reservation for a Friday night at Del Rio's Steak House. My uncle's friend Paul was a co-owner. I called him and explained the sensitive situation, and asked if he could secure us the best table in the house.

"You've convinced that rock star boyfriend of yours to try our steak?"

"No, Paul," I replied. "Beau and I broke up."

"So, this is a new guy, eh? And a meat eater? Good for you."

It may have been a mistake for me to go to work that Friday. I couldn't focus on anything. I was too nervous. But why should I be? I'd just come off a relationship with a major rock star. Surely I could handle a slightly geeky TV host. Still, the jitters were getting the best of me.

Joel's plane was scheduled to land at 1:30 p.m. I didn't need to be at the airport. He'd go directly to the Hilton downtown, a few blocks from my apartment. I'd go home and get ready for our date. He'd pick me up at 7:00 p.m. I had to get through the day without totally freaking out.

I left work a half hour early. The last two hours had dragged on so slowly that I couldn't stand another thirty minutes. Before going up to my apartment, I stopped by the desk and informed the concierge that I had a date coming so Joel wouldn't have any trouble. Not that he should. How could the concierge not recognize his face?

Three outfits lay discarded on my bed. A pile of shoes sat next to it. I had finally settled on a pair of black pants and a royal blue blouse. Someone had once told me royal blue made my eyes pop. I'd picked pants over a skirt because I didn't want to seem like I was trying too hard. But what if I seemed like I wasn't trying hard enough? My hands went to my hair in frustration as I stared at the outfit in the mirror. Then I resigned myself to my pants decision and slipped into a pair of black, sling-back heels.

The clock read 6:59 p.m. when my doorbell buzzed. I stood in my living room preparing my nerves. I'd been ready for a good half hour. But I still believed a little bit in that old rule that dictated I should keep him waiting. I didn't want to seem too eager. So I waited for the second buzz and went to the door, acting as if I had just been putting on the finishing touches.

He was smiling at my door. He looked more handsome than I remembered. My heart fluttered in my chest.

"Come in," I said stiffly, willing my nerves to get under control. We were both weirdly formal in that moment. Maybe he was nervous, too.

The moment felt strange. We were already friends, but the only other time we'd talked face to face was at the party where we'd met. We'd chatted online a few times since then. He was a funny guy. I'd never been nervous around him before. Now there was pressure. There were expectations. It was awkward.

"I like your place," he mused, looking around at the exposed brick and high ceiling of the modern apartment built into a one-hundred-year-old building.

"Thanks. It's probably not as grand as yours." What a dumb thing to say. Grand? Was this a medieval castle we were discussing? So far, I was failing hard.

"Actually, my New York apartment is about this size. Two bedrooms?"

I nodded. He nodded. We stood awkwardly for a

minute and then he said, "Okay, I have a car if you're ready to go."

Like a true gentleman, Joel held the car door open. He slid into the back seat next to me. I was acutely aware of his thigh lightly touching mine.

I told the driver where to go. Joel found it odd that we were leaving downtown, a place teaming with restaurants, to drive to a place twenty minutes away.

"If you want good steak," I explained, "you have to go farther into the city. You have to go west."

"Well, I've heard Omaha has the best steaks, so I'll let you be the boss." He joked to the driver that we could have saved him some time by eating sushi across the street. The driver laughed politely, as he was paid to do.

Joel sighed and grinned at me. Then there was a series of awkward silences punctuated with small talk. Silently, I scolded myself for letting my nervousness get to me. Joel was a casual guy. He had asked me out. There was no reason for me to be worried I would blow it.

At Del Rio's we were greeted by my uncle's friend Paul and shown to a quiet table in the corner. I saw a few heads turn, but maybe I imagined it. People in Omaha weren't used to seeing famous people around town, so they usually dismissed them as some look-alike. That never happened with Beau, of course, because he couldn't help looking like a rock star, not like he belonged in Middle America. And I frequently got the feeling he didn't hate the attention as much as he claimed to.

Joel ordered steak and a bottle of wine. I ordered chicken. We sat for a few minutes thinking of what to say. When the conversation finally flowed it was still stiff and awkward. It was a disaster. Maybe he was only funny on TV or when he had time to think of a reply. Maybe I'd had too much to drink at that party and had thought we'd gotten along better than we had. I was disappointed this might be our only date. So far it was going badly.

Toward the end of our meal, we were interrupted by two older ladies who'd been sitting at the next table. They were on their way out and wanted to tell Joel how much they loved him on TV, and blah blah blah. I wondered if he was relieved for the distraction. Whatever his mood was about the situation, he acted pleasant and courteous and even posed for a picture with the ladies, which they asked me to take.

When the fans were gone, Joel apologized.

"It's alright," I said truthfully. "I'm used to it."

"That's right. Beau Castle." He raised his wine glass in a swift toast and took a drink.

"What does that mean?" I was pretty fed up with the way the date was going. It was clear he was trying hard to make a good impression, but he had so far missed the mark. Maybe I'd only thought he was a nice guy. Maybe he was really good at playing one on TV.

"Nothing. I'm sorry. I didn't mean anything by it. But you did just come out of a relationship with a major rock star."

"And you swooped in and got me." I wasn't hiding now how annoyed I felt. I wanted the date to be over.

"No." He sighed heavily and shook his head. There was a long, awkward silence, and then he said, "Is that what you think? Like I was waiting around for you two to break up?"

I shrugged and examined the bits of food left on my plate.

"I wasn't. I like you. I liked that we were getting to be friends. And then there was a chance to see if we could be more than friends. At least, I'd hoped there was a chance."

"Well," I mumbled. "I'm sorry." I was sorry for misunderstanding him. I was sorry for dragging him halfway across the continent for a lousy date. I was sorry our relationship wouldn't go beyond this night. Our friendship probably wouldn't, either.

The server came, and Joel paid the check. We exited the restaurant through a sea of stares and whispers. I tried not to let my irritation show on my face as I walked quickly ahead of him. The last thing I needed was to be featured in the media as "Joel Ruskin's grumpy date."

The ride home was more awkward than the ride out. When the driver pulled up to my building, Joel got out and stood on the sidewalk with me. He said politely, "I can walk you up."

"That's okay. Thanks for dinner." I felt terrible. But the last thing either of us needed was to extend it with a silent elevator ride. He nodded and I knew he felt the way I did.

"It was good to see you again."

"It was good to see you."

"Are we still friends?"

"Of course." I meant it. We may not have been a match romantically, but I still enjoyed talking to him. Apparently, I could enjoy his friendship best from a distance.

With a hug and a quick peck on the cheek, Joel wished me well and promised me we'd talk again soon.

When I finally got into bed I stared at the dark ceiling. I couldn't get the bad date out of my head. Was it my fault? I replayed parts of the night over and over in my head. This went on for far longer than it should have. I looked at my bedside clock. Midnight. I closed my eyes and tried to breathe deeply. The thoughts crept in again and ran around my brain like mice. I checked the clock once more. 2:00 a.m.

Somehow I eventually managed to drift into a dreamless sleep. Joel's call woke me up around nine. The shrill ringtone shocked me into consciousness. I tried to pretend he hadn't awakened me.

"I'm sorry about last night," he said. "It was..." He paused.

"Terrible?"

"Yes." He laughed. "It was terrible. I was nervous. I was trying to be cool and I think I just came across as a dick."

"Why should you be nervous? You're a TV personality. I'm some girl from nowhere."

"You're an incredible girl from nowhere. I really, really like you, and I didn't want to mess it up. I'm sorry I messed it up."

"You didn't mess it up. I was probably a little cold. I don't know what was wrong with me."

"Can we try it again? How about lunch?"

"Don't you have to catch a plane?"

"Eh, there'll be other planes. I want to make it up to you."

Two hours later, Joel was at my door once again. He wore jeans and a t-shirt. This time there was no car waiting. He had walked over from the Hilton. We were going to have lunch close by.

"That way if one of us wants to run we don't have far to go," he joked.

"I won't run."

We ducked into the deli on the corner and found a booth. This time we were both relaxed. Our conversation was light and much more like we'd been before the awful date. He made me laugh until I was sure my face was red. When a couple of fans approached our table, Joel was obliging once again. When more people started to catch on, we really did have to rush out. At least we were escaping together and not from each other.

Quickly, we walked a few blocks and crossed the busy street. We kept walking until we were in the park strolling beside the water and not being bothered by anybody. This was nice. This was leisurely. I loved this.

"I have to tell you something," he said after a long, comfortable silence.

"Hmm?"

"I have to tell you I am flying out tonight. My plane leaves at 9:00."

"Oh." I stared at the ground as we walked on.

"I'd like to stay..."

"There'll be other planes," I interrupted.

Joel took my hand, and we kept strolling. We had turned back toward my home.

"I wish I could stay, but I have a creative meeting in L.A. tomorrow."

51

Neither of us said much the rest of the way back to my place. We spent the rest of that afternoon at my apartment sipping loose leaf tea we'd picked up at the tea shop on our way back. We talked about ourselves and got to know each other better. Nothing romantic happened between us, and I began to wonder if we were meant to be just friends.

Joel suggested we order a pizza before he had to leave for the airport. I loved that he was casual. It felt natural. I began to forget he wasn't some average guy. And I was beginning to have real feelings for him.

And then it was time for him to go. The day, in contrast to the night before, had been wonderful. I wished we had more time.

He left after another peck on my cheek. So, we were still just friends after all. I sat alone in my apartment–a product of my last failed relationship–and wondered if this thing with Joel was truly what I wanted. He was a nice guy. He was funny. He wasn't a Hollywood type. He liked to relax. He was easy to talk to. And he ate real food. So, the failure had to be me.

It was 9:00 p.m. and Lucy was driving toward the airport, lost in her fantasy of Joel. The music blaring from her speakers acted as a muse for the story inside her head. She knew the way to the airport well, and barely had to think of anything other than him.

She imagined checking her Twitter feed. Joel had tweeted *"I demand a do-over."* He'd posted it public, for all the world to see. It was cryptic. They were the only two people who knew what it meant. Lucy's heart raced.

She imagined commenting with a winky face. Let his fans wonder what was up between them.

Once she was at the airport, she cruised slowly past the airfields and the large building full of people going to or from someplace. She made one trip past the gates and idled in front of the United entrance only long enough to imagine dropping Joel off for his flight back home.

Taped to her dashboard was a photo of him. She kissed her two fingers and pressed them to his two-dimensional lips. Then she exited the lot and drove further down the main road. When she had passed the last runway, she made a U-turn and drove by again. This went on until she finally spotted a plane climbing into the air. She imagined Joel was on that plane and he was looking out the window for her car. A lump formed in her throat. She would miss him terribly.

Then she turned back for home with the film of their love affair still rolling in her mind.

CHAPTER NINE
Omaha - Present

Lucy Bonneville wasn't much help to Elijah yet.
She hadn't given him any useful information. She only
insisted she was innocent and soon everything would be
cleared up. He knew that wasn't true. He'd reviewed the
transcripts of her trial and had seen all the evidence
available. But that information only went so far as to
prove her guilty. There wasn't nearly enough there to tell
her story.

It had been two years since her name had been
entered into the unofficial Celebrity Stalker Hall of Fame.
It had been the top entertainment story for several weeks.
Interest was revived again a year later when she was
convicted of a laundry list of offenses. That's when Elijah
caught on and decided she was his meal ticket.

He'd read and saved every article he could find
online about her. Plenty of them were helpful. Some of
them were sensational. A few were downright lies. He
even found a very early one that reported her name as
Laura Boneville. Those kinds of inaccuracies made him
want to weep for modern journalism.

Online articles weren't enough for him to go on if he
intended to tell her real story. He would have to do the
legwork. If she wasn't willing to give him her story, he
needed to drag it out of the people who knew her. He
intended to walk where she walked; to see the world

through her eyes, demented as that world view might be.

Despite having a pathetic social life, Elijah did have friends. One of those friends was able to hook him up with the judge involved in Lucy's case. That judge gave him somewhat limited access to the evidence against her. But he wasn't using that evidence to solve a crime. He was using it to follow in her footsteps.

Armed with what he knew, Elijah tracked down her former coworker. Her name was Joni and she had probably spent more time with Lucy around that time than anyone. Hopefully she could give him a better idea of what Lucy was like as a person and not as a criminal.

He had arranged to meet her at the Bliss Day Spa where she worked as a massage therapist. The business was in a strip mall with a façade that gave nothing away. When he stepped inside he was greeted with ambient light and sound and the almost overpowering scent of lavender and spice.

The woman behind the high counter smiled and welcomed him. She was slim and pretty with black hair pulled into a long ponytail. Her winged eyeliner accentuated the upward curve of her eyes. He wondered what heritage was responsible for the mocha shade of her skin.

"I'm here to see Joni Silva."

Her professional smile dropped as if she was glad to be rid of it.

"I'm Joni." She looked him over which made his forehead produce beads of sweat. He was suddenly nervous to be interviewing this woman. He would have to constantly remind himself to keep it professional.

"And I'm Elijah Rhee." He reached his hand across the desk in a professional gesture, but she didn't take it.

"I figured," she replied coldly.

"Great." He was skilled at keeping his cool, even around attractive women. "Where can we go to talk?"

"There's a Panera next door. Let's go there." She reached down and produced a handbag which she hefted over her shoulder. Then she stepped from behind the counter to reveal the rounded belly of a woman in the middle stage of pregnancy. Elijah's nerves eased a bit. His professionalism would not suffer.

When he offered to buy her a soft drink and a pastry, she didn't decline. She chose a booth and slid in while he remained at the counter waiting for their order. Within minutes he brought the food to the table and sat down across from her. Then he pulled his phone from his pocket, opened an app, and set the phone between them.

"Do you mind if I record our conversation?"

Joni looked down her nose at the phone. Her brown eyes flitted back to his face. God, she was nice-looking.

"I guess not," she said. "This is about Lucy, right?"

"Yes. You knew her from her uncle's store? Were you friends?"

She let out a short sniff and looked away. "No. We just worked together. She was quiet. Seemed kind of lonely."

Elijah made a mental note of this. A lonely woman with a boring job latched onto a celebrity and couldn't let go.

"Did she have any friends?"

"None that I knew of. She would go out with me and

Leron sometimes and she never invited other people. She never ran into anybody she knew."

"Is Leron your husband?"

"What?" She laughed, but not in a funny way. It was more of a mocking laugh. Like, how dumb was he?

"I'm not married. Leron is my best friend. He worked a couple doors down back then."

"Did Lucy ever have a boyfriend when you knew her?"

Joni took a large bite of her bear claw. She chewed while he waited for her answer.

"She had a couple, supposebly. She talked about a guy named Kevin and then there was Joel." A look of realization crossed her face. "But obviously that was made up. I never met Kevin, so I can't tell you if he actually existed or not. And then she said she was moving to Colorado to live with this guy she'd met. I honestly thought he was real." She chuckled and shook her head, apparently amused with the situation.

"Did she show you pictures of this guy?"

"No, I guess not."

"Did you ever ask to see a picture?"

Joni scowled. His line of questioning was making her visibly irritable. He wondered why that was. It's not like she was the one being scrutinized.

"Maybe. I don't remember. She did say he wasn't on Facebook because he was really private, or something. And one time he was in town. She said she'd bring him by, but she never did."

"He was in town?" This was interesting.

"Yeah. He flew in from New York," she said.

"But you never met him?"

She grimaced again. It was as if she felt she was failing a test. Her tone became defensive.

"No. I remember we were going to the bar that night, me and some friends, and I suggested she and him come along, but she said he probably didn't want to. It was Shifty's. That's a karaoke bar and she said something about he don't like that kind of stuff, or whatever. I don't remember what her excuse was, actually. That was a long time ago. Then one time she went to visit him."

"She went to New York?" The intrigue grew. If Lucy had gone to New York to stalk Joel Ruskin, he was the first one hearing about it.

"Yeah, New York. She said she did, anyway. She was gone for the whole weekend. Took time off. It was a pain in my ass because I had to work that Sunday, open to close."

She put the straw to her mouth and loudly sucked up air from the bottom of her cup. When she raised her eyebrows at him, Elijah knew it was a signal. Silently, he took the cup from her, walked to the self-serve fountain, and filled it again with Diet Coke.

Before he was even seated he posed his next question.

"Did she ever mention Joel Ruskin, the TV host, to you? Not pretending he's her boyfriend, I mean."

"Not that I can remember. I didn't even know who he was until all this was on the news." She looked down at the table and smiled. "Hell, I think Lucy might have made him more famous. Probably helped his career."

"I don't know about that." He lifted his phone

slightly to check the time. The information about New York had put his mind on another track. This interview couldn't end soon enough. Then he'd be ready to follow this new lead.

She still had a bit of her bear claw left. He wasn't going to cut off a pregnant lady in the middle of a snack, so he bought a little time before letting her get back to work.

"Did you ever have any suspicion her boyfriend wasn't real?"

"Only later, after she moved to Colorado. I called the store she worked at."

"Why did you call?"

"Because I was starting to not believe her."

CHAPTER TEN
Omaha – 2015

Lucy spent Friday afternoon carefully packing her suitcase. She packed the black dress she'd worn to her cousin's graduation and some red heels she'd bought but hadn't been daring enough to wear. The other essentials were thrown in and the bag was zipped, unzipped, and zipped again for good measure.

She smiled at the suitcase on her bed, thinking of how amazing a weekend with Joel could be. He would want to make up for their terrible first date. He would invite her to visit him in his hometown. She'd accept on the condition she stay in a hotel and not at his Manhattan apartment. After all, they were still in friend status. She wanted it to be more. She hoped he did, too.

She lifted the suitcase and headed for the door.

At the bottom of the elevator she was met by the frail old woman from down the hall.

"Going on a trip?" She smiled sweetly.

"I'm going to New York."

"Oh." The woman was genuinely impressed. "How exciting. Is it a special occasion?"

"I'm going to see a friend." She wasn't going to tell her she was going for a date. She didn't know what this woman's moral standards were. She might judge her and make their whole neighbor dynamic even more unbearable. The woman only nodded politely.

"My husband took me to New York in the summer. It was 1983. No, '84."

Lucy's eyes widened as she tried not to blow up at the lady. There wasn't time for this.

"Anyway," the woman continued. "It was wonderful. The tall buildings. So much different than here. Of course, Omaha didn't have the skyline it does now."

She couldn't take it anymore. She had to interrupt.

"It sounds great." She tugged on her suitcase. "I'm sorry. I have a plane to catch."

The woman nodded.

"Have a safe trip." Her bony hand patted Lucy's arm. For a second, she gripped it as if trying to steady herself. Lucy smiled feebly and thanked her, taking a step away to indicate she was going.

Once freed from the woman's kind little clutches, Lucy exited the building. She hoisted her suitcase into her trunk, got into her car, and headed east. As she drove with the radio blaring, a Beau Castle song came on. She let out a heavy sigh and pretended as if he had called her on the phone. She turned down the radio slightly and proceeded to have a conversation with no-one.

"I can't talk right now, Beau. I'm on my way to the airport."

"Where're you headed?"

"New York. Just for a couple days."

"Oh, nice. Business there, or pleasure?"

"I'm going to see a friend."

"I didn't know you had friends in New York."

"You don't know everything about me, Beau. In fact, you don't know much about me at all."

"Come on, Love. Don't do that. I didn't call to fight with you."

"Then why did you call?"

"I wanted to hear your voice. I'm on the bus and everybody's doing their own thing. I've had enough of those guys already. Then I remembered when we were together and I used to call you and you'd make me feel better. You were always there for me, Lucy. I miss you."

She missed him, too. She'd stopped listening to his songs and now she missed his voice. She missed watching his videos, intently analyzing every move. Had she made the wrong choice by going with Joel Ruskin? His life wasn't as exciting as Beau's. But he was much more accessible. She had an easier view into his world. True, she missed Beau. She couldn't have it both ways, could she?

"I'm sorry, Beau. I'm almost at the airport. I have to go."

She drove with tears in her eyes. The conversation may not have been real, but the twist in her stomach was. It was a real pain–the pain of leaving Beau behind.

Twenty minutes later she pulled into the parking garage at the airport. With her suitcase rolling behind her, she entered through the sliding doors. Instead of approaching a ticket window as everyone else did, she found an empty bench near the baggage claim.

She loved to watch the carousel turning. She loved to see all kinds of bags and suitcases rolling down the conveyor and then around the huge, silver oval. She loved it when a young man approached a woman waiting there, kissed her passionately, and then retrieved her bag when she pointed it out. That should be her.

Her phone chimed. It was a post from Joel. He said he was flying back home. She smiled. Even with his hectic schedule, he'd made time to let her know. She remained on the bench in the airport, staring off as she thought about him. The people rushed around her, but she was in no hurry to go. Not until the scene in her head was complete.

CHAPTER ELEVEN

I caught an evening flight to New York. Joel was also flying in that night from Hollywood, so I knew we wouldn't be seeing each other until Saturday. That didn't bother me. I'd had a rough day at work. And then there was the phone call from Beau. That had stressed me out even more. The only thing I wanted to do was climb into a big, fluffy hotel bed with crisp, white sheets and fall into a deep sleep.

Because Joel hadn't even told me where I was going, I was met at baggage claim by a driver holding a sign bearing my name. He rolled my one suitcase to the waiting car. I'd packed light, hoping I'd have time to do a little shopping while I was there and because I had no idea what plans Joel had in store.

This wasn't my first time in Manhattan, just my first time there alone. I watched the lively city from the back seat of the black sedan. Omaha was alive on Friday nights, but this place was indescribable. Without Joel here to escort me, I felt the city would swallow me up.

Finally we arrived in front of the Plaza on Fifth Avenue. The driver pulled up to the curb, and the door was opened by a man in uniform. I stared up at the massive stone building, gawking like a misplaced country girl in a romantic comedy. My bags were removed from the trunk and preceded me into the giant lobby.

Joel had booked me into the Carnegie Park Suite,

complete with a living room and two bathrooms. It seemed over-the-top for one person. Still, I had no complaints. I settled in and awaited further instructions. The suspense was almost too much to bear.

When the turnstile in front of her was empty and the departing crowd had cleared, Lucy stood and pulled her suitcase behind her toward the exit. She found her car again in the garage and put the bag back in its place in the trunk. At the exit, she paid the fee and pulled out with the rest of the traffic. Her next stop was Iowa.

She checked into a casino hotel in Council Bluffs, right across the river from Omaha. It was the perfect backdrop for her fantasy with Joel. She loved the sights and sounds of this lively place.

She had chosen a room with a king bed. It was already late, so she stripped off all her clothes and climbed under the sheets. She leaned back on the pile of ultra-soft pillows and opened her laptop. Using the satellite map again, she found the Plaza hotel and dropped herself into the street view to look around.

She wandered Manhattan's streets until her eyes began to cross. When her stomach growled from hunger she obeyed its request and closed her laptop.

From her suitcase she retrieved her outfit for the evening. Before she began to dress, her phone chimed an alert. It was another post from Joel.

"Chivalry isn't dead. It's just been shot in the leg."

She chuckled at his humor. He had put her mind at ease. It was definitely time to let Beau go because she had found someone she could be friends with; a friend she could love.

CHAPTER TWELVE

It was almost eleven the next morning when I finally got a call from Joel. I'd already taken a shower, ordered and eaten breakfast, and was watching meaningless TV from the comfort of a plush loveseat.

"I was beginning to think you'd forgotten about me." I tried not to sound annoyed. I'd been through this kind of thing plenty of times with Beau and I wasn't happy about reliving it. I had never enjoyed the waiting around part, which inevitably was detrimental to our relationship, even if it hadn't been the nail in the proverbial coffin.

"Sorry. I had a conference call. I'm coming over now, and we'll have lunch."

When he arrived, I once again tried to be casual and not rush to the door. I opened it, and he was standing there with a warm smile on his face. He was holding a bundle of three yellow roses like something out of an old romance. He handed them to me and stepped inside.

"Lovely," I said with a smile.

"I know," he began. "So 1950s."

"It's okay. I can appreciate a guy who's a gentleman."

"Then I'll try to be one." He winked, and my knees melted a little.

I placed the roses on the desk. We stared at each other for a minute, not knowing what to say. It was awkward again. We still hadn't established whether this was going to turn into anything romantic. The closest we'd come to romance was a quick kiss on the cheek. Yet, here we were standing in the pricey hotel suite he was paying for. He was obviously trying for romance, right?

"Lunch?" Joel took my hand and ushered me out of the room and to the elevator. When we got to the street I expected to see a car waiting for us. But there was none.

"I walked over," Joel explained. "It's a nice day."

"How far do you live?"

"A few blocks."

"That explains the pricey accommodations."

"Only the best, my dear." He proffered his arm, and I linked mine through it.

We walked through a large crowd of people where only a few heads turned. A couple photos were snapped, but nobody bothered us. It was one of many clues that New York was unlike Omaha in more than just its size.

A few blocks later we arrived at a deli. Joel hopped ahead of me and opened the door. He swung his other arm and bowed slightly.

"M'lady."

"Why thank you," I responded with a fancy accent.

"You see, chivalry isn't dead. It's just been shot in the leg."

I giggled a little too girlishly.

By 1:00 p.m. we were strolling through Central Park with bellies full of sandwiches. Joel was giving me a quick history lesson on the park itself. Then he pulled me off the pathway, and we sat down in the grass.

"Do you want to go to a party tonight?" He plucked

up a blade of grass and shredded it while he talked. "Or dinner? If you don't like parties, we can skip it and just have dinner." He was still studying the shredded grass and acting nervous, like he was asking me out for the first time again. Hadn't I flown here through the sky in a metal tube for a date? Didn't that mean I was pretty much up for whatever date he had planned?

"What kind of party?"

"Uh, it's a cocktail party. A cocktail party at, uh, Tim Fontaine's house."

"Tim Fontaine the TV announcer?"

"Yeah, we've worked together a few times. He's pretty close to retiring. But we don't have to go if you don't want to."

He still wasn't looking at me, so I put my hand over his. When his brown eyes finally looked at me, I wished he hadn't taken my comment about being a gentleman so seriously. Even though he always came across as a nice guy on TV, I'd assumed it was an act. But he really was an everyday, insecure, regular person. A person who hadn't even tried to kiss me yet.

"I'll go wherever you want to go," I replied.

Joel turned his hand over to grab mine. I thought that would be the moment he tried to kiss me. Instead, he pulled me up to stand. We started to walk on the path again, this time hand in hand. The warmth of our palms together sent shots of electricity up my arm. I turned my head away from him so he couldn't see my giant smile.

"Do you have a cocktail dress?"

"Something sexy?" I tilted my head toward him and fluttered my lashes.

"Yes, please."

"I have a little black number."

"Perfect."

Before long we were back at the Plaza. Joel went only as far as the gold and marble lobby. He promised to pick me up later in a car, not to make me walk again. I thanked him for lunch and accepted another innocent kiss on the cheek. The suspense of our potential first kiss was driving me mad.

Luckily, I had planned for a fancy dinner, and had packed my little black dress and a string of pearls. The diamond stud earrings I was wearing had been a gift from Beau. I didn't think much of wearing them on a date, as he probably hadn't thought much of sending them to my apartment days after an explosive argument. And I was almost a hundred percent sure he hadn't picked them out. He had people for that.

Later, I paced the giant lobby waiting for Joel to arrive. He was surprised to see me there when he came through the glass door. Maybe it was because of all the waiting I'd put him through before. I knew my face couldn't hide my anticipation this time.

"I had to get out of that room," I explained. "It seemed a lot bigger when I got here."

"I know the feeling. Next time I'll get you the Park Suite." He ushered me out the door and into the waiting car.

The quick drive to Tim Fontaine's didn't give us much time for conversation. The driver opened my door and helped me onto the sidewalk. Joel followed. When we got into the elevator he turned to me. He looked incredibly handsome in his jacket and tie–more like the guy I was used to seeing on TV. It was easy for me to forget his TV persona when we were sitting in the park or eating in a deli like two regular folks. Now he had transformed into the star everyone loved.

"I haven't told you yet how amazing you look," he said.

My mom had told me I had a bad habit of covering my mouth when I smiled–like I was doing now. I was sure I was blushing.

"Don't cover your smile." Joel took my hand gently from in front of my face and held it. "You have the most beautiful smile."

His other hand cupped my cheek. He was finally going to kiss me. I was finally going to know where this all was headed. As he leaned toward me, we were startled by a well-dressed couple who had to be in their seventies. The old man cleared his throat. Joel quickly stepped back without making contact.

"Going up to Fontaine's?" the man asked when the elevator doors opened.

"Yes." Joel forced a polite smile. He let the couple go first. Then he put a hand on the small of my back and ushered me into the elevator.

"I've known Tim for forty years. I produced those cigarette ads he did way back."

The old woman patted his arm as if to hush him. She smiled politely at us both. She seemed to know what was up.

Lucy strolled through the hallway of the casino

from her room to the elevator. Her red heels thudded on the geometric pattern of the carpet. In the elevator she caught a reflection of herself wearing her black dress. The corset she wore underneath was doing a pretty good job of holding everything in. She let out a heavy sigh. Even dressed up and made up, she was still plain old Lucy.

She arrived at the casino's bar and grille and requested a table for one.

"Would you rather eat at the bar?"

"No," she snapped. She didn't mean to. She didn't like feeling judged for eating alone.

The hostess led her to a table in the corner where she removed the extra silverware and water glass. She was seated between a middle-aged couple with nothing to say to each other and a family with two small children. She did her best not to let them distract her from her daydream. When the server came she ordered a bottle of wine and was again given a look of judgment.

"Can't a woman enjoy wine with her dinner?"

"Yes, ma'am," he said apologetically.

When the server left the table, Lucy smiled across at the empty chair where the ghost of Joel sat. Her heart thudded excitedly in her chest as she thought about what a beautiful moment they could be sharing together. If only real Joel could see the beauty of it too.

CHAPTER THIRTEEN

The cocktail party in the sprawling apartment was interesting to say the least. There were people of all ages and from all different fields of entertainment. Some of them were people I recognized, but most of them worked behind the scenes. Almost everyone knew who Joel was. Those who hadn't yet met him introduced themselves.

Joel kept one hand on my waist while the other hand gripped a glass of wine. Every time my drink was empty, it would be magically replaced with another. I had to remember to slow down or I'd be in real trouble.

There was a brief time when Joel and I became separated from each other. I wandered around the buzzing apartment, trying not to nervously sip my wine down to the bottom of the glass, lest it be instantly replaced. Finally I spotted Joel outside on the balcony talking to an attractive female whom I recognized as one of the models from a popular game show. My heart skipped and jealousy knotted my stomach. I was never good with competition. My first instinct was always to shrink away and cut my losses. This time I had plenty of wine in me, so I pushed myself through the balcony doors and smiled sweetly at them both.

"Lucy!" Joel was overly excited to see me. With his back to the model, he made a face like he needed to be rescued. Then he put his arm around my waist and introduced me to Heidi. She practically ignored me and attempted to continue the conversation I'd interrupted as if I wasn't even there.

"Anyway," she said, "everyone wants to hear it." After touching Joel's arm pointedly, she went back inside the apartment, carried on legs that looked like long, satin stilts. Her leaving did nothing to quell my jealousy, as now I was jealous that I didn't have her amazingly unrealistic body. It was the same issue I'd had the whole time I'd been dating Beau: Why would he bother with a plain girl like me when he was constantly surrounded by incredibly beautiful women?

"What does everyone want to hear?" I asked Joel.

"That song I did for the disaster relief album last year." He said it the way I would say I'd made throw pillows for my couch.

"You're a singer, too?"

He squeezed my waist and laughed. I loved his laugh. I loved the way his eyes crinkled, telling me this laugh was genuine.

"I dabble."

Joel's hand slid from my waist and down my arm so he was now holding my hand. I gripped his hand tightly. This made him smile and shake his head as if to question my intent.

"I'm afraid you'll slip away again," I said in response to his unspoken question.

He pulled me quickly to him and put both arms around me. The city noises seemed to fade away. Looking down and deeply into my eyes he said, "I won't."

"Promise?" I gazed back at him, completely dazzled by his charm.

"I can promise I won't leave you alone again tonight."

He touched my bare shoulder which sent a current of excitement through my body. An involuntary sigh escaped my lips. Joel smiled.

"I think about you," he said softly. "I can't keep my mind on much else. I hardly sleep."

He kissed my forehead. Then he kissed my cheek. Then his lips found my lips, and our first kiss on that balcony in the middle of Manhattan was electric. I became dizzy and feared I might fall right over the railing if it weren't for his strong arms around me.

His kiss left me flustered. When we rejoined the party, my cheeks were still flushed. As soon as we walked back through the door, we were met by Tim Fontaine himself.

"Heidi tells me you're going to grace us with a song." His voice was booming–always the announcer. He clapped Joel on the back and led him to the grand piano.

"I don't think so, Tim." Joel was only halfheartedly protesting. He looked at me to back him up, but I shrugged. I wanted to hear him sing, too.

After a little more coercion, Joel sat down on the piano bench. He rested his hands gently on the keys. My eyes were drawn to those hands. I instantly wished they were touching me so softly. When his fingers began to move I almost felt them moving up and down my bare skin.

Half of the guests gathered around when he began to play. His voice, deep and pure, crooned through the party air and silenced everyone within earshot. I began to wonder why music wasn't his chosen career.

"Let go of the past," he sang. "Someone is here for you."

Then he turned his head to look at me. His hands hit the keys and he smiled. My heart skipped a beat. It could have been the wine. It could have been the magical city. I knew right then I might actually fall in love with this man.

"What you may need," he sang only to me, "is right here in front of your eyes."

I might have imagined he was singing to me. Maybe I put more meaning into it than he had intended. It was a song he sang long before he knew me. What if I was putting more meaning on it? What was wrong with making a moment mine, even if only in my own mind?

When he finished, everyone applauded. Some shook his hand. Another famous musician took over the piano and shared his talent with the party as well, not to be outdone by a TV host.

Joel was finally freed from the spotlight. He found me and once again replaced his hand onto the waist of my little black dress. He leaned in and pressed his lips to my ear. His warm breath tickled my neck and sent shivers down my spine.

"I'm sorry," he whispered.

"For what?"

Quickly, he shook Tim Fontaine's hand, thanked him for both of us, and hurried me out the door. When we were on the elevator, he finally spoke.

"I'm sorry they made me sing."

"I wanted to hear you sing."

"It seems cheesy, though." He ruffled his hair with his hand, making him look slightly less formal and much more endearing. "I mean, we just had a moment on the balcony, and then I'm all..." He finished his sentence with a few waves of his hand. I laughed and caught his arm in midair. This time I was the one to initiate the kiss. That kiss lasted until the elevator doors opened at the bottom floor and Joel whisked me away to the waiting black sedan.

We rode in giddy silence for a few moments. His hand gripped mine like he was afraid to let go.

"Would you like to see my apartment?" he asked.

I turned to him and raised one eyebrow.

"I don't mean it like that." He lowered his voice and wagged his head in a mockingly sleazy manner. "Do you want to come up to my place?" he oozed sarcastically.

This made me laugh. I put one hand on his cheek and leaned in to kiss him again.

"Okay," he said after. "Maybe I did mean it like that."

Lucy left cash for her check and laid her napkin on the table. She walked toward the door. Two middle-aged, bearded men sat at the end of the bar. One of them turned on his stool as she passed. He reached out and grabbed her bare arm.

"Hey," he slurred. "How much?"

She jerked her arm from his grasp.

"Get real." She strode confidently away from him, but stepped wrong on her heel and twisted her ankle. Painfully, she attempted to walk with poise until she was out of sight of the bar. Then she removed her shoes and took the elevator barefoot.

She managed to retrieve and fill her ice bucket. Once back in her room, she tied the ice bag closed and set it on her aching ankle. Her phone chimed.

"Oh, Joel," she complained aloud while reaching for the phone. "For real?"

She checked the display. Joel had posted a link to an interview he'd done the week before. The camera zoomed in on his face as he talked.

"But I assume you have someone to do those things for you," the interviewer was saying.

"I have an assistant, yes." Joel grinned sheepishly, as if he were uncomfortable admitting it.

"Well, that's nothing to be ashamed about."

"I'm not," Joel defended. *"Tracy is a huge asset. She takes care of things I don't have time for. But it's just business. She's not a personal attendant. I can dress myself."*

"So, you don't have an entourage?"

"God, no."

He and the interviewer laughed together. Lucy smiled and nodded as if Joel had been talking directly to her in a private conversation. As he spoke she could imagine his lips pressed on hers. He wetted his lips and she could swear she tasted that glistening saliva in her own mouth. Her hand went toward the screen to wipe the hair from his eyes.

When the video ended she stood up from the bed. She removed her black dress and the restrictive corset which fell to the floor with a thud. After she was fully undressed she climbed under the heavy bedding again and propped herself up on the pillows.

She turned on the large TV, then dialed up the in-room entertainment and accepted the charges for a spicy program. The one-on-one sex made her parts tighten and tingle. She imagined herself and Joel in place of the two bodies on the screen. Her hand played expertly until she was moaning Joel's name in ecstasy. When her orgasm subsided, she lay in the plush bed relishing in her self-gratification. She imagined Joel there next to her, and the endorphins her body had released told her she and Joel were now bound together by this beautiful act.

CHAPTER FOURTEEN

I awoke the next morning with Joel's arm draped over me. The sun was pouring in through the bedroom's giant picture window. My black dress was crumpled in a pile on the floor. I sighed when I thought of the dreadful walk of shame I'd no doubt be taking through the lobby of the Plaza on my way back to my room.

I tried to reach for my dress without waking Joel. He stirred immediately and raised his shaggy head from the pillow to smile at me. The dress was going to have to stay on the floor for a while longer.

Fortunately, there was to be no walk of shame. Joel got up and cooked us a simple breakfast while I sat on a stool wearing his cotton t-shirt. When the doorbell buzzed, Joel didn't even budge. I stared toward the front of the apartment wondering for a split second why he was ignoring his visitor. Then a young woman let herself in and wheeled my suitcase into the living room.

"This is my assistant Tracy," Joel told me, waving the spatula in her direction. "You'll be seeing a lot of her."

Tracy smiled and waved. She fiddled with her smartphone and chatted with Joel about his schedule for the week. Then she bid us both goodbye and left the apartment.

Joel set a plate of scrambled eggs and bacon on the counter in front of me and sat down on a stool. He ate right away as if nothing had happened. I stared at his profile, waiting for an explanation.

"What's with the suitcase?"

"I had Tracy get your stuff for you. I figured you'd want some clothes to wear." He looked down at my naked legs. "Right?"

"Yes," I stammered. "I just..." I didn't know what to say. Was this arrogance or thoughtfulness? Should I be offended that a stranger packed up my room and moved it to his apartment? Should I be mortified that my date felt it necessary to save me from an embarrassing morning-after walk through one of the most famous hotels in the world? Maybe I should, but I was glad to have a change of clothes and, most importantly, my toothbrush.

"Sorry," Joel said between bites. "Was that over the line?"

I shook my head. The eggs were good. The bacon was crispy. It was a comfortable moment, and I didn't want to spoil it. But I couldn't help wondering if Joel's assistant was used to fetching things for his dates in the morning.

"When will I see a lot of her?"

"Hmm?" Joel was pouring us both coffee now.

"You said I'd be seeing a lot of Tracy. When?"

"You know, around."

"My plane leaves at three." It was now Sunday. I wanted to stay. Did he want me to stay? I had work in the morning, and Tracy had reminded him of his busy schedule.

"I know. I hope you're not leaving forever. I had a good time yesterday. I want to see you again." He grinned. "And again."

I smiled back and said, "And if I didn't have a good time? If I didn't enjoy hanging on your arm and letting you dazzle me with your musical charm?"

Joel snaked an arm around me and pulled me off the stool. He slid his hand under the t-shirt and into the waistband of my panties.

"And if you didn't enjoy being ravaged last night," he pointed to the couch, "over there," then to the bedroom, "and in there?"

I motioned toward the entryway. "And over there a little bit. On the way in."

He tried to kiss me, but I wiggled away. He was going to have to wait for me to find my toothbrush and other miscellanies.

"I'm going to use your shower."

"I'll join you."

"I can probably handle the shower on my own."

"It's a very complicated shower." He gave me a sly grin and then chased me into the bathroom.

CHAPTER FIFTEEN
Omaha - 2015

It was Monday. Lucy arrived at the mall with a spring in her step. She was still reeling from the weekend's events. Her temperature rose whenever she thought of Joel. There was a hollow void in her heart which she believed could only be filled by him. Her fantasies had become so vivid she felt it inevitable they become reality.

Joni noticed her euphoric demeanor when Lucy entered the store with two fancy coffees from down the hall.

"I guess you enjoyed your trip, Luce."

Lucy sighed heavily and said, "It was wonderful."

"Really? Did that man of yours take care of you or what?" There could have been a hint of jealousy in Joni's voice. Maybe Lucy was projecting.

Joni had plenty of reasons to be envious of her. She'd been stuck in town working and going to lame bars while her supposedly less attractive coworker was halfway across the country being romanced by a celebrity. She wanted badly to tell her the whole story. Instead she grinned and turned away.

"Wow." Joni stepped around and studied her face. "Did you get laid?"

"Maybe." She blushed. She could rely on a loose

definition of getting laid. If solo counted, then yes, she got laid.

Joni swatted the air dramatically with the magazine she'd been reading, then dropped it on the counter. It was a kind of silent congratulation. She grabbed her coat from the back room and readied herself to leave, but stopped when Leron came bounding in.

"Lucy got laid," she announced to him with zero provocation.

"What?" Leron put his hand to his heart and feigned shock. "I knew you had a glow about you today. I saw you skipping down the hall with those coffees like some kind of coked-up barista."

Lucy covered her mouth with her hand. There was no reason for her to correct either of them. She could let them believe what they wanted to believe. As long as she came out looking better for it.

"Is it as cold in New York as it is here?" Leron asked.

"Um, it wasn't bad." She hadn't thought to check the weather. Hopefully those two would get bored quickly and not ask any more questions. If they found out she had lied about going to New York, she'd never live it down.

"Well," Leron said. "Welcome back to Earth. It's not as exciting here as all that, but a bunch of us are going to Shifty's on Saturday night. You coming?"

"Probably." She meant "definitely", but she didn't want to sound too eager. After all, she was a jet-setter now with a boyfriend. At least that's who she wanted to be.

So, mustering all the courage a shy girl needed to

muster, she put on her best outfit on Saturday night and headed to the bar.

The night was frigid and windy. A strong gust blew Lucy's hair around her face and she stumbled on the step outside of Shifty's. The door banged shut behind her. Through the mess of hair she could see all twenty people in the bar turn and look at her. Now she was a frizzed-up mess.

Joni and Leron were sitting at a large table with the guy from Old Navy and his girlfriend who worked at the shoe store. Before Lucy's presence, they looked like a table of couples. But looks were deceiving. Leron had no interest in women whatsoever, and Joni liked to keep her options open. She always made Lucy sit between her and Leron so guys wouldn't get the wrong idea. Then the two of them would talk over her all night as if she weren't even there.

A dark-haired girl was stepping up to the karaoke stage. Her friends cheered, but the table of mall employees stayed silent.

"She thinks she's Katy Perry," Leron said. This was one of the regulars. Shifty's was like a high school cafeteria. Each occupied table held its own clique. None of the cliques liked each other and took joy in talking shit about the others.

Sure enough, the dark-haired girl began her shaky rendition of a Katy Perry song. Leron and Joni threw up their hands in unison and shook their heads. Leron mouthed, "I knew it."

Lucy nursed a beer while the bar buzzed on around her. People grew louder as the tables filled with empty glasses and bottles. A plastered young man stumbled to their table with a bottle in one hand and a shot in the other. He bent down and handed it to Joni and said something in her ear nobody else could hear.

"I don't drink tequila," she shouted over the music.

"Come on," the guy slurred. "Down the hatch."

"No." She turned from him. He set it in front of Lucy.

"You want it?" he asked. She eyed the cast-off shot. No guy had ever bought her a shot before, Leron excluded, but this one clearly didn't count. It had been intended for someone much cooler than her.

"Lucy don't drink that stuff, either," Leron told him. He was already three beers in and slurring as much.

"I'll take it," she said matter-of-factly. She tried to act like a shot of tequila was no big deal. She'd actually never had it outside of a Margarita. She took the tiny cup from the stranger anyway. Her friends stared at her with gaping mouths.

"Wait," he said. "You need a lime?"

"Nah." She had seen people suck a lime and lick salt off their hand before downing a shot of tequila, but she'd never understood why. She was pretty sure if she tried it she'd do it wrong and give away her inexperience. She wanted to get it over with.

Joni stared at her with wide eyes. Lucy threw the shot back quickly. She willed her face not to react to the burning sensation in her throat. It tasted like nail polish remover. The sides of her tongue tasted like metal. Her eyes threatened to water. She found her composure and smiled at the group.

"Damn girl," the guy said. "Straight up and everything. You're badass."

She grinned. She liked being a badass. It was a good feeling. Everyone would look at her in a different way from now on. She was a changed woman. For a moment.

The guy proceeded to pull up a chair next to Joni. They commenced a secretive conversation. Lucy's heart sank. She had taken the shot, but Joni was still the one getting the attention.

"Shit, Luce," Leron said. "I didn't know you drank tequila."

"Are you kidding? It's my favorite. I drink it all the time."

A few minutes later her head began to feel fuzzy. The bar seemed to have grown a little smaller, yet everyone appeared to be farther away. Another beer was set in front of her. She stared at it intently for a minute before chugging half of it. Then she swiped the song book out of Old Navy's hands and searched for something to sing.

Conversation buzzed around her. She focused as well as she could on the song book, hoping the letters would stop jumping around so she could read them.

After a while the random guy had struck out with Joni and left for another group of women. Everyone else at her table was talking about celebrities. She abandoned the song book for a minute and listened.

"Zac Efron is too still hot," Leron was saying.

"No, no he's not," Joni slurred. "He's still good looking, but he's trying too hard. And he's old."

"That's stupid. How can you try too hard?"

"That Nick guy who works at the movie theater doesn't try and he's hella hot." Joni leaned forward and tapped her finger hard into the table in front of Leron, as if that would help him understand her reasoning better.

"He's body hot," Leron argued. "He's not face hot."

"Wha's that?" Lucy spat in her drunken state. She wanted to get in on this convo, too.

"His body is good," Leron explained, "but he's got a weird face."

"You are mental," Joni shouted. The entire next table looked her way but she didn't care.

"But," Lucy started, let out a silent belch, and started again. "But what if a guy's not body hot or face hot? What's that called?"

Leron stared at her like she had grown a second head. He emphasized his words carefully. "Not hot."

Joni laughed so hard she literally fell out of her chair but caught herself before she hit the ground.

"No," Lucy continued emphatically, "but I mean some guys are hot because they're cool or they're nice or whatever. And maybe because they're kind of cute. But they're not, like, technically gorgeous."

"Like Ryan Gosling," Joni assisted.

"Ooo..." Leron moaned. "Good point. Good point. I'd do him."

"Yeah." Lucy was excited to be having this bonding moment with her friends, even if it was in a deafeningly noisy karaoke bar. "Or like Joel Ruskin."

"Who?" Leron squinted at her as if he could see the answer better in her face that way.

"Joel Ruskin. He's a TV personality. He had a song a

few years ago."

Joni shook her head and downed the remainder of her drink.

"He's like a Ryan Seacrest type," Lucy added.

"He's hot, too." Joni jutted her finger toward her as she said it. Lucy was defeated. How could they not know who Joel was? He was only the most important man in her life.

"Well, he's my boyfriend." The excessive alcohol had apparently eliminated her inner monologue and she was to the point where she was going to say anything that popped into her head.

"Ryan Seacrest is your boyfriend?" Leron asked and giggled.

"No, Joel Ruskin."

"I don't even know who that is," Joni shouted over the applause for the last singer. She did so with her eyes completely closed and then rested her forehead on the table in front of her.

Lucy gave up. She looked at the time on her phone. It was still pretty early. Their night of fun was just getting started. So, she ordered another pitcher of beer for the table.

CHAPTER SIXTEEN
Omaha - Present

A black sedan pulled up to the curb and the passenger window lowered. The driver leaned over the console and said in his most professional voice, "Elijah?"

"Yes." Elijah opened the door. "Omar?"

The driver nodded and Elijah climbed into the front seat. Omar swiped the screen of the cell phone hanging from his dashboard.

"Where you going, man? You didn't put in your destination."

"Actually, if there's a park nearby take me there. I'd like to talk to you about a rider you had a while back."

Omar gave him a side glance.

"What's this about? You a cop?"

"No, I'm a writer. True crime. I'm researching a case for a book. I'll pay for your time."

The driver shrugged.

"Whatever you say. It's your buck."

The car swung left and rumbled into the gravel lot of a city park. The two men got out and headed for a nearby picnic table. Elijah produced a picture of Lucy and his own notebook where he'd written the date and time of her Lyft transaction.

"Do you remember this woman?"

"That was almost three years ago. I drive a lot of

people." He took the picture and studied it. Then he looked at the date again.

"I have a police report saying you picked her up from Shifty's Bar. She was drunk. You had the cops remove her from your car."

Omar shook his head. He knitted his eyebrows.

"You're writing about her. So, what'd she do?"

"She was stalking a celebrity. Claimed to be his girlfriend." He didn't want to give too much away and possibly corrupt the driver's memory.

Then Omar's his face changed.

"Wait. I do remember that lady." He was suddenly thrilled to be having this conversation. "You never forget riders like that. She went nuts on me."

"Can you tell me what you remember?"

Omar shrugged. "Picked her up at Shifty's. I thought she's gonna puke in my car. Her guy-friend put her in and told me not to worry."

"Is that unusual?"

"No, that shit happens all the time. But she was weird, like acting all crazy."

"Crazy how?" Elijah tried to stifle his excitement. This was the kind of information he'd been looking for. What good was a book about a crazy stalker if it wasn't littered with crazy tales?

"First of all, she was wasted. She kept trying to lay down on the back seat. I don't allow that. I told her to sit up or get out."

"Is that why you called the cops?"

"Naw. She seemed harmless at first. She never stopped talking, slurring and stuff. She told me all about this TV guy she was dating. 'Allegedly' dating." He made air quotes. "I didn't believe a word of it."

Oh, this was good.

"What TV guy?"

"I don't know. I never heard of him. She said he lived in New York and she was going to move there to live with him. She asked me if I thought she should."

"What did you say?"

"I told her to follow her heart. You know, shit Lyft drivers say to drunk chicks they pick up and don't want to deal with. She kept going and going about this guy. At that point I kinda wished she would pass out."

Elijah nodded. His pulse was racing. He hadn't expected to get much out of him at all, and here he was getting the whole juicy story.

"She told me she used to date Beau Castle. You know, that rock dude with the tattoos and stupid hair. That's when she started getting really pissed off."

"You called her out on it?"

"No way. Made me laugh, though. She got mad 'cause I laughed. Started yelling that it was the truth and I needed to shut my fucking mouth."

"Did you kick her out?"

"Not exactly. We were already to her building and she was still yelling. She reached over the seat and grabbed my shirt and told me I didn't know anything about anything."

"So you called the cops?"

"Yes, sir. Anyone lays a hand on me in my car I call the police. I got out and called and she was still in the car yelling. I opened the back door and she kind of fell out on the ground. When the cops showed up she was rolling around on the cement crying about something or other."

Elijah looked at the copy of the police report on his phone. "But she wasn't arrested. They just took her inside."

"That's right. She was too drunk to know what she was doing. I just wanted her taken care of. A lady cop took her in and that was it." Omar shifted on the bench. He bowed his head and laughed. "Shit, I told that story to all my friends. That's the only reason I remember her."

CHAPTER SEVENTEEN

For the next two weeks, Joel and I talked on the phone almost every night. We talked about anything and everything. By the end of that two weeks, we pretty much knew each other's life stories. As cliché as it was, I started to feel like I had known him for much longer than I had.

There were a few evenings when he wasn't available, but I didn't mind because those were the nights I could see him live on my TV. Of course, it wasn't the same. But it was something I had to accept. I was sharing him with the world.

I missed him so much. I couldn't take my eyes off the screen when he was on. Millions of people were being entertained by him, but I was holding at least a little part of his heart. Maybe he even thought about me once or twice when he was there. The feeling I had was huge.

Then Joel called on Thursday. He was more animated than usual.

"I want to take you out this weekend. I had a thing to do but it got canceled, so I'm free through Monday."

"I have to work on Sunday."

"How about if I come to you this time? I can find something to do on my own on Sunday and you won't miss any work. I'm tired of talking on the phone. I want to see you in person."

I had to accept. How could I not? I wanted to see him so badly. His excitement put a flutter in my heart. This put me on cloud nine. Nobody could say anything to bring me down.

Friday dragged on like a thousand hours. Joel's flight was slated to land at 7:35 p.m. I was anxious to see him in person and to be back in his arms.

I waited for him at the baggage claim. I didn't even recognize him until he stepped off the escalator and headed toward me with his arms outstretched. He was wearing a baseball cap and glasses, and he hadn't shaved in at least three days. There was a charge in our embrace, like two magnets coming together. Behind him, I spotted Tracy.

"You brought your assistant on our date?" I mumbled so she wouldn't hear me.

"I'm not a hundred percent free this weekend," he said apologetically. "I have a video meeting tomorrow morning. Other than that, Tracy can take care of the business stuff for me. Didn't I say you'd be seeing a lot of her?" He nudged me playfully. Then he grabbed his suitcase as it drifted by.

"I didn't make up the guest room for her."

Tracy, who seemed to have bionic ears, stepped up behind Joel with her own suitcase.

"I'm staying at the Hilton," she reassured me. So far I hadn't seen her without a smile. I pondered if it was a difficult job being Joel's assistant.

Joel was interested to hear about my coworkers' tradition of booze-fueled karaoke performances. Not an hour after we'd left the airport he had already made himself at home in my apartment and even more comfortable in my bed. I'd told him I had already declined my friends' invitation because I would be busy all weekend.

"I've never done the karaoke thing," he told me. His index finger traced an imaginary line down my naked body to my navel. "Maybe it would be fun."

"I don't know if my friends can handle having a celebrity in their midst."

He leaned forward and kissed my lips. "Can you handle having a celebrity in your midst?"

"Pssh!" I pushed him onto his back. "You think you're so special," I joked.

"I'm not special. So, take me to the bar with your friends so I can be a regular guy."

"Wouldn't you rather go on a real date like dinner or something classier than a noisy bar?"

"We've done that classy bullshit. Remember walking in the park, having lunch at the deli? Those were the best times. We're better at casual."

I stared intently at this man in my bed: his soft grin, his brown eyes, and the scruffy beard that acted as an easy disguise. Where were we headed? The last thing I wanted was to get too attached to him, only to find out he wasn't as invested in us to begin with. The only way to know if he wanted a relationship was to come out and ask him, and I was scared the question may only drive him away.

"I like it here," he said, motioning to the window, "in Omaha. It's casual and it's easy. So let's relax while I'm here. Let's do something easy."

"Okay. But, I think if you're planning on relaxing, you're underestimating the cutthroat world of bar karaoke."

CHAPTER EIGHTEEN

Saturday afternoon was as casual as Joel had hoped. In the morning, Tracy came over for his video meeting, and I made myself scarce. When I returned later with lunch, the three of us ate together at my table. After that, Joel and I strolled around the Old Market, with Tracy several steps behind. She was there to handle any potential fan situation, although I thought she was a little small for a bodyguard. No one bothered Joel at all. The hat and scruffy chin were working in his favor.

Tracy was also on our tail when we went to Shifty's for karaoke. I drove this time instead of letting Joel hire a car. If he was trying to be incognito, showing up in a chauffeured car wasn't going to do it.

When we got to the bar, all of my friends were already seated around a few tables they'd smashed together. We sat next to Joni, who looked surprised. I didn't appreciate the shock on her face, however.

"So, you did bring your boyfriend."

"Not my boyfriend," I corrected, probably beet-red in the face. "My date."

"And his friend?"

"Yes. Tracy."

"So, he brought another woman on a date. Is something weird going on here?"

"It's not like that," I protested. Obviously, I wasn't

well prepared for these questions.

Joel sensed my discomfort. He leaned over me and put his hand out to Joni.

"Hi," he said. "I'm Joel. I'm Lucy's date." He emphasized the last word and gave me a side eye. I was hoping he hadn't taken offense to what I had said. He grinned at me. Then he turned his attention to the server who had come to our table.

"You guys want something? Appetizers? Beer?"

Joel perused the single-page appetizer menu on the table.

"Which ones are good?" he asked no one in particular. Everyone at the table shouted out their favorite of the five options. Joel laughed heartily and dropped the menu back onto the table. "One of each," he said. The server stared at him for a minute to see if he would announce that he was joking. He didn't. Onto the order he added a whiskey sour for him and a Bud Lite for me.

The server turned to Tracy.

"You want anything to drink, Miss?"

"That's okay. I'll probably end up driving these two home."

Joel put his arm around me and nodded in agreement.

"Pop's free for designated drivers," the server told her.

"Huh?"

"Soda," I interjected. "You get a free soda."

"Oh. Okay. Coke, then."

"Are you from New York, too?" Joni asked Tracy. Tracy nodded.

"You his cousin or something?" Joni waved her finger between Joel and Tracy. Lucky for us, the bar erupted in cheers as a burly, bald man took the microphone and launched into AC/DC's "Back in Black".

Everything was going well. The booze flowed, and everyone started to forget I had brought two newbies into our group. When the five appetizers came, Joel invited everyone to share them. This made them all happy and made him a hero. Even outside of fame, Joel seemed to have the ability to charm everyone around him. Tonight he was a regular guy who bought them food and made them laugh.

Currently, a confident redhead was belting out a shaky rendition of "My Heart Will Go On" with all her might. In the world of karaoke, some of us were there to have fun, and some of us were there with much more serious intentions. She was one of the serious ones. I figured either she was practicing for something or hoping to be discovered in this obscure Nebraska bar. Or maybe she really, really enjoyed singing.

"Do you sing, Joel?" Joni, who was now plenty drunk, was leaning over my lap toward him and exposing most of her lacy, red bra. She reached over and put her hand on his arm. "Why are you still wearing that hat?"

"Uh," he looked at me questioningly. I shrugged.

"Do you sing?" She was slurring heavily.

"A little."

"Get up and sing." Her arm gave out and she nearly landed face-first in my lap.

The others in our group began to chant for Joel to sing. The redhead grimaced on the last lines of her song, offended that we weren't engrossed in her performance. She finished and rejoined her friends who, so far, had monopolized most of the stage time with their routines worthy of American-Idol outtakes.

"Don't worry," said Leron who then patted Joel on the back. "I put your name in."

Joel and I exchanged glances. I whispered to him that we could leave. He squeezed my shoulder.

"I'd kind of like to do it," he said. "Gotta try new things, right?"

Leron handed him the song book. Joel perused it for a few minutes, wrote down his selection, and handed it to Leron who took it to the DJ. When I asked Joel what he'd picked he grinned and patted my leg. Then he motioned for our server to replace our empty drinks.

While I sipped my next drink, some of my friends got up and shouted a song together. Then the redhead took the mic again. She picked a show tune and got into character.

"She's really into this shit," Leron said. The others laughed. "It's always fun to see the ones who think they're pros."

"Everybody has to start somewhere," Joel said to no one in particular. I put my hand on his arm to show my support. The group fell sheepishly silent, then quickly changed the subject and were rowdy again.

The redhead finished to half-hearted applause.

The DJ announced, "Next up is Joel, 'I Want to Know What Love Is'."

My friends and coworkers cheered for him when he took the microphone. As most drunk people do, they immediately went back to their spirited discussions before he could utter a note. My attention was fully on Joel, who winked at me as he began to croon. He didn't care if they heard because he clearly only meant the song for me. The whole bar talked right over him, but he sang as if he and I were the only ones in the room.

As Joel's voice crescendoed with the music, the room became quieter. Conversations dropped as everyone in the room took notice of Joel's vocal talent. All eyes were on him when, during a break in the song, he took of his baseball hat and ruffled his messy hair.

"Oh my god," Joni hissed at me. "Is he Joel Ruskin?"

I nodded and continued to watch Joel, unable to control the giant grin on my face.

"Are you dating Joel Ruskin?" Leron asked.

I shrugged casually. "I guess."

Joel finished strong, his eyes on me. I smiled, and the whole bar erupted in hoots and hollers. Several people stood up and patted him on the back or shook his hand as he passed. Tracy, the sober one, was already out of her seat and ready to usher us out the door.

Our group was suddenly even more enthralled with my date now. He strolled to the table and put his hand out to me to help me out of my chair. I was hit with a head rush from standing quickly and from the alcohol, noise and excitement. When I stumbled toward him, Joel caught me with both arms and smiled down at my booze-flushed face. He was hardly more sober than I.

Joni was looking on at us with her arms folded across her chest. Leron patted Joel firmly on the back.

"I knew it was you the whole time," he boomed.

"Just wanted to see how long you could keep it up." He rustled Joel's hair like they were old pals, then fell drunkenly back into his chair. He laughed loudly and announced to the others, "We should have had him order us way more food."

We quickly said goodnight. Joel checked that Tracy had paid the bill, and then he dropped an enormous tip on the bar for our server. Everyone seemed to be trying to talk to Joel at once as we made a break for the front door.

Tracy was standing outside waiting for us with her hand outstretched. I handed her my keys and we ran for the car.

CHAPTER NINETEEN
Omaha - 2015

"You missed some craziness last night," Joni said. The two of them were sweeping glass from a large picture that had mysteriously fallen off the wall overnight.

"Did I?" She was aware that several of the mall closers had met at the new bar down the street. After the hangover of the previous weekend, Lucy wasn't at all disappointed she'd missed it. She still reveled in the memories of her fake date with Joel. Joni didn't even realize Lucy had been with them all in spirit. In her mind, Joni was insanely envious and recapping the night that Joel Ruskin showed up at Shifty's.

She imagined the Monday morning news. Channel Six would have thrown in a story about all the Joel Ruskin sightings around town over the weekend.

"Celebrity Joel Ruskin was spotted in Omaha this weekend. Sightings included the Old Market, The Henry Doorly Zoo, and even singing karaoke at Shifty's bar. No word on whether he was in town for business or just visiting our fair city. I guess we'll have to wait and see where he pops up next."

Mostly she was tuned out while Joni talked. The imaginary evening played over the sound of her friend's voice. She watched her with glazed eyes, nodded a few times, but only caught words here and there.

Instead, she was calling Joel to tell him that Omaha had noticed his presence. Of course, the call went to voicemail. She was disappointed to not hear his voice and have this laugh with him.

"Hey, there. Your name is all over the local news today. You're our latest celebrity sighting. There was even a shaky video of you singing at Shifty's. Anyway, I thought you'd like to know you made an impact. Talk to you later."

Her lips moved slightly as she imagined herself leaving him a voice message. Joni didn't notice.

"It turns out," Joni continued, "that guy Brandt from the sporting goods store isn't even gay."

"Really? I totally thought he was." That was still not as nearly interesting as when Joel revealed himself to the crowd.

"I know, right? It's like, nobody should spend that much time and money on their hair if they ain't trying to attract a man. Anyway, Leron tried to put a move on him and he all got up and called him a fag. It was crazy. Then he left and Leron's acting like he don't even care. But he so much did care. I had to drive him home 'cause he got shit-faced after that."

Lucy wanted to add to her message that she missed him and that she couldn't wait to see him again. She wanted to tell him to call her back as soon as he could get away because she wasn't sure how long she could go without hearing his voice speaking directly to her and not through her TV screen. She kept that all to herself, though. She was still guarding her heart.

105

Joni stopped talking. That was Lucy's cue to step back into reality. She shrugged, hoping this was the correct response. It was apparently acceptable because Joni didn't blow up at her for not listening like she had before.

The two of them finished cleaning up the broken glass and went back to their usual Sunday task of sitting on the stools doing nothing. A group of girls wandered in to browse, but they clearly weren't planning on buying anything.

"How's your boyfriend?" Joni posed the question like a sixth-grader would.

"Joel is fine."

"Is he staying at your place?"

"Yep." She leafed noisily through the People magazine that had come in the mail earlier in the week.

"You should tell him to come visit us today. I'd like to meet him."

"I'll tell him."

Joni picked up Lucy's phone from the counter and set it on the counter in front of her.

"Text him right now."

"In a minute." She wasn't paying attention to her. She had stopped on a page in the magazine of candid celebrity shots. There, under a photo of Nicole Kidman in a park, was a picture of Joel Ruskin walking in New York with his mom.

She looked like a typical mom, not necessarily a star's mom. She was a little overweight and wore little makeup. Lucy's heart jumped. She had found another piece of him. For a moment she imagined the three of them having lunch together. They were laughing. There could be no reason Joel's mom wouldn't like her as much as he did.

"Ugh," Joni groaned. "Get your nose out of that magazine. What? Did you find a picture of your boyfriend Beau Castle in there? Does Joel know you have a crush on him?" She hopped off the stool, stuck her face next to Lucy's ear and whispered, "Does he know Beau's your lover?"

Lucy swatted at her with one hand like she was swatting a fly. She knitted her brow. If Joni only knew.

But Joni just laughed and headed out of the store to use the restroom. When she was gone, Lucy carefully cut Joel's picture out of the store's magazine. She tucked it carefully into her purse, and when she got home she taped the small photo to the full-length mirror in her bedroom. Then she smiled at Joel's image and had a lengthy conversation with it. She wished him a safe trip back to New York.

CHAPTER TWENTY

Because of a creepy neighbor and her building's super old washing machines, Lucy preferred to do her laundry at her mom and dad's house. It was also a great time to get some free groceries from their overstocked kitchen. Even with their only child out of the house, they still kept enough food to feed a large family.

Her mom had finished taking photos of her handmade jewelry. Now she sat on the couch next to Lucy with her computer in her lap.

Lucy was eating popcorn and watching HGTV. She liked to get ideas for the house she might one day have. Someday maybe she and Joel would have a place here in Omaha to get away from the fast life in New York. They'd have a yard and a fence and a dog and some kids. Joel would come to prefer the simple life. He would spend all his free days there with her and they would be intensely happy.

On the TV there was a local commercial for a national talent competition that was filming in town. Twenty contestants from the area had been preselected from online video submissions and would be competing onstage in ten cities. The judges would pick two finalists from each city to compete in Hollywood during a live show. Viewers could then vote online in real time. She wasn't interested. She didn't have talent, and she'd already missed the submission period. Then she saw the faces of the celebrity judges on the screen followed by her very own crush. She gasped.

"...and hosted by Joel Ruskin. Hometown Star is coming to your town. Go online for tickets now."

"You should do that, Lucy," her mom said. "You love to sing."

"You don't need talent for karaoke, Mom." It was hard for her to talk. She could barely breathe. Joel was coming to Omaha. He was actually going to set foot in her city. For real this time. She had to go to that show.

She pulled up the ticket website on her phone. Every last ticket was gone.

"How can it already be sold out?" she asked herself out loud.

"Honey, they've been playing this commercial for weeks."

"Really?" She hardly ever watched live TV anymore. When she watched shows on her DVR, she would always skip the commercials at the highest speed possible. For the last few weeks she'd been watching everything she could find on Joel, so it wasn't clear why this was the first she was hearing of the competition.

She began to perspire. How could this be? Was she really going to miss him? She began to tremble, but quickly composed herself. There had to be a way. If she couldn't be in the audience, at least she could still go to the arena. Maybe she'd catch a glimpse of him. Maybe she would see him around town.

It may have been fate bringing him to her hometown. Could it be true? Could she and Joel be destined for each other? And was this proof? There was no other explanation in her mind for this coincidence.

CHAPTER TWENTY ONE

Distractions were hard to find as I waited for the day of the Omaha show to roll around. I stressed over my appearance for several days before Joel came. Everything needed to be perfect. I was manicured, waxed, tanned, and dyed for the occasion. There was plenty of competition for his attention, and I didn't want to get lost in the crowd even though he assured me I wouldn't.

With the taping and the traveling, Joel and I had no time to see each other. I'd thought about quitting my job and touring with him, but we weren't nearly far along enough in our relationship to even consider asking him. And I needed my job. Besides, his schedule was hectic beyond what the camera showed, and I would probably spend most of the time lonely and bored.

At least I had the Omaha audition to look forward to. Until that week, there were only short conversations fit into both of our lives. Each one was a countdown to the day we'd finally be able to see each other again. He reminded me there probably wouldn't be any casual free time like before, but I looked forward to having his arms around me even for a moment if it was all I could get. I wondered, with all the people who would be buzzing around him if I would even get a chance to talk to him at all. How unfair that would be.

Joni was tickled that my famous boyfriend was

coming into town again. I hadn't told her, but there was no way to escape the news of a national singing competition. In fact, she insisted on having a girls' night out on Tuesday to discuss it. I had two tickets to the show, and I'd already told her I was taking my mom with me. She said it was okay, but I still got the feeling she thought there might be a chance my mom would cancel. Suddenly Joni was my best friend, stuck to me like glue. She never let me forget that she was in if my mom backed out.

The truth was, I hadn't told my mom about Joel yet. I hadn't really told anyone, and I'd made my friends promise to keep it a secret. I could only imagine how many people would be camped in front of my building every time they heard Joel Ruskin was in town. This week in particular would have been a madhouse.

"What about your dad?" Joni asked. I had gone downstairs to meet her at the elevator on Tuesday evening. It was her first time at my apartment, and I didn't want her to get lost. "Doesn't he want to go?"

"I could never get him to go to a thing like that. He doesn't even like live theater."

"I bet you could if you told him your boyfriend was hosting."

"Then he'd ask me why I don't bring him home for Thanksgiving like a normal person. And Joel isn't my boyfriend."

"Sure," she smirked. "Whatever."

I let her go ahead of me into the apartment.

"Wow, Lucy! This place is nice." She walked past the couch and gazed out of one of the huge windows. "I would kill for a view like this."

Our plan was to have a few drinks and then meet her other girlfriends at a bar down the street. I opened a bottle of wine and poured two glasses.

"Here's to your fancy place," she toasted.

"Here's to girls' night."

Halfway through our second drink I heard the familiar jingle of a set of keys at my front door. The wine had made me fuzzy, slowing my reaction and comprehension of the sound. Only the concierge had an extra set of keys to my apartment. There was only one other person it could possibly be.

The door had swung partway open before it dawned on me who was on the other side. Joni was looking at me with confusion on her face.

"Do you have a roommate?" she asked.

I shook my head, then hopped up from my stool as the man appeared. Joni gasped and spilled a little red wine on my granite counter.

"Beau Castle," she squealed, but didn't move another inch. She seemed to be frozen to her seat.

And there he was, my ex-boyfriend wearing his biggest smile and tightest t-shirt and dangling a key to my apartment from one finger.

"Surprise," he said and held his hands out to me. I only stared at him, still holding my wine glass. He walked over and hugged me, but my arms never moved. I was stunned.

"What are you doing here?" I must have hissed the words like a snake because he laughed. He always loved getting a reaction out of me.

"Hi," he said, sticking his hand out to Joni. "I'm Beau."

"I know," she squeaked. "What are you doing here?"

"Well," he said with mock outrage. "I used to kind of live here. In fact, there's my picture over..." He motioned to the end table where I used to keep a framed picture of the two of us. "Aw, there was a picture of me right there. Where did the picture go, Luce?"

I was still staring at him. My heart was pounding practically out of my chest. When we broke up, Beau had told me that because the apartment had been a gift he would sign it over to me. I'd asked for his key, but since he still technically owned the place the property manager insisted he have full access. We had agreed he could keep the key until the paperwork was finished, but he wouldn't use it. That was months ago. Why was he standing in my kitchen now?

"Wait." Joni was trying to piece it all together. "This was your apartment?"

"Technically it still is," he replied, eyeing me pointedly.

"It's our apartment. Temporarily." I was trying not to get upset, but I was sure my face was becoming fire-engine red.

"That's true." Beau poured himself a glass of wine. "It was a gift for Lucy." He stepped back over beside me and put his free hand on my shoulder. "She deserves the best."

Joni began to ask another question, but I quickly interrupted her. I wasn't interested in the two of them getting to know each other.

114

"Beau, what are you doing here?"

"I wasn't busy, so I thought I'd pop over from Nashville and see how things are going. Is this a bad time?"

Joni shook her head. She was clearly star-struck. I was annoyed.

"Yes," I countered. "It's very bad."

A million thoughts raced through my mind. What if someone spotted him in town? It would surely make the news like every other celebrity sighting in Omaha. What if Joel found out? He had to know Beau wouldn't come here for any reason but to see me. Worse yet, what if Joel showed up right at this moment? What if he had the idea to surprise me, too? I began to panic. I had to sit down. I sunk into the yellow couch, and Beau followed. Joni perched on the edge of the armchair next to him.

"Are you one of the judges?" Joni asked. Beau gave her a quizzical look. I buried my head in my hands.

"For the show?" She gave Beau a brief rundown of the show and, of course, added Joel's name into the mix.

"Oh." Beau leaned back and was quiet. I looked at him and shook my head.

"You didn't know?" Joni's face dropped. "I guess you probably don't follow stuff like that."

He looked at me. "Are you still seeing him?"

Beau and I hadn't talked much since our breakup. But one night he had called to talk and play the role of the loneliest rock star. It had sounded like he wanted to get back together, so I'd told him about my date with Joel. He didn't seem to mind and had laughed it off. Maybe he'd thought it was a passing thing, or that I could never go for a guy like Joel Ruskin after tasting the fast life with Beau Castle.

When it became clear she was in the middle of a heavy situation, Joni excused herself. She was going to meet her friends at the bar. I apologized that I wouldn't be able to join them. She told Beau a few times how much she loved his music, and then rushed out the door.

"When's he going to be in town?"

"Saturday, probably."

"I'm sorry, Lucy. I really didn't know—about the show or about the two of you. Is it serious?"

"Jeez, Beau. We've only been on a few dates." I stood up and paced in front of him.

"Here in Omaha?"

"Yes. And New York."

Recognition flashed in his eyes, like he remembered our last phone conversation. Now he was getting it. Hopefully he was getting it right.

"You don't think that's serious?"

"Was it serious when I went to Nashville to visit you?"

His face fell. I'd hurt his feelings. I didn't mean to, but he hadn't always been worried about mine.

"I thought so. Serious enough to get you out of that old crappy apartment." He waved his hands around like he was showing the place off. It was a jab to my heart. We'd had an open relationship. That was my idea. I knew a relationship with a touring rock star was open on his end no matter what we said to each other. I preferred not to play games. He had bought the apartment because I was ashamed of mine, and he didn't want to stay in a

116

hotel when he came to visit. It was an arrangement that worked. Until it didn't.

"Besides," he added. "You didn't want serious."

I nodded. When I went to the bedroom to wipe my brewing tears, he followed me. He touched my shoulder, and my heart nearly exploded. I missed him. I missed everything about being alone with him. I didn't miss the drama or the jealousy I that consumed me when we weren't alone.

"We're over, Beau." I tried to keep my voice from quivering. "You agreed to that. You didn't fight it."

"If you love someone," Beau said quietly, "set them free. Right?"

"What's that supposed to mean?"

"I let you go," he said in the saddest tone I'd ever heard from him. "You were supposed to come back to me."

I sniffled and busied my hands, fixing nothing on my nightstand. I hated the mixed emotions that brewed in me when he was around. How dare he come here and try to make me want him again?

"Do you want something serious with him?" He spoke low, as if he was forcing himself to ask.

"I don't know yet."

Beau came closer to me and I finally turned to him. His hand traveled over my collar bone and up my neck. With his hand cradling the side of my head, he bent down until his lips were almost touching mine.

"Don't think about it," he whispered. The heat from his mouth shot through my body and seared my heart. He was irresistible, and he knew it. Finally, he took my agony away with the kiss that I'd forgotten I'd been missing.

CHAPTER TWENTY TWO

When she was leaving for work on Thursday, Beau was sitting shirtless on her couch drinking a smoothie he'd made with all the remaining fruit in her kitchen. Her dream kitchen, that is. The one with the wrap-around marble counter top and stainless steel appliances. He'd asked if the fruit was organic, and without the store stickers there was no way for him to know she was lying.

"I'll be home at seven," she informed the empty sofa. "Will you still be here?" She tried not to sound anxious. The last two nights were incredible, as always, but she wanted to get back to normal. Most of all, she wanted him to be out of town by the time Joel rolled in.

"You haven't given me much time to relax," said the ghost of the rock star.

"Sorry." She noticed then he hadn't looked at his smartphone once since he'd arrived. Usually he was inundated with messages from agents and industry people.

"Where's your phone?"

"In my bag."

He'd only brought an expensive-looking messenger bag. He'd left plenty of stuff in the fantasy apartment before. She'd moved it all into the fictional second bedroom months ago, and it was still there waiting for him to claim it.

"It's been quiet." She crossed her arms and narrowed her eyes at him.

"I turned it off."

"Are you hiding out?"

"Kind of."

"Shouldn't you be doing that on some island somewhere with a beautiful blonde or two?"

He grinned at her. *"I like it here. No sand."*

"What if someone needs to reach you?"

"They can call my agent."

"What if it's an emergency?"

"My agent knows where I am. He has your number."

She rolled her eyes. The conversation was going nowhere, and she had to get to work.

"Well, you'd better find an island before tomorrow because I have plans."

The apparition stood up, his abs rolling and flexing and making his panther tattoo dance. He came so close she thought he was going to try to kiss her again. And he smelled good, like men's body wash after a hot shower.

"Don't worry, Lucy. Your boyfriend will never know I was here." He zipped his lip with two fingers and tossed the imaginary key.

"He's not my boyfriend." She resisted the urge to put her hand on his muscled chest. Work. She had to get to work.

When she turned for the door she reminded herself that Joel was better for her. Beau was trouble, and she didn't need that. Tomorrow, Joel would be here to remind her.

CHAPTER TWENTY THREE

In the morning, there were three notifications on her phone. They were all posts from Joel. The first was a picture of his luggage with the caption, *"Off to Omaha."* The second was a selfie from the plane with his thumb in the air. The third was a re-post from the show's website reminding everyone in Omaha to come on down to see the show. The sold-out show.

The picture from the plane had been posted at 8:05 a.m. The luggage in the first photo had been sitting on a bed whose comforter she recognized from a previous post. It was his bed, which meant he was coming from New York. All she had to do was find the flight around 8:00 from New York to Omaha. Easy.

She quickly showered and slipped into the clothes she'd set out the night before. Her phone blared music on her bathroom counter while she put on her makeup. There was a real possibility she would be face-to-face with Joel and she needed to look her best.

After a hasty breakfast and half a cup of coffee, she rushed out the door. She managed to dodge the friendly old lady and hop into the elevator. She sprinted out of the main doors and across the parking lot to her car.

She could be at the airport in twenty minutes, but her gas gauge was pointing at empty. She drove to the gas station down the street. The service bell dinged when she pulled up to the full-service pump. The usual attendant was immediately at her window and he took her debit card with a smile. Her finger drummed on the steering wheel, willing him to somehow pump the gas faster.

Being in her mid-twenties, there were plenty of things she hadn't done. She hadn't been in a relationship. She hadn't left the country, although her parents had plenty of times without her. She hadn't skied down a snowy mountain. She hadn't paid her own bills. And she hadn't pumped her own gas. Ever. No one had ever taught her how. She figured maybe it was something people assumed everyone knew how to do and now she was embarrassed to ask anyone. So she'd only ever used the full-service pump. She didn't see anything wrong with it. After all, what was it there for if people weren't supposed to use it?

Finally her tank was full and she raced cautiously for the airport while watching out for speed traps. She didn't need a speeding ticket. That was another thing she'd never done. She'd never had a ticket.

The parking lot of the Best Western down the road from the airport allowed a great view of the planes landing and taking off. She was using the airline's app to track Joel's flight. She could see it was getting close. While she waited she scrolled through photos she had saved from his Twitter feed. She paused on one from a professional photo shoot in his apartment. He was sitting on a wooden bench next to a large colonial-style window with white trim. The walls around him were brick. The ceiling had to be ten feet high.

Another photo showed a black grand piano in front of the same window. He had captioned it, *Finally got this baby tuned today.* This was the photo that had prompted her to look into his brief musical career. It's how she had discovered the song he'd performed on the fundraising CD which she'd listened to at least a hundred times by now. That only left her wishing there were more of these musical inspirations she could carry with her and fill her car with the sounds of his voice.

A jet roared overhead, prompting her to check the airline app. Joel had arrived, but it would still be a while before the passengers were deplaned. She continued to browse his Twitter photos, including one taken from his kitchen floor when he was so exhausted from the day he had declared dramatically he may never move from it. She gazed at the dark cabinets and recessed lighting, imagining strolling up to the counter while he made their breakfast.

The phone buzzed. His plane had officially arrived. She started her car and headed out of the hotel's parking lot. She took her time driving the long road past the airport's employee parking lot, to the frustration of a car behind her who swooped around her left side to get ahead.

She pulled up to the curb in front of the airline sign directly behind American Airlines. Ahead of her were a Smart Car and a large, black SUV. She had expected to see a limo. Joel obviously wasn't being picked up in a smart car. Her hands gripped the steering wheel; one more tightly than the other. She adjusted several times until all fingers on both hands were spread evenly and touching the hard plastic with the exact same intensity. Her nerves seemed to be getting the better of her.

When Joel came out the door, she would have missed him had it not been for the photographer who busted out of the doors first. He was snapping shots of him while a large, bald man ushered Joel to the SUV. Joel wore a newsboy cap and thick-rimmed glasses. His coat collar was popped up, and he was clutching it around him to partially cover his face.

She sat up straight in her seat. Blood was rushing in her ears, the sound even louder than the jet engines on the other side of the building. Her palms began to shake and sweat. She couldn't blow this opportunity. She couldn't lose him.

When the SUV pulled from the curb, she was right behind it. Her heart pounded with the realization Joel was right there in that car, in the flesh. If only she could do something to make the car stop and wait for her. Maybe the tire would blow out and she would have to stop and help them. If only she had magical powers, she could pop the tire. She giggled at her foolishness.

Joel's car pulled into the driveway of the downtown Hilton. Lucy passed it and headed for the parking garage. She couldn't leave her car on the curb while she chased after a celebrity.

After she parked she rushed into the hotel, but he had clearly bypassed the front desk and gone up to his room. She sat down in the lobby, pulled up the hotel's website on her phone and searched for photos of their most expensive rooms. The two-room suite was gorgeous with plush carpet and floor-to-ceiling windows. She imagined him up there right now getting settled and waiting for her to arrive.

CHAPTER TWENTY FOUR
Omaha - Present

Joel Ruskin wants nothing to do with the stalker case. Quote: Don't give that lunatic any more publicity.

The text made Elijah hyperventilate for a second. Interviewing the victim of the crime would add depth to his story. Now he was going to have to do without it. If Lucy didn't give him enough, he'd have to dramatize the events of that night. It was disappointing, but not unheard of. Unless he could find another way to get that information.

At this moment, however, he was sitting in a beat-up office chair in the security room of the Downtown Hilton. The cast of *Hometown Star* had been put up here when they came to town for auditions. Elijah had a good feeling Miss Bonneville would show up on their security footage.

A young woman named Su had found the archived footage for him. Now she was manning the controls while he navigated. They'd already been through two days of black and white video sped up to three times speed. He knew the date that Joel had checked in, but he wanted to make sure Lucy hadn't entered the hotel ahead of time for some reason. She was clearly capable of the oddest behavior.

Finally her image appeared on one of the four

sections of the screen. The camera, focused on the front doors, caught her face clearly. Elijah got a rush like he'd won a round of Keno.

"That's her." He thrust his pointed finger at the screen, lifting himself from his chair.

Su gave him an irritated side glance and reversed the video a few seconds. She played it back in real time. They watched together as Lucy entered the lobby. Instead of approaching the desk, she took a seat on one of the guest couches. The only camera viewing her was above her and behind her head. She sat and fidgeted for a long time.

After almost a half hour, Lucy stood up and walked off the right side of the screen. Su hit some keys and switched to a view of the elevator doors. It was clear she'd done this for people many times. Elijah's writer mind could imagine what kind of incriminating information hotel cameras held.

An elevator opened and Lucy stepped in. Su changed the image again to a screen filled with about a dozen nearly identical images of elevator doors. One of those images showed movement, so she hit some more buttons and the four-square screen came back.

This time the cameras focused on hallways on one floor of the hotel. Lucy walked slowly past the room doors. She paused in front of several. At a few she pressed her ear to the door for several minutes. Then she got back onto the elevator and tried another floor.

"Seems like your lady is looking for someone," Su said.

"Yes, she is."

"Is she gonna find him?" By her sly grin she assumed he knew something was about to happen.

He didn't know. The story he was telling only had an end. So far there was no beginning and no middle. Lucy probably wasn't going to tell him everything. He needed to fill in the blanks.

It was obvious she was searching for Joel Ruskin's room. Did she actually make contact with Joel in that hotel? Did she get into his room somehow? What was her plan? The intent of a psycho stalker couldn't be to just say, "Hello, how are you?"

Nothing happened. Lucy didn't find anything. She took the elevator down to the first floor and planted herself back in the lobby.

Su sped up the video again. Lucy barely moved. Then something finally did happen. A familiar form appeared on the monitor.

CHAPTER TWENTY FIVE

I pulled up to the VIP lot at the arena and handed
the attendant my pass. She was pleasant and wished me a
good evening.

"How much did that cost you?" my mom asked from
the passenger seat. She still didn't know why I had asked
her to go with me to the taping of a nationally televised
talent show. I hadn't told her everything was free–the
tickets, the parking, even the sweater I was wearing–
courtesy of the guy that I hadn't told her I'd been seeing
for two months.

I didn't answer her, but pulled into a spot and killed
the engine.

"This is kind of far from the door, Lucy." She
motioned to all of the empty parking spots beyond the
fence and closer to the main entrance. "You couldn't have
picked one of those?"

"We're not going in that door, Mom." We got out and
started toward the back of the building where several
large buses and trailers were parked. "We're going this
way."

She looked thoroughly confused when I handed her a
lanyard and had her put it around her neck. I flashed mine
at the guard and he let us pass.

"Is Beau one of the judges?" She was whispering

loudly enough for anyone to hear. Her excitement when she said Beau's name was a little annoying. She'd enjoyed telling people her daughter was dating a celebrity. She'd been disappointed when I'd told her I wouldn't be seeing him anymore. She'd never given up hope we would reconcile.

"No, Mom."

We walked through hallways and past busy people who paid us no attention. Everyone was working at a seemingly frantic pace. Their movements were automatic, like they'd done all of this a hundred times before. I realized that in every city they had to build a set and then pack it up and move on. It was like a traveling circus.

We came to another door that was blocked by a muscular woman with a clipboard. I showed her my lanyard, but she asked for my name. After checking me off of the list, she opened the door and let us through. Now we were walking down another long hallway. This one had significantly less activity going on. I could hear the faint sound of the audience filing into the arena above us. Mom had a grip on my upper arm now as if I might lose her. She was grinning and looking around like a child in a toy store.

The white doors were all labeled with computer generated paper signs. I glanced around until I found Joel's name. I knocked on the door and then looked at my mom who was still utterly confused. The door was opened by Tracy. She smiled, as usual, and motioned for us to come in, all the while having a conversation with someone through the Bluetooth in her ear.

Joel stood up from a long, leather couch and hugged

me. I introduced him to my mom, who was suddenly speechless.

"I saw you fill in for that morning show host a few months back," she said, finally. "You are funny, Mr. Ruskin."

"Joel," he corrected graciously. He put his arm around her shoulder, which made her smile even wider. "You have to call me Joel."

The two of them continued with small talk for a few minutes. Then Tracy politely interrupted to say, "Ten minutes, Joel."

"I'm happy to have met you finally," he said to my mom. He was laying on the charm pretty thick. "I hope you enjoy the show." He looked at me and said, "I'll see you later?"

"Yes," I replied. "If you're up for it."

Joel winked at me. He shook my mom's hand and then kissed my cheek. We were gently rushed out the door by Tracy. On our way back down the long hallway, Mom began her twenty questions.

"You know Joel Ruskin?"

"Yes."

"How long have you known him?"

"A few months."

"How did you meet him?"

"At a party." I continued to stare straight ahead.

"And he invited you to come to the taping?"

"Yes."

"What did he mean when he said he'd see you later?"

"He meant he'd see both of us after the show."

"Is there an after-party?"

130

We were about to walk into the arena to find our seats. I didn't want to have this conversation with her in there. I stopped walking and turned to her.

"Mom, Joel and I are kind of seeing each other."

She looked stunned. Then spoke. "For how long?"

"It's been like two months, but we've only been on a couple dates. His schedule is crazy."

"Is it serious?"

"Not yet." I sighed like a teenager and rolled my eyes. "We haven't had a chance to get to know each other that well. We'll see how it goes."

"Do you have to give Beau back the apartment?"

I narrowed my eyes at her question. Then I sighed deeply again. She loved my apartment. I wondered if she was comparing Joel and Beau in her mind. Which one did she prefer I date? Not that it mattered.

"No, it's mine." I pushed a heavy door open and walked into the roaring arena. We found our seats in a VIP area with a clear view of the stage.

After a long wait, the lights dimmed and the music boomed. When Joel came onstage he seemed bigger than life. He was not the same man who'd walked with me in Central Park and had brushed my hair from my face before kissing me good morning. The crowd loved him. He even leaned down a few times to shake hands with the audience. I relished my good fortune that I wasn't one of those girls smashed up against the stage trying to get noticed by him. I had him already; at least I had him for now.

My mom enjoyed the show. She kept telling me how cute and talented he was. I could tell she was over the moon that he and I were dating. She asked me a million questions whenever there was a lull in the show.

Although watching Joel work onstage was impressive, I couldn't wait for the show to end. I wanted him to transform back into the regular guy I had been getting to know. It was like onstage he was Superman, but I really wanted to be with Clark Kent.

After the show, my mom and I made our way down to a large room where everyone from the show was mingling and congratulating each other on a job well done. The contestants who had been chosen to move on were posing for pictures with the celebrity judges and with Joel. Mom and I hung back to watch all the action and also to grab some free food. She was star-struck and nervous and couldn't stop herself from chattering on and on.

When the photos were done, everyone quickly dispersed. Joel put his arm around me and asked my mom how she'd enjoyed the show. She gushed at him about his performance. She even gave her opinion on a few of the contestants. Joel was amused. It was going well. Then she gave her opinion of us.

"You two look great together," she said.

I covered my face with my hand. Joel buried his head in my shoulder and laughed. Then he said, "I know I look better with Lucy standing next to me."

I shot him a smile. It was great that my mom approved, but I didn't want Joel to think I was taking whatever thing this was too seriously. I changed the subject.

"We'd better go and let you wrap it up."

"Sorry we can't have more time," he mumbled into my ear. "But I'm beat."

"I understand." And I did.

Joel kissed me square on the lips for everyone to see. Nobody was paying attention, but Mom seemed tickled. Blushing, I let her lead me out of the star-filled room.

CHAPTER TWENTY SIX
Omaha - 2015

Lucy fished a granola bar from her purse and sat down on a stiff loveseat where she had a good view of both the hotel elevators and the front door.

The cushion under her was uneven. She could feel that one of her sitting bones was sinking lower than the other. She shifted and pressed the higher cheek into the cushion until both were even. But the back of her hand had brushed against the coarse fabric of the armrest. She reached around with her other hand and swiped the back of it where she'd made contact with the first. It wasn't right. She'd swiped too high. She had to do it again, but now she needed an extra swipe on the other hand.

While alternately swiping the backs of her hands, Lucy noticed an old man eyeing her from across the lobby. As much as the flesh of her neglected hand burned from wanting, she had to stop. She smiled at the man and turned her focus to the large windows on her left.

The show's venue was right across the street. She could see a small crowd had gathered, even though the show was still three hours away. It seemed silly they would be waiting there so early. The tickets were for assigned seating, and the show was sold out. Either you had a ticket or you didn't. She didn't have a ticket. She'd found a seller online, but the guy wanted six hundred dollars for two tickets, and she knew her mom wouldn't agree to that.

Her phone chimed. It was Joel. *Getting close to show time,* he posted. *Are you ready, Omaha?* She clenched her teeth. How frustrating it was that he was somewhere right above her and practically talking right to her, but she couldn't reach him.

The granola bar hadn't been enough. Lucy was hungry. Skipping lunch had been a mistake. She was afraid to leave her seat in case Joel was on his way out.

A crowd of girls had gathered outside and were peering in through the wall of glass. One of them had ventured in earlier and approached the desk, but the desk clerk had asked her to leave. Lucy had scoffed at her rookie mistake. What made her think the woman would give her any information? She was too obvious. Now the girl stood outside in the cold with her friends while Lucy sat casually on the sofa, her behind sore from sitting too long.

Then the black SUV pulled up. Behind it came two more exactly like it. The crowd of girls was parted by two large men dressed all in black. Her chest fluttered with excitement. The desk clerk eyed her when she stood up and inched forward. She seemed to know what she was up to.

An elevator dinged and out stepped a woman with a headset, a cameraman, and a boom operator who all seemed to be tethered to each other. The camera stayed trained on the elevator as its operator walked backward through the lobby. As if on cue, Asia Simon, the show's only female judge, walked out of the elevator in front of her bodyguard. From another elevator came the rest of her entourage.

Lucy had never been a fan of Asia Simon, but here she was in real life. She looked as much like a Barbie in person as she did in magazines. The impossible heels she walked on made a hard clicking sound which was muffled by all the fuss going on around her.

The girls outside the window were going nuts while the two large men did their best to keep them away from the doors. The camera crew were already on the other side getting every possible shot of Asia walking to the first SUV. She stopped and politely greeted a few of the fans. Then she climbed into the tall vehicle, pulling her mile-long legs in last. The car took off around the corner to the arena across the street.

The scene repeated itself when the other two judges entered the lobby. This time the camera stayed outside and filmed them interacting with the crowd of fans that was growing larger by the minute. They climbed into the second SUV and were off.

That left Joel Ruskin, but the crowd didn't seem to care. Most of them ran across the busy street, dodging cars and giggling. Only two middle-aged women remained. They were both dressed like they'd borrowed their clothes from their teenage daughters. She was embarrassed for them.

The camera crew had come back into the lobby and were now trained on the elevator doors. She stepped even closer, keeping her eye on the desk clerk who was keeping her eye on the two ladies who had crept in the door.

When Joel stepped off of the elevator it was as if

Jesus himself walked on water. Her chest tightened and she thought she would stop breathing forever. He was also followed by a large man in black, but there was no entourage trailing him. He had clearly shaved since arriving on the plane that morning. Now he wore a dark gray suit and a light blue tie. He was smiling.

She stepped quickly forward, but was blocked by the boom operator who was trying to keep up with the camera. She was so close. She'd gotten too far to let him slip out the door.

"Joel," she called. His name fell out of her mouth. She hadn't thought about it. Her brain knew she needed him to notice her. Maybe he would stop and talk to her. Maybe he would shake her hand. More than anything, she needed him to know she existed in this world.

Amazingly, Joel heard her and paused. He turned partway around and waved in her direction. At first he didn't see who he was waving to, but when she waved back he noticed. His smile was warm and infectious, his glance sending laser beams through her body. He had seen her. He had noticed her. She was part of his world now. And then he walked on.

CHAPTER TWENTY SEVEN

Lucy crossed the street to the auditorium. She didn't have a plan. Should she wait here for hours and meet him again in the hotel? Should she wait by the back doors? Or should she go home and be happy that she'd actually made contact?

A group of five women and an eager-looking man rounded the building. They were chatting excitedly. Out in front of the small crowd was a middle-aged woman in a double-x Joel Ruskin t-shirt. She eyed Lucy who was perched awkwardly on a large, concrete planter. The other four stopped walking when she stopped and waited silently for further instruction.

"Couldn't get tickets, either?" the woman asked Lucy.

"No," she answered. "They sold out, like immediately."

"Are you waiting for somebody?"

"No. Just thinking about what to do next."

"Are you a big fan of the show?" The woman's questioning tone bordered on interrogation.

"I'm a fan of Joel Ruskin." Lucy chuckled nervously. She couldn't figure out this woman's motives. "I watch it because he's on."

The woman relaxed and stepped closer to her. She introduced herself and her group. "I'm Belinda. I'm the head of the Joel Ruskin Fan Club, *Joel on the Brain*." She pointed to the individuals that had followed her over. "That's Tammy, Lindsey, Carol, and Miles." She sized her up again, more obviously this time. "Have you ever met Joel Ruskin?"

"I just met him about an hour ago." Lucy grinned from ear to ear and blushed a little. It was an exaggeration, but she didn't want to feel like a loser.

"I've met him seven times," Belinda informed her. "The first time was accidental."

"It was fate," Miles interjected. Belinda rolled her eyes, but let a tiny grin creep up the corners of her mouth.

"We've become friends," she continued, "and he says hi to me whenever he's in town."

"Then why couldn't he get you tickets for the show?" Her question was innocent. She asked it without thinking and certainly without malice. Belinda scowled at her impertinence.

"That's not how it works," she grumbled. Belinda quickly pushed her annoyance aside and composed herself once again. She proceeded to carry on a long, one-sided conversation with Lucy while the rest of the tiny fan club talked quietly amongst themselves. She told her about how she had met Joel Ruskin several years ago in New York when he hosted a show that featured her previous favorite celebrity. She had been waiting outside in the crowd and when Joel came out instead of who she was expecting, he had been gracious and talked to her and her small group of friends.

"He was just starting to get famous then. Not many people in the crowd knew who he was. But I could see he was going to be a big deal. He's so talented."

The others nodded. A tall, awkward woman around Lucy's age spoke up.

"We're having a party later," she said. "You should come."

"Tammy," Belinda scolded. Then she shrugged her shoulders dramatically and sighed. "We're having a get-together in my room after the show," she admitted reluctantly. "I emailed Joel this morning and invited him."

"He said he'd try to come," Tammy blurted. Belinda gave her the stink eye again and she shrunk away.

"I know he'll come," Belinda continued. "He appreciates all of his fans, but he knows how important fan clubs like ours are to his career. Anyway, you can come if you want to."

"Sure," she beamed. She couldn't believe her luck in running into people with connections to Joel Ruskin. This was what she needed to get close to him so he could see they were made for each other.

Instead of waiting outside the venue for several hours, the fan club agreed to meet at a café down the street. Lucy joined them. They ate at a large, round table and talked the whole time. The conversation never strayed from Joel Ruskin. Belinda's devotion was impressive. She knew every detail of his life. She even claimed he'd told her to give him a shout if she was ever in New York.

"I'm saving for a plane ticket," Belinda told her. "I'll probably stay at his place. He has plenty of room."

"Really?" She couldn't help the smile that crossed

her face. Was this woman for real?

"Not like that," Belinda said, her cheeks turning pink. "I have no interest in Joel romantically. I could be his mother."

Lucy stifled a laugh. Obviously Joel would have no interest in Belinda either. Had he really offered to put her up in his home? It was doubtful.

After a few hours the group made their way back to the event center. Belinda was silent as she marched ahead toward the back entrance where several large trailers were parked. When she stopped, the rest of them gathered around her as if she were going to make a speech. She turned to Lucy and gave her a serious look.

"When Joel comes out," she instructed sternly, "I don't want you to make a scene. He's like any other person, and he doesn't deserve to be harassed. He'll stop and talk to me because he knows me, but don't try to get in his face if he doesn't notice you. That's just the way things work. Celebrities are people, too."

She was a bit offended by Belinda's accusatory tone. She'd encountered Joel a few hours ago and hadn't gone all psycho-fan on him. What made Belinda think she was going to freak out now? And who did she think she was, the queen of celebrity etiquette?

From around the other side of the building came the sounds of people filing out of the huge building. The traffic began to pick up as people were leaving. Her heart started beating faster as her moment drew getting closer. She would be respectful and not try to draw Joel's attention from Belinda, but she wanted to make sure he noticed her again. She tried to position herself closer to the fan club leader, but Tammy and Miles flanked her like two eager lap dogs.

Finally, after almost an hour, two large men exited the back doors followed by two of the judges, another man in black, and then Joel Ruskin. He didn't keep his head down the way the other two had. Instead, he waved to the crowd that had formed beyond the temporary barricades that hadn't been guarded when the fan club had arrived. He almost walked right by Lucy and her new friends, but Belinda called out his name enthusiastically and raised her hand above her head.

Joel turned and smiled his stage smile. He recognized her for sure, but he didn't seem a hundred percent happy about it. Then Belinda handed her bulky Nikon to Lucy so she could take a picture of the group. But that wasn't fair. Maybe it had only been a few hours, but wasn't she part of the group now, too? She wanted to protest, to be included in the picture, but they were all posing around Joel now, and she didn't want him to think she was a crybaby. She snapped a few pics and tried to hide her disappointment.

Clearly in a hurry to get away, Joel shook the hands of all of the members of the fan club. He turned toward Lucy and she was sure it was her turn for physical contact. Belinda reached out and touched his arm to get his attention.

"Joel," she gushed. "Don't forget about our little get-together. Room 209. We're headed over there now."

Joel nodded his head quickly. He was walking away and waved back at her. She had no chance now unless she tackled him. She was sure his muscle men wouldn't allow that to get far.

The crowd dispersed but the fan club stayed. They were all awaiting Belinda's next move. She was watching Joel walk away as if he might turn around one more time. But he didn't and soon he was out of sight.

"Well, I guess we'll head over," Belinda sighed. "I'd hate for Joel to get there before we do."

Having had more of a pep in her step when Joel was around, Belinda now put her arm on Tammy's shoulder and walked laboriously toward the street. Lucy hadn't noticed Miles had slipped away, but now he was pulling a car up to the curb where the others stood. Tammy helped Belinda into the front seat, then took out her phone and turned back to her.

"I'll friend you on Facebook," she said. "Then I can send you an invite to the fan club page. It's a closed group. We like to weed out the fair-weather fans." Lucy helped her find her profile and within seconds they were friends.

"Tammy, come on." Belinda's arm hung out the open window. She slapped the outside of the door one time like she was summoning an unruly animal. Tammy quickly got into the back seat and waved at Lucy. Everyone else went presumably to their own cars. She stood alone on the sidewalk in front of the arena.

CHAPTER TWENTY EIGHT

Room 209 was a double queen, non-smoking room with dated furniture and not enough working light fixtures. The group assembled inside and immediately produced piles and piles of well-loved scrapbooks. The members had spread them out on the two beds for display.

The albums all contained photographs, articles, and other Joel Ruskin memorabilia. There were even printouts of emails between the members discussing Joel or recapping their fan encounters with the star.

Most of the Joel snapshots–there seemed to be hundreds of them–were so similar she wasn't absolutely sure they weren't mostly duplicates. Some were candid shots of Joel signing autographs at meet-and-greets or at events. She saw pictures of Joel with the group or with individuals from the group, including people she hadn't met. In every one of these Joel's pose and expression were the same: standing straight, stage smile, one hand in his pocket and the other around the shoulder of the lucky fan. Nearly every photo was at a meet-and-greet or outside the back exit of a venue.

Belinda had acted as if she and Joel were friends, but none of these pictures were the casual kind you would take with a friend. They were all staged. In all of them Joel was clearly obligated.

She moved toward the dresser where an object had caught her eye. It was a large, rectangular vase. She picked it up carefully. Every side of the ceramic pottery featured multiple pictures of Joel Ruskin that had been apparently cut out of magazines. There was a glossy seal painted over the pictures, giving it a smooth finish and keeping the pictures safe.

"I made that," Tammy said. She kind of sneaked up on her, causing her to almost drop the gaudy vase.

"It's nice." She set it back gently onto the dresser. Next to where it had been was a gift basket stuffed with snacks and four glass bottles of orange soda.

"What's this?" Lucy asked, motioning to the basket.

"That's for Joel." She touched each item in the basket without disturbing the careful arrangement. Lucy nodded but said nothing.

"He needs his Goody pop," Belinda said from her spot on the edge of the bed. Everyone in the room laughed. Lucy didn't get the joke, but grinned politely.

Tammy leaned toward her as if to share secret information. She spoke at full volume when she said, "It's a joke between us and Joel."

"Between *me* and Joel," Belinda corrected.

"Right," Tammy conceded. "Back when MySpace was a thing, Joel had put up a picture of himself drinking a can of Orange Crush and the caption said he needed his Orange Crush. Then Belinda commented that Orange Crush isn't as good as Orange Goody. He actually replied and told her he'd love to try it someday."

Lucy looked in Belinda's direction, but Belinda was staring off at the opposite wall as if she wasn't paying any attention to the conversation wherein she was the subject. Miles was leafing noisily through a ragged scrap book. He finally found the page he was looking for and thrust it toward Lucy and Tammy.

"Here it is," he said, pointing at a printout of a screenshot which was protected by a plastic sheet. Sure enough, there was the grainy picture of Joel with the orange soda and his and Belinda's subsequent back and forth.

"So right after that," Tammy went on, "Joel was hosting the Miss Teen Chicago Pageant. Belinda knew somebody who worked at the center and she had her put four six-packs of Goody pop in his dressing room." Everyone laughed again.

"Now we do that any chance we get," Miles told her. "If we can get Orange Goody to Joel, we do it."

"What does he think of all that pop?" Lucy asked.

"He loves it," Tammy said, but she didn't seem sure. "I bet."

"He sent a thank you card," Miles said. He flipped a few more pages of the scrapbook and, sure enough, there was a hand-written note from Joel Ruskin and an envelope addressed to Belinda. The writing on the envelope was not the same as the writing on the card, so it had clearly been addressed by someone else.

"He has your address?" Lucy asked Belinda.

"Of course he does," she replied peevishly. "I send him gifts all the time from the fan club."

Belinda turned away, indicating the story was over, and everyone went back to their small talk. Lucy couldn't think of anything to say to anyone. Many thoughts and emotions were churning inside her brain. Joel had clearly recognized the group, or at least Belinda, outside the arena. But how did he really feel about her and the soda and the fan club?

A knock at the door signaled the arrival of pizza. The boxes were stacked onto the desk in the corner. Belinda reminded everyone to refrain from touching photo albums with their greasy pizza hands. Miles lifted the lid of one of the pizza boxes and was immediately scolded by the leader.

"Not until Joel gets here," she bellowed. His face fell and he stepped away from the food.

Not until Joel gets here? Lucy was sure there was no way in hell Joel intended to come to this shindig. What would his reaction be if he walked into this hotel room and was greeted by piles of pictures and delivery? Where would he even sit?

Finally, after fifteen minutes or so, Belinda apparently got hungry and gave the go-ahead to dig into the pizza. The fan club members swarmed around the desk. One by one they each found a place to stand with their backs to the wall so they could eat their slices without endangering the memorabilia. Lucy ate hers outside the bathroom door.

A tall woman approached her. She had a wild mane of dark curls and wore men's double-bar glasses. Her t-shirt was clearly home-made. In the center was a picture of herself with Joel. It was bordered with a shiny gold ribbon. Above that, his name was embroidered in large letters.

"How long have you been a Joel Ruskin fan?" the

woman asked her.

"Oh, a while," she fibbed. What would this group do to her if they found out she was newly obsessed? She was sure they wouldn't think her worthy of their celebratory pizza. Why should she care? She was the one destined to be with Joel, not any of them.

"I'm Barb." She wiped her free hand on her high-waisted jeans and stuck it out for her to shake. "I've met Joel twenty-seven times. All of my pictures are over there in the blue binder." She motioned toward one of the beds. "They're all dated and in order. I made this shirt myself."

Lucy nodded and told her it was very good. Technically it was. Everything was neatly placed and stitched well. She'd literally never seen anything like it. And Barb seemed to be a genuinely nice person.

She told her the name of the small South Dakota town she'd come from. Her heart went out to her. Barb probably didn't have anyone in that small town to share her Joel obsession with. But neither did Lucy, and she was constantly surrounded by people.

"Have you met Joel?" Barb asked.

"A couple of times." Her face turned a little pink. She suddenly felt underqualified to be there. These people all seemed to be fan warriors, devoting so much of their time and money to following this man around middle-America.

Silently she scolded herself for thinking that way. They had no idea the connection Lucy had with him. They didn't know the truth that lived only in her mind. If they knew the intimate moments she'd spent with him, that she was his only true love, would they be jealous?

Tell them, her alter-ego screamed inside her head, wanting to be recognized. *Tell them who you are. You're that mystery girl seen with Joel Ruskin. You're probably in one of these pictures.*

She inconspicuously scanned the nearest splay of candid shots. None of them showed Joel with an unknown female. There was no scene she could imagine herself into.

What if they did know? Would they be astonished? Would they kick her out or would they treat her like royalty? Because they ought to. If Joel was their king, Lucy would soon be their queen.

A while passed and everyone became absorbed in their conversations. The pizza boxes were now empty and piled next to the tiny waste basket. Then a cell phone chimed a notification. Miles pulled his from his pocket. Another phone alerted and then another. Lucy's phone beeped, too. She took it out and swiped the screen. It was a Twitter notification from Joel. Every face in the room dropped as they viewed the same photo she was seeing. Mutual high speed disappointment. Joel and his crew were gathered around a table in a contemporary restaurant. *Swanky eats with the crew. Thanks, Omaha!*

"Well," Belinda said angrily, breaking the disappointed silence. "I guess Joel had a better offer." She slammed down the framed photo she'd been holding, not at all hiding her anger at the star's supposedly insensitive behavior.

The others stared at her as if awaiting instruction. Lindsey began nervously tidying up the room. Tammy gathered the photo albums into a few piles. Belinda put her hand to her forehead and closed her eyes.

"I'm tired," she said breathlessly. "Everyone please go."

The others looked at each other questioningly. Belinda waved her hand dismissively and leaned back onto the headboard of the bed where she sat. Everything on the beds was claimed by the owners. Quietly they all retreated into the hallway. All except Tammy who stayed behind to tend to Belinda in her agony.

Outside the room the group muttered to each other, unsure of where to go next. She didn't know these people. They didn't know her, so they didn't invite her to tag along wherever they were going. In fact, nobody seemed to notice when she turned and walked down the hall to the elevator.

CHAPTER TWENTY NINE

OMAHA, NE—Joel Ruskin, who was in Omaha this week filming auditions for the upcoming program Hometown Star, was admitted to an area hospital shortly before noon today. He'd just finished an interview with our morning crew. It's reported the TV personality is suffering from a severe case of food poisoning. "Joel started feeling sick on set before the interview," a producer reported. "He's a true professional. He finished the show, and then we consulted the medic."

Lucy read the news story online right before her shift ended. She couldn't believe her luck. Joel's stay in Omaha had been extended by, no doubt, the hands of fate. It was unfortunate that fate hadn't told her which hospital had taken him in. There were at least ten major hospitals in town which meant she'd have to check them all until she found him. He could recover and be released by then. How frustrating she was again so close yet so far away.

She began with the hospital closest to home. As she parked in the garage, she rehearsed what she was going to say. She had bought a large bouquet of daisies in a vase and had requested a white delivery box to keep it steady in her car. Delivered flowers always came with a white box. A white cotton shirt and black pants were generic enough that she didn't have to explain she was simply there to do her job.

As soon as she killed the engine, her phone chimed. Finally, it was a post from Joel.

Guess I'm staying in Omaha. #badfish

Perfect. He was comfortable enough to use social media, but not well enough to go home. This bought her more time, although she might arouse suspicion by trying to deliver flowers in the middle of the night. It was already eight o'clock.

When she reached the passenger door to retrieve the flowers, her phone chimed again. She sighed heavily and considered not even looking. Joel was slowing down her hunt with his posting. But she did look, and she was glad she did. This time he had posted a selfie from his hospital bed. He was wearing a light blue gown with tiny geometric shapes. His hair was sticking up in places. He looked tired, but not sick. And he was grinning. There was no caption.

She studied the photo harder for clues. Amazingly, in the corner of the picture was the only evidence she needed to find Joel. On the tray beside his bed was a burgundy folder. Only the edge of it was visible, but on it was the hospital's logo in white. It was unmistakable. She had been there before. And she could be there again in ten minutes.

Ignoring the posted speed limit, Lucy rushed through scattered traffic. If ever she had a reason to risk getting a ticket, this was it. Joel was waiting for her. Destiny was holding him, so she couldn't be late.

Despite the cold outside, Lucy was sweating when

she entered the hospital. The flowers were heavy and obstructed her vision on one side. She had to move quickly. A posted sign told her visiting hours were almost over. When she got to the desk, however, nobody was there. She set the box on the counter and waited. Finally, a guard approached the desk. He looked to be in his seventies and, judging by his slow pace and his wide girth, probably not effective as security.

"Receptionist went to get something." The chair groaned as she sat down with a huff. "Can I help you?"

"I have a delivery for a patient. Joel Ruskin."

The guard waited patiently for the computer to wake up. He tilted his head back and peered through his bifocals. With one finger he typed in his password. Then he looked at her.

"Who again?"

"Ruskin. R-U-S-K-I-N."

His finger clicked the keys one at a time. R. U. S. K. I. N.

"Joel." Her heel tapped impatiently on the tile. She tried to be calm. She resisted reaching over the desk and turning the screen to get a better look.

The guard leaned closer to the screen. His eyebrows went up. He looked at her and then at the screen again.

"Says 'no visitors', ma'am."

"I'm just delivering." She had hoped the outfit would have been enough. She regretted not somehow fabricating a name tag.

"I can take it for you," he said slowly.

She couldn't argue. What would she even say? At least she was in the right hospital. The guard had confirmed he was there. There was still hope she could find him. Maybe she could pass as kitchen staff, grab a tray from a room, and wander the hospital undetected.

She slid the box a few inches toward him to signify her defeat. He pulled a sticky note from the drawer and slowly wrote a number on it, 619. Then he stuck the note to the box and waved her away.

Could it be real? Could he really be that absent minded? The guard, without realizing it, had given her Joel Ruskin's room number. She thanked him sincerely and headed back toward the parking garage as if she were leaving. Instead of going through the automatic sliding doors, she took the elevator up and scurried through the lobby's second floor to the hospital's main elevators.

The sixth floor was buzzing. People were leaving their loved ones for the night. Nurses were checking their rounds. The two nurses at the main desk barely acknowledged her presence. She walked with purpose and tried to act like she belonged there.

When she passed room 617 her heart began to flutter. Her neck was on fire from the nerves. She was almost to his room. This was the part she hadn't practiced. What would she say when she saw him? What would be her reason for walking into his room? Her legs were beginning to feel like Jell-O.

619. The door was slightly open. The hallway was virtually empty. She pushed the heavy door. The hospital bed came into view. Its back was raised slightly. Joel's messy hair covered the white pillow. He was facing the window, ignoring the barely audible TV. As she crept inside her heart was pounding out of control. Sweat

beaded on her forehead. She was afraid Joel could hear the thudding of her pulse which pounded in her ears.

Suddenly, the door hit something metal hiding behind it. There was a terrible screeching noise. Joel turned slowly. He looked straight at Lucy who was frozen in place. She was sure he'd be mad at her for sneaking into his room. If he yelled at her, she was sure she would cry. She didn't want him to see her cry.

"Hi," was all he said. It was a question, like, What are you doing here?

"Sorry," she said lamely. She took another step toward him, wondering what she would say next. He wasn't shouting at her to get out. He wasn't calling security. Did he recognize her from before? Was it okay because he knew her? Could it be he knew she was the one for him? That they were meant to be?

A voice from the doorway at her back halted everything.

"Can I help you?"

She turned to see the nurse. She wasn't just any nurse. She was a young and extremely beautiful nurse with brown, wavy hair and artificially tanned skin. Why was she a nurse? She could be a model. Lucy immediately hated this nurse for caring intimately for her Joel. She hated her for her Florence Nightingale ways.

"I was delivering flowers," she stammered. She looked around the room. There were balloons. There were a few gift bags, but there were no flowers. The nurse scowled and motioned for her to leave. Lucy turned, ashamed, and walked quickly down the hall. Joel didn't stop her. He let her go.

"Wait a minute," called the nurse who already had the phone in her hand. Lucy kept going. She pushed the elevator button a dozen times. It wasn't coming. She stepped back and scanned the area for a stairwell. When she spotted it she ran.

Holding the metal railing, she hopped down the stairs two at a time. Adrenaline propelled her forward and she laughed out loud, assuming she had escaped free and clear. Then she heard the loud clank of a door pushing open on the floor below. A security guard stepped into the stairwell and looked up at her.

"Hey," he shouted as he climbed the stairs toward her.

Lucy let out an involuntary yelp. Spinning around to retreat back up the stairs, she twisted her ankle and fell down hard. A concrete step bruised her thigh and sent blinding pain through her body.

The guard approached more slowly now. He simply stood over her for a minute and glared. When she attempted to get to her feet, he took her by her upper arm and didn't let go. Another guard emerged from the staircase above. The two escorted her down to the first floor without a word.

Before opening the stairwell door to a hospital full of patients and visitors, the guard released her. He folded his arms and glared at her again.

"You have any I.D. on you?" he asked.

Lucy pulled her wallet from her pocket and produced her driver's license. What did he need that for? He wasn't a cop. But she was too nervous to find the words to protest. She handed him the plastic card.

He read her name out loud. The other guard wrote it on a tiny notepad. They exchanged looks, then both stared at Lucy again.

"Are you a patient at this hospital, Lucy Bonneville?"

For a minute she thought of saying yes. But he'd be able to verify it wasn't true. So she told the truth.

"No."

"What are you doing here?"

Like a child, she looked at the floor and mumbled, "Visiting Joel."

"Visiting Joel Ruskin?" He chuckled. His colleague snorted. She hated the way he said Joel's name, like she shouldn't want to see him. If she could prove their relationship, he'd have a different attitude. But she couldn't. She had no proof.

"Well, Lucy Bonneville," he said, "I don't want to see you in this hospital again. You're banned for life. Unless you come in on a stretcher, don't ever show your face here again."

The other guard chimed in. "We'll be watching out for you. Trust me, you're not the first. We have a whole wall of banned individuals in the security office."

He then stepped around her and pushed the heavy door open. She turned and stepped out into the bustling lobby. A few people turned to look at her with curious faces, but most didn't notice the woman being ushered out by the guards. They watched her walk the long hallway to the parking garage.

Once inside her car she nearly had a nervous breakdown. Her arms and legs began to shake. The adrenaline from the experience was starting to wear off and if she weren't sitting in her car she would have fainted. She smiled before her emotions completely overtook her. Her hands went to her face to push back the tears that flowed.

Despite the outcome, she had come close to Joel. This time they'd been alone together. Surely fate had allowed things to fall into place so easily. She really was meant to be with him. The universe was giving her a sign to hold on. It wasn't the right time yet. Now her future with him was much more certain.

CHAPTER THIRTY
Omaha – November 2015

Black Friday, as always, was a nightmare. The mall had been open all night for stores that wanted to take advantage of the crazed shoppers. But Gobo's kept regular hours.

When Lucy got home that night she fell onto her couch and let the mail in her hand fall to the floor next to her. She had worked ten hours. She'd eaten two meals huddled in the back room of Gobo's. She'd gone to the bathroom only twice because it took so long to get there only to find maintenance couldn't keep up with the hectic traffic and general grossness of the shoppers.

The new issue of People magazine lay in the mail stack. It wasn't hers. The mail carrier must have put it in the wrong box. She snatched it up to check the address on the label. Then she began to flip through the pages.

She stopped on a page titled *New Couple Alert*. There were photos of four celebrity couples. Half of one of those couples was Joel Ruskin. He was posing at some kind of event with his arm around a woman who looked vaguely familiar. The article said her name was Michelle Bruin, and she was an actress on some show Lucy had never watched.

Her palms began to sweat. Her heart was racing, and she could feel her face flaming.

How could he do this to me? she thought. *She's not even that pretty. Her dress is disgusting. It looks cheap. What in the hell would he want with her?*

Her stomach dropped. She felt like she could vomit. Emitting a low, desperate wail, she fell onto the floor and rolled onto her back. Her chest heaved as she tried to catch her breath. Had all the air been sucked from the room?

He'd found someone. He was no longer available. She turned onto her side and slapped her hand on the magazine. She studied the smile on his face, which she now perceived as smug and mocking. He was looking right at her, like he was flaunting this woman only to upset her. It was a sickening display. She hated him. She had thought he was better than that; better than falling for a shallow, brainless actress. With this woman in the picture, there was no way she could make him love her.

"Why didn't you tell me you were seeing someone else, Joel?" The bare walls of the apartment echoed back at her.

Standing from the carpet, she tore the page out of the magazine and ripped it into pieces. Her eyes stung with tears. She didn't hold back. She'd read online that he would soon be in Las Vegas filming a Christmas special. She imagined arguing with him on the phone while he was in a hired car on his way to the airport.

"I'm not dating Michelle." He sounded annoyed. Was he annoyed he'd been caught cheating? *"It was a publicity thing, nothing more."*

"And why can't I be part of your publicity thing?" She paced around her apartment holding her phone in her

160

hand but not speaking into it. Instead she shouted at the empty air. "Am I too homely? Too middle-America?" Or had he been taking advantage of her the whole time? She wiped away a tear and tried not to let her voice quiver. Surely he could hear she was angry, but she wouldn't let him know she was devastated.

"Stop it, Lucy. You know none of that is true. Michelle and I have the same agent. Our agent thought it would be a good boost for her show to be seen with me. He wanted to get the media talking. I promise you it was nothing more than that."

She could barely get the next words out. "I think we're better off not seeing each other anymore, Joel. It's too hard to maintain this... well... this whatever it is, halfway across the country."

"Come on, Lucy," he pleaded. *"You know I don't want that. I miss you. I want to see you and keep seeing you. We can make this work."*

"I don't think so, Joel." An unintentionally loud sigh escaped her lips. "I can't do this anymore. I deserve someone who can be there for me all the time. You deserve someone, I don't know, someone who lives in your world."

Joel began to speak again, but she interrupted him. "Let's not drag this out, Joel. I've made up my mind."

He was quiet for a minute. Then he finally said, *"Okay. If that's what you want."* His voice was calm, but he sounded defeated. *"I'm at the airport now. I have to go."*

And that was the end of it. She tossed her phone onto the bed and threw herself face-first into her pillow. She cried uncontrollably for a half hour. Her heart was broken. Her head was pounding. She'd lost him and she was afraid she would never find happiness again.

CHAPTER THIRTY ONE

Her melancholy lasted through Christmas.
Although she was surrounded by family, Lucy's heart was numb. She didn't even have an imaginary boyfriend to give her a virtual gift under the glow of an outdoor Christmas tree. Every time she saw a couple enjoying their holiday hand- in-hand, she regretted deeply that Joel Ruskin had let her down. And he'd picked the worst time to do it.

As they did every year, her cousins and aunts and uncles gathered at her mom and dad's house to exchange gifts and eat all day. She wasn't in the mood for any of it. The others buzzed around laughing and speaking words that sounded like dull noise to her. She had moved from the couch in the formal living room because people wouldn't stop sitting down next to her and engaging her in conversation. Almost every adult had attempted to brighten her spirits. She only shrugged at them like a sullen teenager.

Soon she had retreated to the family room where her cousin's kids were watching a holiday special on TV. None of them had any interest in bothering her. She again sat in silence and watched the images on the screen without really seeing them. Until the program shifted to a shot of the Christmas tree at Rockefeller Center in New York.

Her stomach fluttered. Tears sprang to her eyes. She was supposed to be there with Joel in New York enjoying all the splendors of the holiday season. She wanted to sink into the couch cushions and suffocate herself. It wasn't only because Joel wasn't there for her on Christmas. It was because no man was. No man ever had been.

When all of the festivities were over, her only desire was to hunker down inside her apartment and wallow in her sorrow. She stopped by the grocery store on her way from her mom and dad's house and bought all the junk food she could anticipate wanting. Once comfortably in her pajamas, she threw her bedding onto her couch and settled in for the night.

Unable to help herself, she re-watched one of Joel's recent interviews on YouTube, imagining herself as the one he was talking to. She focused on him so intently that a hard knot formed in her stomach. She couldn't let him go, regardless of how he'd hurt her by being photographed with that woman. It didn't make sense that she could feel this way if he wasn't truly her destiny.

Her head went to her hands and she tried to shake the pain of yearning she was feeling for this man, this stranger. She knew him well. She knew he was the only one she wanted. If he'd only let her, she would dedicate her life to him. The feeling of frustration overtook her and she slumped down into a fetal position. How could something be fated yet impossible at the same time?

Joni sympathized with Lucy over her breakup. She and Leron took her out the weekend after and got her nice and drunk. They'd ended up at a nightclub downtown where both Joni and Leron picked up hot guys and Lucy had to get herself home in a Lyft. The next day she had a hangover so bad that Uncle Gordon had to take her shift at the store.

With a head full of rocks, she pulled herself to her couch. She turned on the TV but found nothing good to watch. Then, as if by fate, she spotted Joel Ruskin's name in the description of an afternoon talk show. Although she was still mad at him, she selected the program anyway. She would at least like to hear what he had to say. And maybe she had a longing to see his smile again.

The show was already well underway. A woman in workout gear was demonstrating how to make a smoothie to ease a hangover. She chuckled at the coincidence.

"Antioxidants are key," the woman was saying. She had shoved a few bananas and strawberries and even carrots into a blender. The result was a pinkish goop the host praised as delicious.

After the commercial break it was finally Joel's turn. The host, Lauri Rock, introduced him and ushered him to the guest couch. He smiled and waved at the camera. Lucy's heart melted as if he had been seeing her instead of a studio of middle-aged women.

"Think you could use that hangover cure?" Lauri Rock asked him when he was settled. Joel laughed and shook his head bashfully.

"Definitely not today," he said. *"Maybe in the near future."* The audience laughed. The camera cut to a woman who was covering her laugh and nudging her friend. Jealousy fired in her chest. She had the urge to

165

slap that woman.

"What are your plans for the New Year?" Lauri Rock inquired. *"Anything special?"*

"I do have some projects down the line, but I'm taking a few months off. I bought a second home in Colorado and it needs some tender loving care."

The audience hollered at the mention of this. She wasn't sure why his revelation elicited that response. Maybe they were prompted to do so. But she was definitely excited by it. Colorado, after all, was only around ten hours away by car. Her family had driven there once when she was in middle school. It was their one and only road trip–something her dad had wanted to do on a whim. After that trip none of them wanted to spend that much time in a car together ever again. Planes were to be their permanent form of interstate travel.

"Did you build a house in Colorado?"

"No, I bought an old farm house. It's a bit of a fixer-upper."

"Really? Are you into home improvement? Are you handy?"

Joel chuckled again.

"I try to be. Sometimes it's nice to get my hands dirty. We'll see what happens."

Her interest was piqued. Joel hadn't been on her radar since he'd broken her heart. She'd stopped the alerts from his Twitter feed. She immediately went to her laptop to search his recent Tweets. There was no announcement of a new house, but he had twice mentioned the snow in Colorado *(#whatwasithinking)*.

Next she tried searching for articles about his home

purchase. Nothing turned up. Frantically she searched for even the smallest clue. It proved to be hopeless.

She turned on his Twitter alert again. Joel had always tweeted openly, as if nobody was paying attention. It was hard to imagine he didn't realize that, of his 100,000 followers, a few of them might be watching very closely.

Colorado was close. If she was patient, she could find him. She could go to him. First, they had to get back together.

CHAPTER THIRTY TWO

It was two days after Christmas when I got his call. Joel, whom I hadn't spoken to in almost a month, was speaking to me with a hint of groveling in his voice. He asked how I was and how my Christmas had been. I was cordial, but suspicious. This call definitely had an ulterior motive.

"I'm going to a New Year's party," he told me. "It's a big deal."

"Good for you," I interrupted. I wondered why he felt the need to share this news with me.

He chuckled a little as if he thought I was acting like a pouting child.

"I want to ask you to be my date."

"What about what's-her-name? Are you already over her?" I sat down on my kitchen stool and grabbed an orange from the fruit bowl. I could have squeezed it to death with the resentment I was holding in.

"Lucy," he pleaded. "I told you, we only went out that one time. I'm sorry. I should have told you."

"Yes, you should have."

There was silence. I finally broke it.

"I don't think we should start this again, Joel. We're better off as friends."

"Then, let's go as friends. Come on. Do you have plans for New Year's?"

"No," I admitted.

"Then make plans with me. Wouldn't you like to be surrounded by classy people in a swanky ballroom instead of drinking beer in a bar in Nebraska?"

"Classy people like you?" I teased.

"Hell, yes. I'm as classy as they come."

I caved. He had charmed me into it. The truth was, I didn't have anything planned, and I'd rather ring in the New Year at a fancy party than alone in my apartment.

There was no fancy Plaza hotel for me this time. Even though we were attending the party as "just friends", I stayed at Joel's apartment in his guest bedroom. I had flown into New York late at night and had taken a cab to his place. He'd been waiting for me and greeted me with his usual wide and infectious smile. I tried to ignore the feeling of longing that smile gave me. It told me to jump into his arms so I could feel his warm body on mine again. But I was standing my ground. I didn't want to rekindle our going-nowhere relationship that spanned too many miles.

Instead of making love like in the past, we sat at his kitchen table and talked long into the night. He told me about a few projects he'd been considering for the New Year. I talked briefly about my mundane life back home. It was a nice and easy conversation; the kind friends have.

The next morning we were back at that kitchen table, and he was cooking us eggs. I was starting to think he didn't know how to make much else.

Before I'd left Nebraska, he'd told me not to bother bringing a dress for the party.

"New York is full of dresses," he'd told me on the phone. "We'll find you one."

"On New Year's Eve?"

"New York doesn't shut down for holidays, babe."

He'd called me babe in a silly way, not in a possessive way. He'd said it the way he'd said it back when we were friends, before we dated. I was relieved we were friends again. I'd been missing his emails and his phone calls. I'd resisted many urges to send him a message to say hi.

Now it was New Year's Eve and I was sitting in his kitchen freshly showered with nothing to wear to a formal party. I felt like I should remind him of the fact because he must have forgotten. Then the buzzer rang. It was the concierge announcing someone with a unique name. When he turned to me, Joel's face showed his excitement.

A few minutes later Joel opened the door for a flamboyant man and a woman pulling a rack of dresses. They were both dressed in a way that told me they believed they were the height of fashion. He was overly tanned, and her arms were so thin I thought I might break one when she shook my hand.

Sa'Jay and Mindii were apparently professional shoppers for the very wealthy. I'd heard of personal shoppers, but I'd never been quite sure of what they did. It appeared what they did was buy a bunch of dresses based on Joel's description of me and then make me try on all of them to see which ones I would keep. So, for the next hour I put on these heavy and obscenely expensive gowns and paraded through Joel's living room to see

170

which one the four of us liked best.

Eventually, I chose a short, black, kimono-style dress with gold sequins on the hem. Sa'Jay and Mindii selected jewelry to match and a pair of black pumps that made me nervous for the safety of my ankles. I learned, though, that the jewelry and shoes were not mine to keep. They were on loan and needed to be returned in pristine condition. No pressure.

Later in the day, a woman showed up with two black cases. She was there to do my hair and makeup. Joel was putting his coat on to leave when she started massaging some cream into my scalp.

"You're not going to endure this with me?" I asked him.

"I have some errands," he replied. He started to lean down to me, and I thought he was going to kiss my cheek. Then he stopped, as if remembering we were just friends, and stood straight again. The truth was, we'd been having such a good time being together in his apartment all day we'd both forgotten we weren't still together.

"You didn't have to do all of this for me, Joel. But I appreciate it."

"Lucy, you deserve to be spoiled." With that, he turned and rushed out of the apartment.

CHAPTER THIRTY THREE

Joel and I arrived at the party in a black limousine. He wasn't a limo kind of guy, but the night wouldn't have been complete without it. We waited our turn in line behind a half dozen other cars like ours. When it was our turn, the driver pulled up and my door was opened. I was helped out of the car like Cinderella out of the carriage. Most of my concentration was dedicated to not falling off of my four and a half inch heels. Joel held my elbow and whispered into my ear that I looked stunning. I smiled because I believed it was true.

The party was littered with famous people. I couldn't turn around without seeing someone I recognized. We were on the top floor in a hall that seemed to be completely enclosed in glass. Outside, the lights of Manhattan sparkled like a million stars. Blue lights illuminated the glass ceiling where a net full of balloons waited to be dropped at midnight.

Joel slipped his arm around my waist and guided me through the crowd. He introduced me to various celebrities, telling me their names without needing to. I was repeatedly star-struck, but did my best to keep my composure.

We ate four courses at a round table with a late-night talk show host, a composer, and their wives. I mostly smiled and nodded, afraid whatever might come out of my mouth would sound either ignorant or lame. So far these celebrities in my midst hadn't a clue I wasn't one of their kind.

After dinner a band took the stage and the music picked up. People danced. Joel put his hand out for me. I obliged him as a friend and we managed to cut a rug without looking too silly. But the next song was a ballad. We could have left the dance floor, but Joel didn't budge. When we were dancing slow and close, I wanted more. I wished there was some way we could work things out. I still wasn't ready to move to a giant city to be with someone I felt I hardly knew.

As we swayed, our bodies drew closer together like gravity was pulling me to him. He smiled down at me but didn't say a word. Maybe it was the wine, but I felt like I was falling and I needed him to catch me. His hand was firm on the small of my back. It seemed to hold me to him.

"I need some air," I whispered and stepped away from him.

Joel turned away with my hand still in his. He led me through the crowd to a glass door. Soon we were out on the balcony, like we'd been at the party the first time I was in New York. This made me dizzy, so I stayed close to the window, fearing I might fall over the railing to my death. I put my hand to my head to stop it from spinning.

"Are you okay?" Joel put his arm on my shoulder. I nodded.

"It's the wine," I said. Then I laughed. "Maybe two glasses was enough."

"Do you want me to take you home?" His face

showed genuine concern.

Home. Take me to his home? To my home? Would he take me all the way back to Omaha where I could be alone and forget the magical spell the city and the holiday had me under? Could he reverse my decision to accompany him to this fancy soiree with the ridiculous notion we could be just friends? Because while he seemed to be doing a great job of maintaining our platonic relationship, I was failing miserably.

"No." I composed myself, turned to him, and bumped his shoulder with my fist. "It's all good, buddy."

He smirked like I was being funny but he wasn't enjoying the joke. His gaze lingered and I couldn't figure out the expression on his face. He put his hands in his pockets and turned toward the balcony.

"Do you hate New York?" he asked, his back to me.

"No." I was confused. I'd never said a bad thing about the city. What was he getting at?

"You can't imagine yourself living here?"

"Sure, if I could afford it. But I don't have the experience to get a job where I could make enough to get by. And it's busy here all the time. I don't know how long I could handle the constant stream of people." I kept on talking. For some reason I felt like I needed to. It seemed Joel had something heavy on his mind, something I didn't want to know, and if I kept talking I wouldn't have to.

When I finally ran out of steam, Joel turned around to face me. He tapped his wrist where a watch would be if he owned one. Then he held the door and motioned for me to step inside.

The dance floor was still full. The room was buzzing

with music and laughter. Joel walked ahead of me toward our table. Before we could get there, we were met by a server bearing a tray of champagne glasses. She reminded us there were only three minutes until the New Year. Joel took two glasses, handed one to me, and gave me a wink.

"Any wishes for the new year?" he asked me. He had to shout over the excitement of the party crowd.

"Maybe," I answered coyly. "I think I'm not supposed to tell my wish."

"Isn't that for fountains and candles? I don't think that applies here."

We both laughed awkwardly and clinked our glasses. Practically everyone in the room was standing now and waiting for the countdown to start. A giant display on the wall showed midnight was less than a minute away.

"What do you wish for?" I shouted. He smiled broadly and put his free hand on my back. When he pulled me to him I nearly spilled my champagne.

"A midnight kiss," he answered.

The crowd was now counting down from ten in unison. As their merriment swelled, my stomach fluttered. Joel looked down at me with such intensity my knees nearly buckled. Then the clock hit zero, the crowd shouted, and Joel pressed his lips to mine with more passion than "just friends". My hands went to the nape of his neck where I gently held onto his hair to keep us from falling apart. Balloons fell onto our heads and all around us, but we stayed locked in that kiss with the world screeching around us. It was a new year. My wish had come true. But did I really want it? I wanted it in the moment, but would I want it in a day?

CHAPTER THIRTY FOUR
January 1, 2016

Lucy awoke on the first of January alone in her own studio apartment. There had been no great New Year celebration, no four-course dinner, no marvelous kiss from Joel Ruskin at midnight. They hadn't rushed back to his apartment and made passionate and desperate love in the first hours of the New Year. She'd spent the evening drinking a bottle of sparkling wine, watching Dick Clark's Rockin' Eve and eating a pint of ice cream in solitude.

Her hangover was real, but her fantasy lingered in her mind. She imagined waking in Joel's bed. He was still sleeping when she tried to get up. But the pain in her head knocked her back down. Her stomach turned over and threatened to spew its contents onto his satiny down comforter.

Joel rolled onto his back. He squinted to look at her and smiled. A happy moan escaped his throat when he reached for her half-naked body. She dropped her head back onto her own pillow and reached for the extra one on the bed. She pretended it was him and cuddled against it.

"I want to die," she mumbled into the pillow. He laughed. Then he got out of bed, stumbled briefly, and headed for the kitchen in his boxer shorts.

She got out of her own bed and crossed the studio apartment to the kitchenette. Luckily, there was plenty of fruit in the bowl on the counter. She took the blender out from the bottom cabinet.

When she added the ingredients and turned on the machine, it was Joel's hands she saw. He poured the pink liquid into two glasses and handed one to her.

"Hangover cure," he announced. *"Antioxidants are key."*

"What is it?" She held the glass cautiously. The other one sat half full on the counter.

"Bananas, strawberries, pineapple juice, carrots, and some other stuff."

She raised her eyebrows at him. Her stomach turned again, but she tasted the smoothie anyway. It actually wasn't that bad. She drank it all and soon after began to feel much better. Her stomach still ached, but at least she could see straight.

Joel led her back to the bed where they sat quietly drinking the miracle hangover cure. They gazed out the huge windows of Joel's apartment watching the snow fall on New York City.

It was a beautiful scene; one she wished she could wake up to every day. Then she scolded herself for thinking that way. Their drunken night had no meaning. Waking up this way was the result of something that shouldn't have happened in the first place. Although, in her heart she held on to the tiniest shred of hope.

She was elated to have Joel back in her life. She had missed his company inside her head. She wanted to see his face again for real. So she pulled out her laptop and typed his name into her search engine. What showed up was exactly what she had been waiting for.

Joel Ruskin Buys Home in Spring Fork

The article was from the Spring Fork, Colorado Chamber of Commerce website. The exact location of the home wasn't mentioned but, just as Joel had said, he had purchased a farmhouse and a few acres on the edge of town for only $300,000.

She browsed the town's website and links to local businesses. It was a tiny town in the mountains. There was a quaint main street lined with shops. She pulled up the Earth map and dropped herself into the street view to "walk around". Unfortunately, the street view didn't go far beyond the main row. She could see nice, large houses behind the shops, but she wasn't able to turn down those streets.

The town, although friendly to tourists who happened to pass through, appeared to be guarded from the outside world. Visitors were welcome to stop by for the day, but the little village didn't even have a motel. This was a problem for her, as she would have to find an alternative living arrangement to be close to him.

By lunchtime I was feeling a hundred percent better, so we headed down the street to the deli for lunch. The snow had stopped, and the sun was shining. We both walked with our hands in our pockets, not knowing how to act. We were supposed to be just friends. But it clearly hadn't worked out. Now I was unsure of what was going on. I was still convinced we couldn't make a relationship work. So, were we friends with benefits? Was I letting

Joel take advantage of me? Did he think I was taking advantage of him?

When we returned from lunch, I couldn't take the tension anymore. I had to be on a plane back to Omaha in a few hours, and I needed to know first where we stood.

"Was last night a mistake?" I blurted.

Joel, who was sitting on the couch, stared at me for a long moment. Then he patted the seat next to him. I hesitated, but then sat by his side.

"Last night was the best night out I've had in a long time." He took my hands. "It had nothing to do with the fancy party or the drinks," he paused for a minute and tilted his head to catch my eyes. "It wasn't even the sex." He grinned. I blushed. "It was you. I enjoyed being with you. We could have been in a dive bar somewhere or sitting at home in sweat pants. I would have loved being with you no matter what." He pulled my hands to his heart, forcing me to look him straight in the eyes. "I miss you, Lucy, when you're not here. I love being with you." He kissed my hand. He gazed hopefully into my eyes. "I love you, Lucy."

My heart must have stopped because my body seemed to be frozen for an instant. He'd never said this to me before. He'd never even let on he felt this strongly about us together. I let him kiss me. Then I pulled away and dropped my gaze to my hands.

"I miss you, too." I thought for a minute. I was opening a door that I wouldn't be able to close again. "And I love you. But it doesn't change the way I feel about us. Dating you is hard. You're always working, and I'm alone. I don't want to be alone."

"Then marry me."

I looked at him to see if he was joking. His face was serious. He stared intently at me, unblinking, waiting for me to reply.

"What?" The word barely escaped my lips.

"I'm not kidding. Marry me, Lucy, and then neither of us has to be alone. I bought a house in this little Colorado town in the mountains. Whenever we get tired of New York we can hide away from everybody there. And you can come with me when I'm working. We won't have to do this long-distance thing anymore. I love you. I'm tired of missing you."

"I don't know." A million thoughts were racing through my mind. I loved him, but did I love him for real, or because he was new and we had a good time together? Would I love him a year from now? Would I hate his crazy, jet-setting life? Would I feel trapped in this apartment in this overcrowded city or lost in that hideaway mountain town? He was a good guy. We had plenty of things in common. Hadn't I spent all these years searching for someone like him? Now he was handing me the very thing I'd been hoping for. How could I turn him down?

"We haven't known each other long," I said, already knowing what my answer would be. "Don't you think we'd be rushing it? What would people say?"

"Do I ever care what people say?"

"A little bit."

"Not about this. This is my own life, not some staged show. We haven't known each other long, but it doesn't make any difference to me. There are people I've known for years who don't make me feel the way I feel when I'm with you."

I searched his face, still afraid it all might be an elaborate joke, that at some point he would shout, "Gotcha!" Instead, he got down onto one knee in front of me and took both of my hands in his.

"Lucy Bonneville," he began, "will you be my wife?"

When I said that I would, he nearly tackled me. His kiss was filled with happiness. In that moment I truly believed we would be happy together.

Naturally, I missed my flight back home. We went out to celebrate our currently secret engagement. He chose an exclusive and outrageously expensive restaurant where everyone greeted him by name. The chef, famous in New York and probably the world, came to our table himself to ensure his creations were being enjoyed. We drank champagne again. Joel rarely took his eyes off of me. He was beaming. I'd truly never seen him this happy.

"Let's get married on Valentine's Day," he suggested.

"That's a month away." I was stunned. I'd expected a full year to plan something like I'd always envisioned. "I can't plan a wedding in a month." It also didn't give me much time to reconsider this crazy life decision I'd made at the tail end of a hangover.

"It doesn't need to be big. We just need our family for the ceremony. We'll do it in Vegas or on the beach. Whatever you want."

"Why does it have to be so fast? Can't we take our time?"

"It's just," he shook his head. "It's just that I don't want it to be a big media thing. I don't want E! News to cover it. I don't want paparazzi buzzing around for months trying to get the scoop. I want this to be just for us, and I'm afraid the more we stretch it out, the crazier it will become."

I had to admit I liked the romantic implications of running off to get married without letting the world know. The thought of having photographers crash our wedding or ambush me on the street was frightening. Joel's logic won me over. We were going to be married in Las Vegas on Valentine's Day in the presence of our family. I was going to be Mrs. Joel Ruskin, New York resident.

CHAPTER THIRTY FIVE
Present

A simple scan of Lucy's Facebook profile had turned up an interesting lead for Elijah. Fortunately, he didn't have to leave the fair city of Omaha, where he'd already spent three full weeks of his life, to interview the woman he had discovered. He only needed to dial her up on Skype.

When Belinda answered the video chat she looked exactly like her profile picture. She had a round, grumpy face framed by thinning hair of an undeterminable color.

Elijah assumed her unpleasant demeanor was due to the subject of his call. It was understandable that a self-proclaimed superfan would be appalled by the actions of one of their own who stepped over the line.

Hopefully she would cooperate, because he was running out of time and options. And the aforementioned stalker hadn't given him anything useful as of yet.

"Hello, Belinda," he said with as much forced enthusiasm as he could muster.

"Hello, Mr. Rhee." Her tone was pleasant and did not match the expression on her face.

"So, as I said in my email, I'm calling you about Lucy Bonneville. You know who that is, right?"

"Of course. Who doesn't?"

"Obviously." He could think of plenty of people off

the top of his head who didn't know who she was. It's not like she'd been stalking the Pope. Still, if he had his way, true crime readers all over the country would get to know her well.

"You run the fan club *Joel on the Brain*?"

"Yes." Pride. He could see it in her eyes. She smiled, then, like she was more than happy to share what she knew. Perhaps there wasn't much else going on in her small town in Iowa. Maybe this interview made her feel useful.

"Was Lucy a member of the club?"

"No." She drew the word out. It needed to be emphasized. The fan club had no ties with that crazy woman. "We met her at the *Hometown Star* taping in Omaha. She was alone, so we kind of took her under our wing. We do that. It's what Joel would want us to do. Shepherd the lost."

Elijah nodded. Shepherd the lost? Were they a fan club or a cult?

"She was friends on Facebook with one of your members, Tammy. So, she didn't know Tammy before the *Hometown Star* show?"

"No. Like I said, she was there alone and Tammy took it upon herself to invite her into the group. I didn't approve it, but it kind of happened. She joined us for lunch and then at my hotel later for a little party we were having."

"What did you know about her at that point?"

"She said she had just met Joel that day. Other than that she didn't say much. She kind of kept to herself. I was upset to find out later she was using us."

Well, wasn't that the pot calling the kettle black?

"What do you mean?"

"I told her Joel and I have been friends for years. I had no idea she was trying to get closer to him by getting close to me. If I had known what she was capable of I never would have let her in the group."

He tried not to let his skepticism show on his face. What was she talking about? She was a middle-aged factory worker from some town in Iowa nobody had ever heard of. Joel Ruskin was a native New Yorker with a career that was presently on the rise. He let the comment slide. She wasn't the subject of his inquiry, after all.

"Did you have any interaction with her after that day?"

The woman scowled. Had he said something stupid?

"I assumed you wanted to talk about the video."

"Video?" Elijah racked his brain. Then he sifted through his notes.

"The video she sent me from the house." She clicked her tongue and sighed. Her tone was like that of a teacher scolding a child who couldn't comprehend a math problem. "It was all over the Internet right after it happened. But nobody credited me, so I guess you wouldn't know it was me she sent it to."

He vaguely remembered something from the evidence files that had been sent to his email. No, he hadn't put the pieces together. Now he was going to have to find it again and study it more closely.

"I'm sorry," he said sincerely. "I didn't realize that video was sent to you. Did you two talk regularly?"

"Never. I'd forgotten about her until Tammy told me

she moved to Spring Fork. She read that on her Facebook profile. I messaged her to find out why."

Good. The story was finally starting to unfold. He rubbed his hands together excitedly under the desk.

"And what did she tell you?"

"She said she and Joel had gotten to know each other and she was helping him remodel his house. She said things to try to get me to believe they were hanging out on a regular basis."

What? There was no way that was true.

"This was before she sent you the video?"

"Obviously." She rolled her eyes. If only there were a way to reach through the screen and strangle this woman.

"Did you believe her?"

She laughed. "Of course not. She'd only met him once. I've known Joel for many years. If he was going to ask for help, he would have asked me. He knows I'd do anything for him. Plus, sometimes she would say he was with her in Colorado when I knew for a fact he was somewhere else completely."

"What do you think was her purpose in Spring Fork, then? Why did she go there?"

"I'm sure she planned on seducing him. Some women think they can use sex to get what they want. But Joel isn't that type of person. He would have seen right through her."

Elijah shuddered. Seduce him how? He couldn't fathom how she'd come to that conclusion. Anyway, it wasn't helpful.

"Do you have any idea why she did what she did?"

Belinda rolled her eyes and then closed them.

"Because she's crazy?" She opened her eyes and leaned closer to the monitor. "She does not represent the typical Joel Ruskin fan. Joel's fans are respectful and would never do anything to hurt him. He knows that. It's why he's so open with us. Well, he used to be. Until this happened. Now he's not even on Twitter anymore. I sent him cards and flowers when he was in the hospital, but he didn't respond to anything. I hope he can recover from this. He needs time."

It was clear the woman had nothing more to tell. He was anxious to move on to his next lead.

"Well, I appreciate your input. You've been very helpful."

"Do you think you'll talk about *Joel on the Brain* in your book?" Her face was hopeful, like a child's almost.

"Maybe," he lied. "I'll keep in touch if I need more info on that."

When the call ended he sat back and breathed a heavy sigh. He was tired and dreamed of getting into the hotel bed and watching trash TV for the rest of the evening. First he needed to get to the mall before it closed.

CHAPTER THIRTY SIX
Omaha - 2016

When Lucy walked into Gobo's her attention was on her smartphone. Joel had tweeted a picture from his New York apartment. A stocking hat and scarf were draped over the back of his leather sofa. *Headed for the mountains #inovermyhead*

"Heads up!" Joni threw a stuffed bear in her direction. Lucy dodged it, but glanced at it on the floor. Its belly said "Happy New Year" in red letters. Joni had spent New Year's Eve bar hopping with not one, but two dates. One of them must have tried to get a leg up on the other by bringing her the kind of little gift girls are supposed to like, the kind men buy at Walgreens on their way to pick up the girl. Clearly Joni thought enough of it to throw it across the store and leave it in the dusty corner.

"What'd you do for New Year's?" Joni asked.

"Party." Her nose was still buried in her phone. She'd somehow missed a picture Joel had posted overnight. It was a selfie from his bathroom. His hair was wet and his chin was covered in at least two days of growth. Her thighs tensed. The thought of him out of the shower sparked her dirty imagination. She didn't even pretend to listen to Joni's recap of her night out. Instead she stared at the photo and pictured the towel that must have been around his waist and imagined pulling it off of him.

"Can your party top that?" Joni was staring at her with her hand on her hip. She'd already taken her coat out of the back room and was putting it on.

"What?" She looked up from her phone. "I wasn't listening." Since Joel had professed his love and had promised his life to her, she was much less amused with Joni's life and her ramblings. Where she'd once been desperate for Joni's friendship, it was no longer necessary.

"Seriously, Lucy." Joni's tone was disgust. It was the tone she used when she wanted to convey to her that she was miles beneath her and she only let her hang around her and Leron out of pity. "Sometimes you get on my last nerve."

"I'm leaving," Lucy said matter-of-factly. "I'm moving out of town."

"Are you kidding? Where?"

"Colorado. Joel bought a house. He wants me to move in." She dared not mention their engagement. She'd promised Joel she would keep it under wraps. Joni would have spilled it, no doubt.

"Who's going to work at the store?"

"Gordon will have to find someone."

Joni scowled at the framed reprint on the wall next to her. She was thinking. Stunned.

"Luce, how long have you known this guy?"

"Like four months, I think."

"And you're going to move in with him? Do you think that's a good idea? You guys were broken up the other day. What if you get there and he leaves you high and dry?"

Really? In all the time she had known her, Lucy had been trying to become the kind of person interesting enough to get Joni's attention. She'd never cared about her personal life at all. Now suddenly she was judging her for this? She had no right to have an opinion on her choices.

"We're in love, Joni. We don't need years to figure that out." She wanted badly to tell her it wasn't just love, that they were getting married, committing forever. But maybe that would make things worse.

Joni sighed and looked at her phone.

"I have to go," she said. "Let's talk about this later, okay?"

She smiled to herself when Joni was gone. This was the exact reaction she'd imagined anyone would have if she'd suddenly up and married a man she'd only dated for a few months. It was the reaction People magazine would have when they got ahold of the news that Joel Ruskin had married an unknown store clerk from Nebraska who he'd only met the summer before. And when they found out he'd practically stolen the girlfriend of Beau Castle, that she hadn't even moved out of his apartment, the story might even warrant the cover.

When it was time for her dinner break, she pulled the store's gate and put up a hand-written sign declaring she would return in thirty minutes. Before going to the food court, she stopped at Helzberg Diamonds on the corner and had the ladies take out some engagement rings for her to look at.

For the rest of her shift, she searched Pinterest on her

190

phone for the perfect diamond ring. Finally she found it; a two-carat solitaire surrounded by a halo of smaller diamonds set on top of a filigree, white-gold band. It was $40,000; much fancier than anything a mall store could offer. She pinned the photo to a board she titled Joel along with a few ideas for the garden reception she and Joel were planning for the spring.

The next step was to find a job in Spring Fork. Infiltrating the tiny mountain village proved to be difficult. Every potential employer she emailed wanted to know her reason for moving there. One even suggested she try the ski resort nearby. That wasn't an option for her. The resort was an hour away from Spring Fork. She needed to be close.

Within days she had found the perfect job. It was a gift shop on the main street called Starshine's Boutique. It appeared to be a small hippie shop that sold everything from crystals to clothing. The owner, who went by Moon but whose real name was Melanie, was excited to talk to her on the phone. Lucy had told her she was moving to Spring Fork for a change of scenery. Moon said she loved her free spirit, and she thought she would be perfect for the shop. She seemed to be the only person in town receptive of outsiders.

Her new bohemian gig lead her to the solution to her lodging problem. Moon hooked her up with the only boarding house in town. It was apparently another of Spring Fork's hidden amenities. She didn't even know boarding houses existed anymore, but apparently in a sheltered community, they were a necessity.

Uncle Gordon took Lucy's news surprisingly well.

She had thought she was indispensable at the store. It turned out Uncle Gordon agreed it was time for her to move on.

"You've always been my favorite employee," he told her. How ridiculous. She had always been one of two employees and a relative. "I'll be sad to see you go, but you can't work in the mall forever. You're old enough to get out and see the world. Colorado is much more interesting than Nebraska. Although, I don't know if January is the best time to move there."

Her parents, however, weren't as accepting of her decision.

"You're going to pack up and move to some mountain town because you feel like it?"

"Mom, I'm twenty-six. Don't you think I should have an adventure for once in my life?"

"Lucy, you can barely take care of yourself. Now you want to move thirteen hours away where you don't know anybody?"

"Dad, I can take care of myself. I've been living on my own for two years."

"We pay your rent! We're not going to pay for this silly excursion of yours."

Fire sprung into Lucy's cheeks. Yes, they gave her money, but that didn't mean they owned her. They couldn't stop her from going.

"I have a job in Spring Fork. I can pay my own board."

"And your cell phone bill?"

"Sure." She focused on her feet. She was a grown adult and her parents were making her feel like an irresponsible child.

"You're going to drive to Colorado by yourself?" her dad demanded. "Well, I'm not coming to get you again in the middle of the night like I did that time you supposedly got on the wrong party bus and went halfway to Missouri."

Her mom sighed and said, "What are you going to do with all your stuff?" Nitpicking. Whenever Lucy got a lofty idea, her mom would pick apart the logistics until she didn't even dare to bother. She wouldn't let her talk her out of it this time. And she had no doubt her parents would continue to pay her rent, despite what her dad said.

Joni and Leron, however, seemed prepared to wish her well. Joni had obviously made peace with the idea of Lucy running off with a guy she barely knew. Of course, she wanted to know all the details. That turned out to be the longest conversation she had ever had with Joni in which she herself was the main subject.

"Joel bought an old farmhouse and we're going to renovate it," she explained.

"That sounds terrible," Joni said as she leaned against the counter inspecting her new manicure. "Why would you want to do all that manual labor? Tell him to buy a new house you don't have to break your back on."

Lucy shrugged. She tried not to appear offended.

"So that's all you're going to do out there? Free labor for some guy?"

"No. I got a job in a little tourist shop."

"Ooo," Joni teased. "Big step up from selling fake art to soccer moms."

Lucy rolled her eyes. She wished she had a better lie.

Then Joni got that serious look again.

"You haven't known this guy that long," she said. "Are you sure you're ready to move in with him?

Joni was the type of person who would do things on a whim, which is why Lucy was surprised again by her concern. Maybe she did care. Maybe she'd cared all along, and just kept it hidden well. It touched her heart and made her regret her decision a little bit.

Still, Joni admitted she was happy for her. She and Leron even took her out for farewell drinks. By the third drink Lucy was truly beginning to rethink leaving her friends. Joel was worth it. He had to be.

CHAPTER THIRTY SEVEN
Omaha - Present

After almost three years of her absence, it was hard to find a person in the mall who remembered Lucy. A couple of people knew about her from the news. Nobody admitted to knowing her personally. Most of the employees he encountered hadn't worked in the mall back then.

Finally, Elijah's luck changed. A forty-ish woman with an asymmetrical haircut and bright red glasses approached him in the food court. She'd heard he was asking about that lady that stalked a famous guy.

The nametag on her black suit said "Robin," but she introduced herself anyway. It also said "Helzberg Diamonds," but she clarified that as well.

"I'm the manager," she said. "I've been there for five years. Manager for one."

Elijah chose the quietest booth possible and motioned for her to sit. She hoisted her Louis Vuitton handbag onto the table and slid into the seat.

"So," he began. "You actually remember her?"

"Oh, yeah. She came in one day and wanted to look at rings. I recognized her from that art store down the hall. Sometimes I'd see her in the food court. She said she was engaged or getting engaged." She waved her hand in the air and rolled her eyes. "I don't remember.

But she wanted to look at the biggest diamond we had. That was a two carat, I1, round diamond. It was $15,000."

"You have a good memory."

"I love diamonds." She smiled. Elijah nodded. The rocks on her hand had made that point already.

"So, you showed it to her?"

"An associate and I took her into the diamond room to show it to her. We don't like to show merchandise that big on the main sales floor."

"Is it normal for women to come in looking for engagement rings alone?"

"Women will come in and try pieces on or browse through the glass. Usually they're with somebody else. Even if they're just thinking about getting engaged they at least bring a friend with them. I guessed because she worked in the mall it was convenient to hop over."

"Were you suspicious she had other motives?'

"Like that she wanted to steal something? That's why we have two associates in the diamond room when we show those high-end pieces. She really seemed like she wanted to just look at it, though, not steal it. Plus, she had to know we knew her from the mall and we have cameras everywhere. A grab and run wouldn't be smart."

Robin appeared to get even more excited when talking about their safety measures than she had when describing the diamond. He wondered why she didn't have a job in security.

"Did you think she was lying about getting engaged?"

She nodded and chuckled. He imagined she and her

coworkers might have had a good laugh after Lucy left.

"We kind of thought she might be. Or at least that she was exaggerating how much he would be able to spend. She actually said he would probably want something bigger and asked if we could special order something."

"Did you special order something?"

"No. She said he would take care of that."

Of course she'd said that. The delusional behavior Robin was describing was consistent with what he'd already uncovered. The picture of her was becoming clearer; a lonely woman making a fictional life for herself, trying to make it real. Her delusions had begun to insert themselves into her everyday life. She was just the type of character who could captivate his readers and fling him into the literary spotlight.

He excused himself calmly, fighting the urge to run straight out of the building and back to his hotel so he could get started on writing Lucy's story. But there were still holes to be filled.

CHAPTER THIRTY EIGHT

Without even any further discussion I found myself living with Joel in New York. I hadn't really moved in so much as I'd never left. We weren't married yet, but we were certainly beginning our happily ever after.

"I want you to sell the apartment."

Joel's statement was so out of the blue that I stared at him for a few seconds. He hadn't been home for more than ten minutes. I'd spent the day shopping because I'd had nothing else to do. I didn't know anybody else in New York. Not well enough to spend the day with them anyway.

"We need someplace to stay when we go to Omaha to visit my parents."

"We can stay with them."

I gave him a stern look. He didn't know my parents. He'd met my mom, but he had no idea what it would be like to live with the Bonnevilles. Sure, they had plenty of room. But I intended to spend more than a few nights at a time in my hometown.

"What if we want to stay for a while? You might have some long boring job out of town. I don't want to stay in New York where I don't know anybody. And I'm definitely not staying with my parents. That's out of the question."

Joel sighed, walked over to me, and kissed me on the tip of my nose.

"Fine," he said. "Sell the apartment and buy a house. I'm not totally comfortable living in your ex-boyfriend's place after we're married. Although I'm sure that would be a great story for TMZ."

He had a good point. I could imagine the headline: *Joel Ruskin Steals Former Beau Castle Love Interest, Squats in Omaha Apartment.*

"Okay, but I don't want a huge house. I want someplace cozy."

"Whatever you want, my dear." He kissed me again. Those kisses turned into deeper kisses. Soon we were in bed for the night.

Before I drifted off to sleep, I made up my mind to fly home as soon as possible to look for a house. I'd already quit my job because I knew I wouldn't need it. My future with Joel was as good as set in stone. In less than a month, I would be his wife.

It was another week before I returned to Omaha to tidy up all the loose ends. My life had basically been put on hold while I was in New York. Joel and I had given the news of our engagement to my parents via Skype. They'd taken it well, despite the seeming urgency of our pending wedding. Of course my mom had asked me if I was hiding a pregnancy. Who wouldn't? What Joel and I were doing seemed crazy. But we felt there was no reason to wait any more.

When I got back home, my mom revealed she wasn't completely thrilled we were getting married so fast. It had nothing to do with us personally. She tried to talk me into slowing things down.

"I have one daughter," she told me. "That gives me one chance to plan a big wedding. And you want to elope?"

"We're not eloping, Mom. Eloping is going to the courthouse and not telling anybody you're doing it. The wedding will still be up to your standards." I told her she could plan as much of it as she wanted. Party planning was her thing and had never been mine. The less I had to do the better.

Next on my agenda was to visit my former place of employment. I'd basically walked out on my job, meaning Uncle Gordon had to work more hours in his own shop until he could find my replacement. I knew Joni wouldn't be happy about that. Gordon was an easy-going guy, but nobody likes having the boss watching over their shoulder.

Joni's face lit up when I entered the store. Then her brows dropped and she glared at me.

"Where have you been? Did you really just up and quit? Your uncle said you moved to New York."

"I did," I answered sheepishly. "I am. I'm in the process. But Joel works all the time, so I'll be back in Omaha every once in a while."

Her face softened. She put her arms out in front of her and came in for a hug. She'd never hugged me before.

"I'm happy for you, Luce," she gushed. "You and Joel are cute together. And he's so rich! You better not let that one go."

I felt guilty that I couldn't tell Joni about our engagement. But Joel and I had agreed the fewer people who knew the better. And Joni wasn't the best secret keeper. I was sure most of the things I'd already told her had made their way into someone else's ears.

As I looked around the store, a pang of sadness tore at my heart. I was going to miss Gobo's. I'd worked there for a decade. I'd never worked anywhere else. And I had no idea what I'd be doing in the future. I definitely wasn't going to sit around the apartment all day waiting for Joel to return.

And I would miss Joni. Even though I hadn't known her for long, we'd become good friends. I'd never had a best friend, but she was the closest I'd come. We both had tears in our eyes when I said I had to go. There were many more things I needed to take care of.

Lucy browsed the real estate website for open houses in Omaha. There were a few million-dollar homes Joel could definitely afford, but she wanted something quaint, something homey, something her mom and dad would love whenever they came to visit. There was a gorgeous, three-story, brick home in Dundee for under $700,000. She imagined strolling through the tree-lined neighborhood and what the house would look like all decorated for Christmas. It was open from noon to two. She would have to dress the part.

Wearing her only black business suit, Lucy walked through the front door of the century-old house. She gasped at the sunlight pouring through the windows atop the sweeping staircase. She'd always wanted this type of grand entryway in which to greet her guests and to send off her adoring husband on his way to the airport for another tour.

A cheery, blonde woman with a wide, plastic smile greeted her when she stepped into the formal living room. She handed her a flyer.

"What brings you out today?" Her voice was squeaky and forcibly cheerful.

"I'm getting married," she answered. "We'll be living mostly at his place in New York, but we want a home in Omaha to be near my family."

The agent's eyes widened along with her impossible smile.

"Oh," she said, "what does your fiancé do in New York?"

"He's in the entertainment business." She ran her hand over the shiny blackness of the grand piano. She pictured Joel seated there, crooning a tune he'd stayed up all night writing for her. Then she turned her back on the agent and headed for the kitchen.

"What does he do? Would I know who he is?" The agent was genuinely interested. She skipped after Lucy so quickly it was obvious she was dying to know.

"I can't say," she whispered loudly. "Our engagement hasn't gone public yet."

The agent looked her up and down and then simply smiled with disappointment in her eyes. Then the front door squeaked open and two sets of footsteps echoed through the foyer. The agent excused herself to greet the new prospective buyers. Lucy, in her suit and heels that click-clicked on the wood floors, was free to inspect the mansion and daydream away.

The open house had enough traffic that the agent

forgot about her. She carefully inspected each room, imagining Joel living there with her. This was definitely the house they would make into their home. There would need to be some changes, but Joel didn't need to worry about any of that. This one would be her home. He would more or less be a guest in it, as infrequently as he would be in Omaha.

The real estate agent entered the bedroom as I ended my call with Joel. I'd told him I had the perfect house in mind and he'd given me his blessing.

"Do you have any questions about the home?" she asked. Her tone indicated she was actually trying to hurry me out the door. Clearly she didn't think I had any interest in the house. Or maybe she thought I didn't have the means to pay for it.

"No," I replied. "I'd like to make an offer."

The woman's sculpted eyebrows raised. She let out a tiny, surprised giggled, waited for me to indicate I was joking, and then realized I was serious.

"I look forward to doing business with you."

Lucy was in the master bedroom laying on the chaise lounge and staring at the ceiling. She'd let her imagination get away from her and had lost track of time. That's when the real estate agent came into the room and let out a startled yelp at the sight of her.

"Miss," she said breathlessly. "You scared me half to death. The open house is over. I didn't even realize you were still here."

"Sorry." She stood up and slipped her feet back into her high heels. She rushed past the flustered agent. Obviously her story was blown. The woman didn't even bother to ask her if she had any intention to buy the house. And so she hurried out of the beautiful old mansion with her proverbial tail between her legs. Fortunately, she had more than a dozen pictures of the rooms on her phone that she could refer back to in her future daydreams.

CHAPTER THIRTY NINE

The Bonnevilles and the Ruskins arrived in Las Vegas on the afternoon of February 13th. We all settled into our rooms at the Bellagio. My penthouse suite overlooked the fountain below. Tomorrow night I would share the suite with my husband. Tonight, however, I would keep with tradition and sleep alone as a single woman for the last time.

The room was so big I didn't know what to do with myself. My mom was running around fussing with my dress and making sure we both had everything we needed for the ceremony. I was standing in the living room of the suite staring at the white couch and wondering what the price tag was on this whole trip. I'd grown up comfortably. Even living on my own I'd never had to worry about money. My parents had plenty of it, but nothing like what Joel had. Barring some unforeseen event, I'd never have to worry about a price tag again.

My mom snapped me out of my pre-wedding trance. First on the agenda was a grand dinner in a fine restaurant. I was thrilled and nervous to meet Joel's parents and his two younger siblings. Would they even like me? Would they be disappointed Joel wasn't marrying a fellow celebrity? And how strange that I was meeting my future in-laws for the first time on the eve of my wedding?

As it turned out, I couldn't have asked for a nicer family. Joel's mom was thrilled to meet me. His parents were regular people whose son had made a successful career of being charming. Our parents got along well. By the end of dinner they were like old friends. While they were chatting I caught Joel smiling at me from across the table. I could tell we were both equally relieved it was going well.

Our wedding was beautifully simple. Just our family and a few friends were there. Joel's sister Beth was my maid of honor and his brother Jeff was his best man. Both of our mothers cried. I didn't feel guilty about not inviting my work friends. I was pretty sure they didn't care much about me before Joel came along anyway. And I was ready to start a brand new chapter in my life and leave the old one behind.

My dress was champagne-colored with long, lacy sleeves. The back was open and ten strands of pearls cascaded from shoulder to shoulder and all the way down to the small of my back.

It was finally time. I wrung my hands nervously. My dad kissed me on my cheek before we walked through the doors for the ceremony. When I approached Joel, his eyes widened and his smile couldn't be contained. In that moment, I knew we would be happy for the rest of our lives.

Joel's publicist had insisted on letting a few carefully selected journalists in on our secret ceremony. They had to wait outside until after we'd said our vows. Then they rushed in and shouted our names while snapping what seemed like a million pictures. They asked me to turn and show the back of my stunning gown. I mimicked the women I'd seen on the red carpet. I was going to have to get used to being part of the story instead of the unknown woman on the sidelines.

When we had our first dance the photographers were allowed to take a few staged pictures. But then they were ushered out and the party was once again private. As a surprise to me, Joel had hired a band he knew I liked. I held on to him as we danced for the first time as Mr. and Mrs. Ruskin. It was a relief to know that now he really was mine and I was his.

CHAPTER FORTY
Spring Fork, Colorado - 2016

Spring Fork was accessed by what Lucy believed to be a far too treacherous mountain road. The other drivers didn't seem to think so as they impatiently lined up behind her slow-moving vehicle. There was no passing allowed on the narrow road, so they had no choice but to tolerate her white-knuckle driving. She was sure one slight turn of the wheel would send her careening off the side of the mountain and leave her impaled on one of the pointy trees below.

For this reason, she decided the only way she was driving that road again was to leave Spring Fork forever. She would drive to the Tall Pines Ski Resort and Lodge for anything she couldn't get in town. The neighboring town had a Walmart and plenty of amenities for tourists and resort employees. In the coming months she could even roam around the employee village and think about becoming one of them. She needed to be in Spring Fork. She needed to be near Joel.

Her new home was an old hotel that was built in the nineteenth century. It was now a boarding house with one floor for men and one for women. Stepping into the First Spring Boarding House was like stepping back in time. Red carpet covered the steps of the grand staircase which lead to a long hallway of heavy doors. Each room was small with a bed, a dresser, one window, and a sink in the corner. The bathroom was three doors down from Lucy's room and across the hall. There were two stalls and two showers. This made her morning routine rather difficult. If she wanted a hot shower, her best bet was to take it at night when the young tenants were down in the dining room drinking and playing cards and the older ones were already in bed with the lights out.

As soon as she was settled, she updated her Facebook profile to reflect her move. For the first hour her mom was the only person who liked the post, although Lucy knew she didn't truly approve of her taking off to a strange town. Finally she was alerted to a comment. It was from Joni.

Enjoy your new digs. Say hi to your hotty boyfriend.

Joni didn't really mean she thought Lucy's boyfriend was good looking. It was part of her online image to talk like that and to make others think she had interesting friends.

"Why isn't he on your Facebook?" Joni had asked before she had left Omaha for good.

"He doesn't do social media. He's a private person."

"Well, try to get a selfie with him when you get up there. I want to see what your man looks like."

She had promised she would. It wasn't a lie. She fully intended to insert herself into Joel's life. Then she could take all the pictures of him she wanted.

The next person to comment on her announcement was Tammy from the fan club.

Spring Fork? What are you doing there?

There was no way Tammy didn't know about Joel's new house in town. Any true fan had to know, even a mildly obsessed one. She tried to think of a vague response. Or maybe she wouldn't respond at all. Before she could make up her mind, she was alerted to a private Facebook message. It was from Belinda.

When did you move to Colorado? Because Joel Ruskin just moved there too. Weird coincidence?

She didn't like her accusatory tone. She replied, *I just got here today. Joel asked me to come help him renovate his new house. I like the town, so I decided to stay.*

Why would he do that? How does he even know you?

Her body heated with mild rage. Who did this woman think she was? Did she think she owned Joel? Was she the only person who could be his friend? He hadn't even shown up to her lame-ass pizza party.

I ran into him after the show in Omaha. We started talking online and he liked my ideas for the house. Since we're friends it's no big deal to come here and help him.

That was that. There was no further reply from the fan club leader. Obviously she hadn't liked her answer. Good. Maybe it was jealousy. Well, she was going to have to get over it.

No one in town had seen any sign of Joel Ruskin. Not that she had asked. But in small towns, when someone famous was in town, everyone knew.

Moon was a laid-back boss, probably more so than she should be. She had told her she'd appreciate it if she could be at the shop by nine, but she didn't want her to fight her body if it ever wasn't ready to begin the day at that time. Other than that, she only asked that she respect the store's brilliance by governing her own actions.

"I'm not here to be your slave keeper," Moon had

told her on her first day.

This no-rules policy wasn't a problem for her. She didn't have to struggle to be there at nine. She was an early riser most of the time anyway. And she didn't know anybody else in town yet, so there was nothing else for her to do but sit in the shop and wait for customers.

The business model didn't work so well on the store's other employee, Cory. He was a skinny guy with tiny, thick glasses. He'd originally told Lucy he was twenty-six, but it turned out he was only twenty. He wasn't into Moon's peace and love philosophy, but he'd grown up in town and this was apparently the only job he could get.

Cory talked non-stop. He talked about anything that interested him as if his brain couldn't keep it all in. One day he talked about nothing but woodworking and how someday he'd like to move to Denver and be a cabinet maker. The next day he wouldn't shut up about a shark movie on the Sci Fi channel. Whenever she would try to change the subject, Cory would change it right back again. Even when she was beyond comfortable listening range, she could hear his voice drone on as if she were still listening.

Then finally he said something that actually interested her.

"Did you hear about that TV guy that moved into town?"

Her ears perked up. She'd been tuning him out, but somehow this got through. She tried to act casual.

"What guy?"

"Joel Pumpkin or something like that." He began tearing at the hem of his t-shirt.

"Joel Ruskin?"

"Yeah. He's on TV."

She stepped closer to him.

"Have you seen him around?"

"Yeah." Cory turned to stock the handcrafted soaps Moon had made on her stove over the weekend. "Did I tell you I wrestled an alligator once?"

"When did you see him?"

"I didn't really wrestle it, like get on the ground and whatever. But they had, like, its mouth taped shut and they let people touch its tail."

"Cory, when did you see Joel Ruskin? Was he in the store?"

"Yeah, he was in the store."

"This store?" Her palms started to sweat. She couldn't believe she might be standing in a spot where Joel had stood. If Moon was right, she could be standing right in the midst of his lingering aura.

"Naw. Beekins." Cory was referring to the family-owned supermarket a few blocks away.

"When?" She wanted to tear the information out of his brain with her bare hands. The suspense was killing her.

"Yesterday."

"Yesterday?" The word came out as a squeak. Joel was in town. He had been on Sunday, surely he still would be. She checked her phone. He hadn't even tweeted about it. In fact, he hadn't posted anything in a week. No wonder she'd missed his arrival. Her heart was pounding. She had to find him. Why wasn't he tweeting? All she needed was a clue.

CHAPTER FORTY ONE
Spring Fork, Colorado – Present

"Mountains are stupid."

Elijah repeated the mantra to himself again and again as he drove the narrow roads into a higher altitude. He'd flown from Omaha to Denver and was now on his way to Spring Fork. If Ruskin had bought a second home in Malibu like a normal person, this part of the journey would be much more pleasant.

After too many hours in the rental car, he reached his destination. The town was clean with a main street of old buildings made new again. He got the impression it was a popular final destination for rich retirees.

The Blue Diamond Bed and Breakfast was cozy and inviting. When he checked in he informed the friendly owner, Mrs. Diamant that he was on a business trip only. He wouldn't have time for sight-seeing or any of the hiking trails that were mentioned in the house's brochure.

Only a half mile from the Blue Diamond was the First Spring Boarding House. He needed to see where Lucy had lived. There was no better way to make her real to his readers than to seek out the mundane details of her life in this place.

Even though it was April and still well below his temperature of preference, Elijah decided to walk there. No use in putting more mileage on that rental than he needed to.

The lobby of the boarding house was wall to wall dark wood. There was an ornately-carved, long counter across from the front door. On the wall behind it were keys hanging on pegs and at least two dozen open mail slots. They were numbered for each room.

Elijah felt like he had somehow stepped into a time warp. Until the proprietor of the establishment emerged from the back room.

"Hi." He was Elijah's age; probably in his mid-thirties. His reddish beard rested on his bowtie. The hair on his head was buzzed on the sides, but long on top and expertly set into a solid wave. In his earlobes were black gauges with hollow centers. Was he dressing to match the old house, or had he bought the house to fulfill a hipster quota?

"I'm Elijah Rhee."

"I know." He nodded. Was he a hipster or a psychic? Then it occurred to him that this guy probably didn't see many new faces. "I'm Baron."

Elijah consulted his notes.

"Dustin Baron, right?"

"That's right. People call me Baron. Nobody calls me Dustin." He stepped from behind the counter and pointed at a velvet sofa by the window. "Let's sit down."

Elijah sat on the couch. Baron took a seat on a high-back chair opposite him.

"You own this place?"

"My parents do. I live in Denver now. I'm a wedding photographer. But they're in the Bahamas this month, so I'm looking after the house."

"I messaged you about Lucy Bonneville. You were here when she lived here?"

"Indeed. I was working here full time back then. That was right before I moved away and started my career."

"You worked at the desk?"

"Yep. Took care of the front-end operations. Clerical. All that stuff. I was at that desk eight hours a day, six days a week."

"Do you remember her?"

"Yes. Sort of. She was quiet. She worked at Moon's shop."

Baron took out a folded sheet of paper. He spread it out on his lap.

"I was thinking about it over the last few days. I jotted down some notes."

Elijah nodded. He appreciated the planning. Hopefully those notes included personal information about Lucy that he could actually use.

"Did you ever have a conversation with her?"

"No. Just gave her the tour when she moved in. I can give you the tour when we're done here if you want."

Elijah nodded.

"She never gave me any trouble," Baron continued.

"Was she ever behind on her rent?"

"Never." Baron glanced at his notes. "She had automatic withdrawal from an account with the name Nancy Bonneville. Always went through fine."

"Are residents allowed to have guests in the rooms?"

"Yes. We also have a lounge area here on the main floor and a rec room in the basement." He rose from his seat. "Do you want to see?"

Elijah nodded and followed him down the hallway to a wide staircase. He continued his questioning as they descended.

"Did Lucy ever have guests that you know of?"

"Not that I know of. I don't remember anyone asking for her."

They exited the stairs into a large room with wood paneled walls, couches, a pool table, and a big-screen TV. It looked cozy. Elijah wondered if Lucy was ever social enough to venture down.

"So you don't know if she had any friends or if she was in a relationship?"

"I assume she did know other people in the area. Sometimes I wouldn't see her come in for days."

Finally they were getting somewhere. He wanted to know exactly how many nights she spent away from the dorm. How long had she been going to the yellow house? If only there was some physical record of the nights she didn't check in.

"Do you keep track of your renters' whereabouts?"

"Not really. But I'm always at the desk in the morning when everyone is up and moving around and leaving for work. And we serve lunch, so people come for that, too. I see the same faces like clockwork. There were periods of time when I wouldn't see her at all. I started checking her room when it got dark to see if she was still living here."

"You went into her room?"

"Of course not." Baron approached a couch and fluffed one of its cushions, then returned it to its place.

"I'd look at the bottom of the door to see if the lights were on. There seemed to be a lot of nights when they weren't. I mean, that's her business, but I wanted to know if I should be worried about her."

"Do you have security cameras in the building?" He looked around at the ornate molding that lined the basement ceiling. No electronic devices were visible.

"No. Not at all. Spring Fork is a pretty safe town, Mr. Lee."

"It's Rhee."

CHAPTER FORTY TWO
Spring Fork - 2016

Two days of wandering around Spring Fork turned up nothing. She had taken long lunches, hoping to run into him on the main street. After work she had driven around town looking for the least local-looking vehicle. Nothing. She couldn't find him.

Then, on Wednesday afternoon, Lucy's phone chimed her salvation. Joel had posted a photo. He was wearing overalls. His hair was covered in dust, and he had a sledgehammer in his hand. Behind him was a pile of wood and huge marks on the wall where cabinets had once been. The caption simply said, *Before.*

Minutes later, her phone chimed again. Another photo. This one said, *After.* Joel was standing in the middle of his newly remodeled kitchen in Spring Fork, Colorado. She stared at it, committing it to memory. The kitchen was all white with glass doors on the cabinets. It had a country feel, but modern as well. Her frustration boiled. She was close to him, staring into his kitchen, but she couldn't reach him because she didn't know where he was.

Over the next month, Joel posted updates on the progress of his new home. She saved every photo to her phone's memory. In some photos, she could see the adjoining room. In others she could see through the windows and noticed if the room faced the road or the thick trees in the back. From these pictures she could put together a rough blueprint of the house. She was pretty sure she could find her way around easily. He hadn't posted a single picture from the outside. She still had no clues to tell her where his house was. She was starting to get angry with him for being inconsiderate.

Weeks passed and still she had no better clues. One day, while Lucy was dusting the shelves of Native American statues and jewelry, she received a notification from her phone. A loud sigh issued from her chest. Joel hadn't posted anything interesting in days. He'd gone back to New York a week ago, and now most of his posts were about work.

It took a few minutes to finish the shelf. Each figure needed to be facing the door, not straight ahead, but looking a little bit to stage left. She adjusted each one almost undetectably until they were perfect.

Then she checked Joel's post. There were two. One she must have missed when she was in the bathroom earlier. *Back at it.* There was a picture of Joel and a friend in overalls apparently standing in the living room of his Spring Fork house. The room was otherwise empty and the wood floors were bare.

The next post was just words. *Taking a break for lunch at Boney Mahoney's. Great food.* She dropped her duster. Boney Mahoney's was two doors down. She went there for lunch all the time. She threw a glance at Cory and then rushed out the door. Why hadn't she checked her phone right when he tweeted?

The lunch rush was dwindling. She tried not to break

through the door of the small diner. Still, everyone turned to look when she went in. Her face flushed, and her hair was most likely in a wild state. She looked around, but Joel was nowhere in sight. How could he be gone so quickly? Maybe his post had been delayed. Maybe he was hip to her following him and had tweeted after he left. Whatever the reason, she made up her mind she was going to have to stake out the place every day until she caught up to him.

Now she stood in the middle of the half-empty diner with a disappointed look and several locals staring at her. She went to the counter and ordered a milkshake to go. Her stomach had sunk, leaving her no appetite.

Milkshake in hand, she wandered back onto the sidewalk. She'd left the store quickly and without a coat. The sun was shining, but the temperature was only in the twenties. The cold cup seemed to freeze to her hand. She was about to walk briskly back to work when two men across the street caught her eye. They were both wearing stocking hats and thick scarves that covered part of their faces, but she recognized Joel immediately. His hands were in his pockets, and his shoulders were shrugged up to his ears. He and his friend were walking quickly down the block. There was a shiny black car parked on the corner, right in their path.

Immediately, she ran to the shop. She set her cup on the counter and went for her coat, but then stopped. A heavy feeling nagged at her. The cup. The permanent coffee ring on the reclaimed wood counter. She went back and lined them up. Damn it, she didn't have time for this.

Cory was sitting at the register eating a cup of noodles. He watched her silently.

"I'll be back later," she told him. She was out of breathe. The outside air was still stinging her lungs when she spoke. She busted out the back door into the ally and ran for her car. When she pulled around the corner to the main street, she was in time to see the black car pull away from the curb. There wasn't any other traffic, so she let them get half a block in front of her.

Snowflakes began to fall onto the windshield. She kept following as the snow began to fall harder. They drove for ten minutes until they were out of town. Then the car turned onto a blacktop road. She slowed down to give the other car more distance. It was one thing to follow him on the main road, but he'd know something was up if he noticed her here.

Her wipers were going full blast. The snow was coming much faster now, making it hard for her to see. She'd let Joel's car get too far, and now she'd lost him. To the left of the road was a ranch with a white fence. On the right side were trees. Finally, she came to a clearing in the woods where a driveway veered off to the right of the road. The snow had settled softly, but there were tire tracks on the driveway. Her heart pounded. This was his home.

She pulled over a few feet beyond the driveway. She took her new binoculars from the glove compartment and lowered the passenger window. The road was lined with a thin barrier of trees. She peered through them. There was a large yard beyond the trees, and she could see a yellow house at the end of the driveway. The black car was parked in front of the enclosed porch.

It was an old farmhouse with weathered, yellow siding and white trim on the windows. There was a matching detached garage at the end of the driveway. It was hard to tell how much land was behind the house, but it was bordered by trees. She was stunned by the rustic surroundings. It was a far removed from the Manhattan high-rise.

The snow was beginning to let up. It had left a dusting on the lawn. She imagined Joel in the car with her. He was driving and had pulled off the road onto the gravel driveway.

"This is it," he said.

"It's..." She paused to find the least offensive word. Joel was beaming with pride. He'd found this grand hideaway before he'd asked her to be his wife. Now he was sure they could make a happy life here. So what if she couldn't picture herself settling into the quiet small town life? It would only be part of the year anyway. She could probably get used to it. "It's cute."

"It is." He sighed. *"And if we decide to have a family..."* He trailed off and gazed at her with anticipation. She shifted in her seat. During their month-long engagement, they hadn't talked about having kids. In fact, there were a lot of important things they hadn't discussed before tying the knot. Certainly he didn't expect an answer to his implied question right here in the yard of their new country home. She forced a smile.

Lucy got out of the car and hurried down the slight incline to the trees. Her canvas sneakers were highly unsuited for traipsing through snow, but that was her fault for not anticipating the normal mountain weather.

She surveyed the acreage, wondering if it was possible to continue without being seen. There was a decrepit shed nearly hidden in the trees about twelve feet to her left. She pranced toward it, knees flying high, trying to keep her cold feet dry.

From beside the shed she could see a long row of windows. She raised the binoculars and peered into the newly remodeled kitchen. Joel and his friend were standing talking to each other. The friend was making large gestures with his arms, and Joel was laughing, his shoulders shaking. She loved his laugh. She could almost hear it in her head. He should be laughing with her.

"You don't like it?" He was clearly disappointed in her lack of genuine enthusiasm.

"It's great," she fibbed in a whisper. Not that either of the men would have heard her way out there. "I've never lived in the country before."

"We're not that far from town. Besides, I figured you're from Nebraska..."

Lucy dropped the binoculars to her chest. She turned her head to glare at the emptiness beside her where Joel's image stood with a hopeful expression. Sure, they hadn't been together long, but did he know nothing about her?

"I'm not from that part of Nebraska, Joel. I grew up in the city. The most time I've spent in a small town is when my dad would stop for gas on road trips when I was a kid."

"I'm from the city, too." He put his hand on hers. *"We'll probably be a little out of place here, but at least we'll be out of place together."* He leaned in and before

he kissed her he said, *"I want a taste of the simple life."*

When she looked back at the house, the two men left the room. She inched forward. She was tempted to creep up to survey more of the house, but was beginning to feel the cold all the way to her bones.

Perhaps she should knock on the door and claim her car had broken down on the road. It seemed legit considering that's where she'd left it. But how stupid would they think she was when they found it to be in working order? Besides, she looked like a mess. There was no way she wanted Joel seeing her like this. She trudged back along the trees to the road, leaving shallow tracks all the way. She would find another perfect time to visit.

CHAPTER FORTY THREE

Joel and his friend didn't visit Boney Mahoney's again that week. Lucy watched out the window every day for the black car. She ate Boney Mahoney's egg salad sandwich for four days straight, hoping Joel would saunter in and sit down right next to her. But it didn't happen.

Meanwhile, Joel kept posting photos of his progress. He'd painted the front hallway and polished the large, wooden staircase. The living room was full of new furniture and featured salvaged antique light fixtures he'd ordered from a picker online.

Then came the worst news she had read in a long time. Through a series of tweets that spanned a half hour or more, she learned that Joel had accepted a small roll in a movie starring and directed by a close friend of his. *Sunny California for two months, baby! Goodbye snow. Hello sunshine.*

She was devastated. Joel was still in town for now, but he would be leaving Spring Fork until April. She would have to survive the rest of the winter without him. What was the point of living in this miserable mountain town if he wasn't there? And maybe he wouldn't come back in the spring. Maybe he would go back to New York and never finish the work he'd started on the farmhouse. She was suddenly angry with him for being fickle.

"Just go ahead and abandon this little pet project you started," she exclaimed out loud. Then she looked up from her phone and around the shop. An old woman was browsing near the front. If she'd heard her, she didn't let on.

While the other young tenants in the boarding house took to partying at night, Lucy used her spare time for reading. The local library had a few wealthy donors, so the selection of books didn't disappoint. Her current choice was a novel in which a woman had murdered three of her husbands without ever arousing suspicion. She was engrossed in the current chapter which had the wife poisoning Mr. Number Two by grinding up glass and putting it into his food.

A thought occurred to her. If Joel couldn't make it to California in time to shoot the movie, would his friend recast him? He had said he had a small part, so it wasn't likely they would stop production for him. It was possible Joel could miss his opportunity if he were, for example, in the hospital with a mysterious illness. The nearest hospital was in Tall Pines by the ski resort. It might be enough to keep him around for a little while longer. And she was sure a small town hospital would be much easier to access than the one in Omaha. She could have him right where she wanted him.

Although she had Saturday off, Lucy still made her way to Boney Mahoney's for lunch. It had become a habit now, one she hoped to break when Joel left for the West Coast. Because she didn't have to work, and because she was in a sour mood, she ended up sipping Coke in the corner booth for more than an hour. She was the only customer left in the diner. Only the cook and one waitress remained.

When the door chimed, Lucy barely looked up. She had been staring at all of Joel's home pictures, trying to piece them together in her mind. Then she heard his familiar voice. She looked up. At the far end of the diner sat Joel and his friend and two other men in matching baseball caps. The waitress politely interrupted their conversation to take their order.

Another group entered the diner right away. They were five middle-aged women who giggled like high-schoolers. They had their ski bunny gear on, so they had probably come from the resort. Maybe they'd come to see the quaint little town and shop for some local treasures, but they'd apparently found more than they'd bargained for. It seemed they'd followed Joel in.

The women squeezed into a booth across from Joel. One of them leaned over and stuck out her manicured hand. Joel had to lean over his friend to shake her hand. He smiled graciously and didn't seem to mind at all. While the women gushed, the waitress hurried back to get their order. A couple of seniors, seemingly oblivious to Joel's celebrity, entered the diner and sat down. Now the lone waitress was overwhelmed. Lucy was invisible.

The cook was busy filling tickets. The waitress was busy taking orders. And everyone else was busy gushing over Joel. The cook put up the first orders and rang the bell. Lucy had clearly heard Joel order a BLT. Now there it was under the heat lamp waiting to be carried to his table. But the waitress was still occupied with the old couple. The women were taking selfies with Joel. The whole diner had been thrown into chaos.

It was no trouble for her to stand up from the corner booth and snatch the BLT. She sat back down and placed the sandwich in front of her. From her pocket she fished the small baggie that had been in there for days. She had ground the glass into a fine powder and picked out any large chunks. Now she sprinkled it discreetly into the mayonnaise of Joel's sandwich. She quickly replaced the plate under the lamp before anyone noticed it was missing. Then she went to the back hallway as if she were headed to the ladies' room and sneaked out the back door. She rounded back to the front of the building and jogged across the street. There was a bench there that faced Boney Mahoney's. She sat down to watch her plan unfold.

Joel was raising his hands to the women as if to politely tell them to give him space. The waitress brought the tray and handed the plates around. Lucy couldn't see them clearly, but she knew Joel would be getting the BLT. They chatted with her for a minute more. Lucy willed her to move on. She was growing impatient.

When Joel lifted the sandwich to his mouth, her heart beat faster. Instantaneously, she wanted to slap it out of his hands, but she also couldn't wait for its effects. It happened more quickly than she had expected. Joel immediately covered his mouth with a napkin. The men around him looked concerned. His friend motioned for the waitress who came right over. There was commotion. Joel handed her the plate. The cook inspected it at the counter. The waitress began to cry. Joel shimmied out of his booth and went to comfort her. One of the men with him was motioning angrily to the plate, but Joel, with his arm around the upset waitress, seemed to talk him down. One of the women snapped a picture with her iPhone and another was taking video. The cook asked the five of them to leave. The old couple, still without their food, sat watching the whole thing unfold with looks of total confusion.

And that was it. Joel never ingested the glass. He never got mysteriously sick. He didn't go to the hospital. Her plan had failed. Whoever wrote that book she'd read was a damned liar.

CHAPTER FORTY FOUR

Boney Mahoney's was closed for the next two days. The sign on the window said they were closed for remodeling, but there were rumors flying all around town. Cory said someone had found something nasty in the food. Moon had heard the place had some kind of infestation. She was worried it would spread to her shop, so she'd had the exterminator come and spray just in case. Others claimed they'd been shut down by the health inspector and even that they'd had a fire in the kitchen. And of course, there was a video those ladies had taken that was flying all around the internet.

Lucy kept her mouth shut and listened. She knew that diner had been closed so they could scour every inch of it for the source of the mysterious glass. It was a consequence she hadn't considered. The diner was losing money, and it was her fault. She felt bad about that.

Apart from feeling guilty, she was disappointed. Joel had clearly noticed the glass when he took his first bite. Maybe she should have ground it into a finer powder. Would that have done anything at all? If he had ordered a milkshake she could have slipped it in. He probably would have gotten a few sips in before noticing anything was wrong. He might not have noticed at all. It was too bad he hadn't ordered a milkshake.

By the following week Joel was tweeting from

Hollywood. She had failed to stop him from going. Now she had to imagine she'd gone with him. She had to insert herself into every scenario he laid out. Living in the tiny mountain town was excruciatingly dull. It was certainly no life for the wife of a celebrity.

On her day off, she drove to Joel's house. She parked on the road like before and ventured through the trees. Using the same path as before–along the tree line and behind the shed–she crept up to the back of the house. The snow was long gone, so her feet stayed dry this time.

There were no cars on the property, but it was still possible someone could be lurking inside. She approached the kitchen windows and standing on an overturned planter, pulled herself up to look inside. The kitchen was immaculate. No signs of life. The back door was locked.

She did the same around the side of the house. The living room looked like a magazine photo. The walls and even the mantle had been painted bright white. A dark gray couch and matching love seat skirted a red Persian rug. She smiled. She approved of his choices. She could even imagine they'd chosen the furnishings together.

The screen door on the enclosed front porch was unlocked. She stepped inside, causing a shiver through her whole body. She was inside Joel's home. Well, not technically inside, but she was on his porch, and that was, so far, close enough. There were a few paint cans in one corner. In the other corner were an old yellow table and a kitchen chair. She ran her hands over them. These were things Joel had chosen to keep. He hadn't thrown them in the dumpster out front. Maybe he thought they gave the porch character–helped preserve the house's old charm.

The front door was yellow with antique hardware. It was, unfortunately, locked. She had seen people in crime shows open locked doors with credit cards. That appeared to be impossible here. She wished she'd studied up on lock-picking. Apart from smashing a window, there was no way in.

She walked around again to the side of the house. She tried some windows, but the house was shut up tight. This meant she was limited to peering in through the windows, instead of going inside and immersing herself in Joel's essence.

The sound of tires on gravel caught her attention. She ducked down behind a shrub and watched two trucks come up the driveway. They stopped in front of the porch, and four men got out. Two of them had been with Joel and his friend at Boney Mahoney's on the day of the ground glass incident. One of them retrieved a set of keys and led the way through the front door. She could hear them talking loudly inside. They'd left the front door wide open.

Shortly after the men had arrived, a small cargo van came up the drive. One of the men came out and instructed the driver to pull around to the back door. Soon they were transferring bathroom fixtures into the house.

She waited on the side of the house for at least an hour. It was cold, and she hopped around to keep warm. She told herself it was worth it to be patient.

And it was. Once the van had been unloaded, the men began pounding away on the second floor. She crept around to the back door, which was also standing wide open. She'd ripped some cardboard from a box near the stairs and now shoved it into the latch strike on the door frame. Her heart pounded. It was exhilarating. She channeled her inner James Bond.

With that in place, she sneaked back through the tree line and to her car. Those men might be there all day. It was best for her to come back at night.

CHAPTER FORTY FIVE

All Lucy could think about was getting back to Joel's house. Her hands trembled on the steering wheel as she drove back there in the dark. Her yellow headlights cut a path down the narrow country road. The night was as black as ink–low clouds and no moon. It was spooky how the night seemed to know her ill intent and was determined to slow her down.

She pulled partway into the drive and let her lights linger on the front of the yellow house. If anyone was there, she could again act like she'd pulled in by mistake.

There were no cars and no movement other than the light swaying of naked branches. She backed onto the road again. This time she cut down to her running lights and slowly crept forward until she had almost passed his land completely. Once on foot, she cut through the neighboring field and entered his property from behind the shed. She kept her flashlight as low as possible so as not to attract any attention, although there appeared to be no attention to attract. It was nearly nine o'clock, and surely all the farmers were in bed for the night.

Because Lucy had jammed the latch, the back door gave way easily. She shook her head at the incompetence of the workers. Those idiots hadn't even checked to make sure the doors were secure before they'd left for the day.

Entering Joel's home was like entering a sacred

temple. She was enveloped in his spirit. He had chosen this place to live and now she was inside. The wall she ran her fingers along was a wall he had touched. The smell of the interior had been smelled by him. It was a dusty smell, but with a hint of warmth and a hint of comfort. And paint. She thought of him on a ladder, painting the living room where she now stood. She saw him raised on a ladder without his shirt, reaching high to get the top of the wall. His jeans rode down low on his hips, revealing the waistband of his Jockeys. She imagined him calling for her and asking her for a favor. Maybe he needed a glass of water. She walked to the kitchen, again keeping the flashlight pointed low so it wouldn't be visible from the outside.

There in the kitchen was a large, high-top table where he'd no doubt sat and eaten his breakfast. He'd surely sat on one of the stools over a bowl of Raisin Bran–a box of it sat alone on the counter–and composed on his phone a Tweet that made him smile to himself. Then her phone would have chimed and she would have read his Tweet and smiled to herself. He wouldn't even have known he had affected her world. They had been previously linked by this heavy lump of metal in her pocket. Now they were linked by this house. Because she was inside of it, and he had been inside of it. His ghost was around her. It came up behind her and laid its hand on her shoulder which made her close her eyes and shrug into it with a contented smile.

"Are you happy here, Lucy?"

"Of course I am. You were right. This house is perfect for us." She meant every word of it. The little mountain town had grown on her since he'd come. After weeks of living among the plastic stars in Hollywood, Spring Fork was a welcome change to the simple life. And any place was paradise with him.

She turned around on the stool to face him. He kissed her tenderly and then with more passion. Then he took her hand and led her out of the kitchen. The sparkle in his eye told her they were headed back to the bedroom. She followed him up the stairs.

The bathroom on the second floor was half finished. All of the fixtures had been installed, but the walls and floor were naked and covered in debris. There was the beginning of a beautifully modern bathroom; a circular, frosted shower stall, a cone-shaped pedestal sink, and a brand new toilet. She wondered how long it would take for them to finish the rest. How long until she had the house all to herself?

Finally, she reached his bedroom. It obviously hadn't been touched up yet. The walls were a putrid shade of light green. Heavy maroon curtains covered the windows. There was an attached bathroom with an antique bathtub. Several of the wall and floor tiles were broken or missing. He must be saving this sanctuary for last. It made sense that he would want to wait for her opinion on the room where they'd wake up together every morning. The sun would beam through those huge windows and gently wake them both.

"Sheer curtains," she said out loud. She imagined seeing the breeze blow through them from the open window.

She stroked the comforter on the bed. This was

obviously new, but he hadn't bothered to make the bed. One half of the blanket was still tucked neatly under a spare pillow. The side where he slept was pulled back and left disheveled. She touched the white sheet where he had laid and then lowered herself onto it. She was close to his body, close to him in his most vulnerable state. It sent a shiver through her.

Joel's ghost appeared again. She was daydreaming of the next morning. She had slept there in pure bliss.

"Good morning, Beautiful."

He entered the bedroom with a tray that he set on the table next to her side of the bed. The sun was shining through the large windows, casting a heavenly glow through the sheer, white curtains.

"Joel, you shouldn't have." She ran her fingers under her eyes, hoping to wipe off any lingering eyeliner that may not have come off during their mutual shower the night before. She wanted to look her best for him every morning for the rest of their lives.

"I really didn't," he said and shrugged.

She looked over the tray. There were two pieces of toast, a jar of jelly, and a glass of orange juice. She giggled and kissed him on the cheek for his effort.

"Looks like we need to do some shopping," she said.

"Well, get dressed and we'll go into town."

She groaned and sunk back into the warm bed. In the city, they never had to actually go to the grocery store. She ordered what she wanted online and Joel's assistant had someone pick it up. Sometimes she ventured to the farmer's market, but that was more fun than trudging through the florescent aisles of a big store. But assuming

Spring Fork's one supermarket probably wouldn't adapt to the online trend anytime soon, she knew she had to get used to doing it herself again.

"Come on." He pulled her arm from under the fluffy comforter and tugged. *"It'll be fun. We'll be one of those cute couples who goes grocery shopping together and picks out fruit while holding hands."*

"Do you want to wear matching outfits?" she teased.

"Only by accident." He yanked on her arm again. *"Let's go."*

The fantasy faded, and Lucy was again alone in the dated bedroom. Her breathing became shallow. There was a tight knot in her throat. She was here, in Joel's actual bedroom, and still she couldn't grasp the one thing she wanted: him.

CHAPTER FORTY SIX

Visiting Joel's house became a nightly activity. On the second night, there seemed to be no progress on the bathroom, but she knew the workers had been there. They probably got paid by the hour. Would Joel have a fit if he knew they were milking the job?

On the fourth night they had it completed. She cautiously turned on the light for a minute to see how it looked. The room was bright and clean and nothing at all like it must have been before it was torn apart.

Five nights in she discovered they had started working on the master bathroom. It obviously needed a makeover, but she was getting restless. She'd been getting back to her room later every night which meant she was dragging to work every morning. Cody noticed how tired she'd been and wondered aloud if she'd been "partying too hard?"

"Yes," she'd replied sarcastically. "Partying hard in this metropolis. It's like being in Vegas."

Evidently, one of the workers had noticed the jammed back door and had fixed it. This was no problem. She had already found a box of keys in an otherwise empty kitchen cupboard and had tried all of them. She now had on her keychain a key for both the front and back doors. It was careless for Joel to not have changed the locks. She would have to talk to him about that.

By Sunday night both bathrooms were finished. They had also changed out the fixtures and appliances in the newly converted laundry room and added a half bath in the closet under the staircase. The foreman had left the house keys on top of a manila envelope on the kitchen counter, meaning their job was done.

Joel's recent Tweets indicated he wasn't coming back to Spring Fork anytime soon. He was enjoying filming his small part. Mostly he seemed to get a kick out of hanging out with his friends on the set. She didn't mind. She thought of herself as the cool kind of wife who would let her man spend time with his buddies.

Now that the workers were gone, she had free reign of the house in the daytime. She had already scoped out multiple places she could hide in case someone dropped by. The only person who would stay too long was Joel, and she was keeping tabs on him with her phone.

It was unfortunate that Joel hadn't fully moved into the house yet. He'd only left a few things in the drawers in his bedroom. Nothing was very personal. Still, his scent was all over the neat pile of t-shirts in his dresser drawer. Lucy had pulled one out and had it pressed to her nose when she heard the pop and crackle of tires on the gravel driveway. She ran across the hall to the empty bedroom and looked out.

An older model SUV approached and parked in front of the porch. A woman in a postal uniform got out with a package under her arm. Lucy lost sight of her when she neared the front door. When the doorbell rang, she considered answering. Would this mail carrier know she didn't belong there? She obviously didn't know no one was home. Why was she delivering a package, anyway? Joel got all his mail at the post office.

She decided to play it safe and stay hidden. The screen door on the porch creaked open and slammed shut. Then there was a rap on the main door. Then a pause. Then another.

"Just go away," Lucy whispered.

Another minute passed in silence. Finally, the screen door creaked and slammed again. Lucy watched the woman get into her car without the package and drive away.

When the SUV turned onto the main road, she leaped down the stairs to the front door and flung it open. The package had been placed on the old chair with a sticky note on top.

Thought this might be important. Amy

The package was addressed only to Joel Ruskin, Spring Fork, Colorado. It was marked FRAGILE in red ink and was heavy. Lucy carried it inside and locked the door. She set the box on the kitchen table and checked the return address. No name, just an address in Iowa.

She retrieved a box cutter from the utility drawer, sliced the box open, and tucked the cutter into her pocket. A top layer of packing peanuts spilled out and stuck to her shirt. She waved them off onto the floor. The next layer was bubble wrap. She peeled it back to reveal three cylindrical objects packed in brown paper.

"You've got to be kidding me," she groaned after unwrapping the first one. It was a glass bottle of orange Goody soda. Then another. And another. There was a second layer of wrapped bottles, equaling six in all. A note card had been tucked between the two layers.

Just a little housewarming gift. Enjoy lovely Colorado. Hope to see you soon. Belinda and the Joel on the Brain crew.

"This woman is insane," she said across the table to where she imagined Joel shaking his head at the ridiculous gift. "You need to tell her to stop."

"I can't. She's a fan."

"You don't need fans who don't know boundaries." She lifted her phone over the table and took a picture of the bottles and their packaging.

"What are you going to do?"

"I'm going to tell her to stop."

"Lucy, don't." He took the phone gently from her hand. *"She's just being nice."*

"Fine." Lucy placed the bottles haphazardly into the box. She picked it up and headed for the back door.

"What are you going to do?"

Without answering, she hopped down the rickety back steps and strode across the lawn to the broad side of the barn. She dropped the box onto the grass and pulled out one of the bottles.

"Thanks for the pop, Belinda." She hurled the bottle at the garage. It shattered against wood. Then she did another and another, fueling her adrenaline.

"Leave my Joel alone." She screamed as she threw the last bottle. The weathered siding now dripped with orange syrup. Glass glittered in the dirt. She smiled at her accomplishment and returned to the house, the box still on the grass where she'd left it.

When she dropped back onto the couch, she was

panting from the workout. She pulled up Belinda on her phone and composed a message.

Joel says thanks for housewarming gift. Goody? Really? Maybe you could be more original next time.

She laughed to herself and selected the photo she had taken of the bottles on the table. Then she thought better of it. If she sent that picture to Belinda, it could get to Joel. Her cover would be blown and she'd be kicked out of his house. Instead, she sent the message without the picture. Belinda would still understand that Lucy hadn't been lying about being there with him.

An icon appeared instantly, indicating Belinda had read the message. Three dots appeared and then were gone. Lucy chuckled again. Belinda must be deciding how to reply.

"Maybe an apology?"

The dots appeared again and then, finally, a message.

I don't know how you know that, but don't think I believe you for a minute, you stalker.

Anger welled up in her. What did she need to do to prove to this woman that she and Joel were living together? Take pictures of the house? Fine. She snapped photos of the living room. She ran up the stairs and took pictures of his bed.

"You want to see where he sleeps?" She flung herself backward onto the mattress and took a selfie. Then she went to his bathroom and took a shot of her reflection in his bathroom mirror.

She sunk into the chair in the corner of the room and scrolled through her photos. Her chest heaved as she tried to catch her breathe. The fury coursed through her and burned her neck and ears.

"Lucy."

She ignored him.

"Lucy," Joel said again.

She looked up from her phone and saw him standing there in the light of the window. He stared down at her with concern on his face.

"What are you doing?"

"I'm going to prove it to her. She thinks she knows everything. She thinks she knows *you*. She doesn't know you. I know you. I have you. She can't."

"Of course she can't." He kneeled in front of her, putting his hands over hers. *"Only you can. You don't have to prove anything."*

He was right. She softened her hands and let the phone drop to the floor. Then she followed him to the bed and curled up beside the shirt she'd been nuzzling earlier. Let Belinda believe what she wanted. Lucy was on the brink of having everything she ever wanted.

She spread one out on the bed and removed her own shirt. When she put on his it was almost like being wrapped in his arms. She unclasped her bra and pulled it off through the sleeve. Her nipples hardened when the cotton touched them. Her hands went to her breasts. She closed her eyes and imagined they were his hands. Then she removed the rest of her clothes and slipped underneath the covers of Joel's king bed. She turned her head to press her cheek against his pillow as she spread her legs, imagining his fingers exploring her. Her loud moans of pleasure echoed against the high ceiling of the room. The next time Joel laid in this bed his body would mingle with what she had done there.

CHAPTER FORTY SEVEN

The morning sunlight slowly woke Lucy from a satisfying slumber. She stretched and reveled in the plush gratification of the down pillows and comforter on Joel's bed. This was definitely the luxury she'd expected from him. She turned toward the empty side of the bed and curled into a fetal position. The king-sized pillow took the place of Joel in her fantasy. She spooned it with dazed affection. A satisfied moan escaped with her breath. This place was heaven.

Her phone chimed from the nightstand. When she retrieved it, she saw it was already after nine o'clock. She had to be at work by noon. Her stomach groaned with hunger.

"I'll make breakfast," she announced to Joel the Pillow. Then she kissed it softly before pulling her naked body out of his bed.

The tiny, white bird on her screen alerted her that Joel had posted. After pulling on her clothes, she opened it to read the post. He mentioned he was attending a televised charity concert that evening. *Gotta get the tux ready. #penguinsuit*

She skipped down the slick, wooden staircase. Their first formal event as husband and wife. She could barely contain her excitement. She had to find a dress and go to the salon. Joel would be encouraging her to go all out. He spared no expense when it came to keeping his brand new bride happy.

After a light breakfast of one egg and one piece of toast, and after cleaning up any trace of her presence in the kitchen, she settled onto the couch in the newly decorated living room. It took her about half an hour to narrow her online dress search down to two that she loved. One was a basic strapless but in a gorgeous royal blue. The other was a flapper-style, short, gold dress covered in black lace and silver beads. After she had finally decided on the blue dress and had saved the photo to her phone, she packed up the few things she had brought and hiked back to her parked car.

On her way to the car she heard the ping of her phone letting her know she had a Facebook message. When she was behind the wheel she checked the alert. It was Belinda. She found it interesting that the woman would send her private messages but seemed to have no interest in officially adding her as a friend on the site. Still, she opened the message to see what she wanted.

Any sign of Joel in town?

He's in L.A. Lucy was perturbed. Hadn't she already told her she and Joel were now friends? *I'm watching the house while he's gone.*

Really? That's interesting.

What the hell was Belinda getting at? Was she insinuating Lucy was a liar?

Actually, I probably shouldn't tell you this because it's not public yet, but Joel and I are dating. I moved in last week.

You expect me to believe you're dating Joel Ruskin?

She huffed audibly. She hated this woman. She had half a mind to block her messages altogether.

I don't care what you believe and what you don't.

He has big plans tonight. Why would he leave you in Colorado? Why wouldn't he take his girlfriend with him?

Damn it. She hadn't considered Belinda would know as much about Joel's plans as she did. But why wouldn't she? He practically tweeted his whole life these days.

He wants to keep our relationship quiet. And it's none of your business.

Whatever you say.

She told herself again she didn't care if Belinda didn't believe her. Soon her lies would become truth and she could prove that jealous bitch wrong. She'd prove all her doubters wrong.

She went to work still high on the rush of spending the night in Joel's house. Even Belinda couldn't bring her down. She was uncharacteristically friendly and helpful with every customer that walked in the door. She was anticipating the party that would happen that night in her head. She imagined the press being there and the twinkling of the camera flashes.

Later that evening, in the privacy of her room, Lucy wrapped herself in her bed sheet and paraded the imaginary red carpet. Unfortunately, her room only allowed for a short stroll, but she had enough space to pose with Joel for the paparazzi.

"Mrs. Ruskin, who are you wearing?" Cameras flashed. *"Joel, over here."* Flash. *"Lucy! Lucy!"* Flash. Flash.

The concert was televised on network TV. She

watched on her laptop while reclining in her bed. She scoured every shot of the audience for Joel. Then she finally spotted him. It was a quick shot of a famous musician, but behind him was Joel, and next to Joel was a woman. That woman put her hand on Joel's shoulder. It was a split second, but she saw it happen. She saw that woman put her hand on him. Then her awful mind imagined that woman's hands everywhere.

She was blind with fury. How could Joel do this to her? Again? She had given him everything. She had moved her whole life for him. Now she was stuck in this stupid mountain town, and he was off in Hollywood having a great time with some other woman. She slammed the laptop shut and tucked it under her bed. The ancient bed frame creaked as she threw her body around the mattress with rage, flopping and punching and moaning wildly.

Then came another Facebook message. It was Belinda again. She had seen him, too.

Seems your boyfriend is off with another woman.

Lucy didn't respond. Forget Belinda. Forget Joel. She screamed so loud it was inevitable she would get a visit from her landlord.

CHAPTER FORTY EIGHT

The next day, Joel's new romance was one of the lead stories on the Yahoo! homepage. The gossips of the Internet were excited for the new celebrity couple. There was a picture circulating of the two of them and speculation of their body language. She was disgusted by it. She'd worked hard to be the one for Joel. She'd come all the way to Colorado for him. She'd spent hours and days taking care of his house. How could he throw that all away to be with someone else?

Sydney Panting was a brunette TV actress whom he'd apparently met at a charity fashion show in L.A. She was pretty, but not drop-dead gorgeous. She had the typical fake smile. She most likely had the typical fake breasts. And she probably spent more time in the gym and the salon than she actually spent with her boyfriend. With that kind of life, how could she give Joel the attention he needed? How could she be better for him than Lucy?

She didn't even want to go back to the yellow house now. Just the thought of setting foot in his home made her heart sick. She'd made it her home too. She'd put her mark on it because she thought they'd be happy there forever. Obviously he wasn't who she'd thought he was. He was shallow enough to be trotting around with a Hollywood girl. She had seriously misjudged his character. How could she move on?

The following months were empty. Lucy merely existed in each day like a robot, with no goal and no plan. Every day she contemplated her purpose. Joel had taken that away from her.

And then it was spring. The sun was shining, drawing everyone out to enjoy the weather. Moon propped the shop's door open to encourage the tourists to wander in. She professed her love for spring whenever a new face crossed the threshold.

Lucy didn't care much about the changing season. She'd had more of Spring Fork than she could take. Ever since Joel had officially announced his new romance on morning television, she grew more suspicious every day that he was never returning to his newly remodeled farmhouse.

Her initial anger had subsided a bit. She had to admit Joel and Sydney seemed genuinely happy together. So, instead of seething over every picture of the couple together, she imagined herself in Sydney's place instead. She chose to live vicariously through the despicable woman that had stolen her man.

Joel and Sydney often publicly exchanged tweets that suggested they weren't able to spend much time together. He seemed to be working all the time. She was in middle of filming her sitcom's third season and had to spend most of her time in L.A. When they were together Joel would post sugary-sweet selfies of the two of them or announce something adorable that Sydney had said. Their happiness and insanely busy schedules indicated the farmhouse in Colorado was the last thing on Joel's mind.

Now it was spring, and Lucy sat on the stool behind the counter while Moon was gone, "basking in the freshness of the day." She, on the other hand, could only think of moving back to Omaha. Her dad, she knew, would point out how backward it was to spend the winter in the mountains only to return to the unforgiving humidity of the Nebraska summer. She didn't care. Her spirit was broken, and she wanted to go home.

She was disinterested in the couple that wandered into the store. She didn't even look up, but was aware of their presence. He had on a newsboy cap and she was wearing a bohemian skirt, like the kind hanging on the rack outside the door. Moon had run down to the diner to grab some lunch. Lucy kept her eyes on her smartphone.

"Joel, look at this." The woman skipped toward the shelf of moccasins.

Joel. Lucy looked up. The man in the newsboy cap was him. The woman was her. They were Joel and Sydney. In her store. Breathing the same air she was breathing.

The phone toppled from her hand and hit the wood floor with a bang. She bent down quickly to pick it up. She didn't want to see if Joel had noticed. It wouldn't do her any good to be noticed by him with Sydney there, even for something as stupid as dropping her phone.

A funny rattling noise caught her attention. When she looked up, Joel was picking up a four-foot rain stick that had been leaning against the wall. The beans inside tumbled melodically when he rotated it. He grinned.

"I haven't seen one of these in forever." He seemed

to be talking more to the stick than to his girlfriend who was now on the opposite end of the small store. He turned toward Lucy and pointed the stick at her as though it were an extension of his arm.

"How much is this?" he asked.

She stared at him for what seemed like a full minute. Joel Ruskin had spoken to her voluntarily. True, he was only asking her a question as a store clerk, a nearly inanimate object, but he was speaking to her nonetheless. And for a long moment she had no idea how to respond. Her brain had shut down, maybe misfired. She got herself together and stepped forward. When she put her hand on the extended rain stick, she was acutely aware their two bodies were now connected by this polished cylinder of wood. Was it possible for her to send all of her energy and love through the wood and into him?

There was a small, white sticker at the end of the stick closest to her. She cocked her head and read it out loud. "Thirty-five dollars." She should say something interesting about the rain stick. She should tell him the Aztecs believed the stick could summon the rain. She should tell him she loved the sound of rain on a roof on a warm summer night. Her mouth couldn't form any more than the facts.

Joel smiled awkwardly at her and gently pulled on the stick so he could lean it back against the wall. Then he turned and walked to Sydney. He put his hand on the small of her back and stood with her as she perused a rack of clearance t-shirts. It was as if in two seconds he had forgotten Lucy existed. Her eyes burned from the jealousy that welled up behind them. Here she stood, a fat and drab part of this chintzy shop. And there he was with his hand intimately resting on another woman's unjustly perfect body. There was no competition between them. Sydney Panting won hands down, as she probably always did and most likely always would.

The two of them faced the front window of the shop. They were having a quiet conversation. Sydney laughed and touched his arm. He turned around and headed toward Lucy again. Then he picked up the rain stick and brought it to the counter while his girlfriend wandered out the door to browse the rack of bohemian skirts on the sidewalk. With both hands he laid the long stick across the counter. She smiled at him and started his order on the computer.

"Is this all for you today?" The words were automatic. She said them several times a day. She was struggling to treat him like any other customer. Now was not the time to act star-struck.

Joel nodded and pulled his wallet from his pocket. Basic black. Nothing fancy. He used cash. This was good. Later she would exchange her own bills for these and keep them forever. They would smell like him. When he handed the money to her she tried to brush his fingers with hers, but only fumbled the cash onto the counter.

"Sorry," she whispered. He grinned awkwardly at her again. She finished the transaction and waited for his receipt to print. Then she thought of the yellow house. How long had they been in town? Had they already stayed the night?

"Are you in town for long?" Her ears flamed. She hoped the question wasn't too lame or too obvious. She was actually impressed with herself that she'd had the courage to speak directly to him. His awkward grin turned into a polite smile.

"Just got in yesterday," he replied. "Don't know how long we'll be around."

"Well, stop in and see us again."

"Will do." Joel nodded, took his receipt and his new rain stick, and went outside to locate Sydney.

Lucy was beside herself. She had to sit on the stool again or she might have fallen onto the floor. For a few minutes, when Sydney was out of the store, she had literally been alone with Joel Ruskin for the second time. His smile up close was a thousand times more powerful than it was on TV. She had looked right into his eyes. They were beautiful and caring and honest and amazing. Then disappointment set in. He hadn't recognized her at all. They'd met twice and he hadn't shown any sign she was familiar to him. The thought began to crush her.

The yellow house. They'd definitely spent the night in the house. They'd no doubt slept in his bed. One of them had slept in the exact spot where Lucy had slept. The imprint of her body had made contact with the body of one of them. But which one? She had to know.

When Moon returned from lunch a few minutes later, Lucy told her she wasn't feeling well. Cody would be there in less than an hour, so Moon didn't mind letting her go early.

"Go nap in the park," the boss told her. "The sunshine will do you good. Vitamin D is a natural healer."

The last thing she wanted to do was lie down in the

255

park. Instead, she hurried down the sidewalk looking for the celebrity couple. There was no sign of them. Ten minutes later she sat on a bench hoping for a miracle. She wondered how she hadn't known Joel was back in Spring Fork. Then she remembered she'd turned off the notification on her phone.

Sure enough, only a day ago Joel had posted a picture of Sydney sitting in the chair on his front porch drinking a beer. *My lady doing the country life.* And only five minutes ago his post read, *Rain sticks. Who knew they were still a thing? #mynewtoy*

The last post had elicited several fan comments such as, *How bout a demonstration?* and *My granny haz one*, as if anyone cared.

Lucy tapped the star on her screen so she'd be notified of his posts again. How could she have abandoned him? It was only thirty seconds before her phone alerted her to his recent post. This one was a photo of a bottle of wine on a white table cloth. *Wine with lunch? Why not?*

She jumped up and headed to her car. If Joel and Sydney were just sitting down for lunch, they wouldn't be back to the house for a while. A plan was hatching in her brain. She needed to make one stop.

CHAPTER FORTY NINE

The yellow house was cozier now that its renovations were complete. Lucy admired the expensive paintings on the wall in the dining room. She ran her hand along the smooth surface of the heavy table. It was definitely better suited now for a couple of TV stars.

The stairs still creaked a little when she climbed to the second floor. Joel's bed was unmade. A suitcase sat open at the foot. The things inside belonged to Sydney. She moved some items aside and found a slim, black case. She flipped it open to reveal jewelry: diamond earrings, gold rings, and a diamond tennis bracelet.

She lifted the bracelet and held it out at arm's length. She saw Joel sitting across from her in a nice restaurant. They were seated in a spot where they could be seen but not disturbed. Joel took her hand and looked into her eyes, smiling as if they were on a first date. He was as charming as he'd been on her first trip to New York.

"What?" She tilted her head and spoke to the blank wall. "Why are you smiling at me like that?"

"Can't a man smile at his wife?"

"You're like a cat who caught a mouse. What are you hiding?"

"Nothing." Lucy held out her hand, palm down, and imagined Joel kissing it. Her other hand came up slowly and draped the diamond bracelet over her wrist.

"How could I ever hide anything from you?"

She gasped and put a hand to her heart.

"What's this?"

"Just something to remind you that you make me happy every single day."

"You didn't have to..." She trailed off. Her words couldn't express how happy he'd made her already. She didn't need expensive gifts to understand what they had together. But what a beautiful gift it was.

She tucked the bracelet into her pocket and threw her arms in the air in an imaginary hug. His imaginary breathe on her neck drew goosebumps on her skin. Then she replaced the jewelry case under the clothes where it was found.

Another suitcase stood upright in the corner. She lifted it. This one was empty. Its contents had probably already been put away in the dresser drawers. Either Sydney wasn't planning on staying long, or Joel was tidier than she was. Perhaps she usually had people to do that stuff for her.

She wandered into the master bathroom. The toothbrush holder near the sink only held one toothbrush. It had to belong to Joel since Sydney obviously hadn't unpacked anything yet. She figured she might never brush those nasty fangs anyway. Such a disgusting person. How could Joel even want to touch her?

The bristles of Joel's toothbrush were dry. She stroked them with her thumb, sending tiny flecks of tried toothpaste flying through the air. She wetted the brush and began to brush her own teeth. Back and forth. Slowly. Back and forth. She closed her eyes to savor the moment. This was closer now. This was closer than she'd ever been to Joel. He was literally in her mouth. And the next time he brushed his teeth, she would be in his.

When she finished in Joel's bathroom, she headed to the hallway to begin her preparations for the night. The door to the attic was down the hall from the master bedroom. The staircase was steep and narrow. A round window looked out over the front of the house but let little light into the small attic. Her new lantern had three settings so she didn't have to use more light than she needed. She set her backpack on the floor and went back down the stairs to the attic door with a hand drill she'd bought at the hardware store. She drilled a hole through the door near the knob and made it big enough to see through. This would allow her to check that the hall was clear before opening the attic door.

Next, she set up camp in a corner of the attic. She laid out a sleeping bag and opened her laptop. She opened the audio program, but the house was too quiet. She found an old hardcover book in a box in the corner and hurled it down the steps. Perfect. The microphone she'd hidden in Joel's bedroom picked up the sound of the book hitting the door at the bottom. If she were more tech savvy she would have set up a video camera instead. She was going to have to get by with just sound.

Then she sat and she waited.

Joel and Sydney got in late that night. According to Joel's Twitter feed they'd had a good time with some locals at a bar. Lucy wanted to kick herself. She could have been one of those locals. She could have gotten to know both of them and eventually nudged Sydney out. Instead, she was asleep in Joel's attic. The house's old floorboards woke her up when the couple got to the second floor. She immediately opened her laptop to listen to them.

"And their faces when you picked up the check," Sydney was saying. "As if they didn't expect you to."

"Are you kidding me? Those drinks were cheap. A round for everybody here was like two drinks at the Rainbow Room."

Lucy opened a window on her laptop and searched the Rainbow Room in New York. She gazed at the photos of the posh club. She wanted to be there with him. She wanted Sydney gone so she could take her place, so she could be on his arm at fancy clubs and restaurants. It was only fair. Somehow it had to happen.

There was some shuffling in the bedroom. Sydney's heavy heels clunked to the floor. Then she said simply, "Get this."

The room was quiet for a minute and then Joel said, "Your hair is soft." He paused. "And smooth. I've always loved this hair." His voice was muffled as if his face were buried in her dark tresses.

"Are you trying to seduce me?" she cooed.

Then Lucy heard more shuffling. This turned into heavy breathing and a little bit of moaning. At first, she was disgusted. Her neck burned with jealousy. Then she remembered how recently she'd been in that bed. She smiled because Sydney had no idea. Sydney thought she was the only one to put her female stink on those sheets.

Lucy listened intently to Joel's sounds of pleasure

and quietly inserted her own.

CHAPTER FIFTY

Lucy rushed past some locals on the sidewalk and into the shop. She was already over an hour late. Moon was taking inventory, a job she'd assigned to Lucy. Unfortunately, Joel and Sydney had slept in that morning and she hadn't been able to get out of the house. She knew she was stupid for not thinking of it before. But when Joel was involved, it was hard for her to think of anything else.

"Sorry, Moon. I overslept."

"It's okay," the older woman replied without looking up from her task. "Sometimes our bodies tell us we need more sleep." There was an unconvincing edge in her voice. She most certainly was irritated with her tardiness. But Moon wasn't one to break her peace-loving image. When she had her count, she excused herself curtly and went to the back room.

Lucy pulled out her phone and leaned on the counter. She scrolled through her Facebook feed to see what was going on in other people's lives. She rarely posted on social media. She'd rather people think she was a private person than know she was an uninteresting one.

She clicked on Joni's profile to see what she'd been up to. There were inspirational quotes over pretty stock photos. A week ago she'd mentioned meeting the love of her life but then never posted about him again. And there were several pictures of her and Leron and some friends one night at Shifty's.

She missed them all. She missed being in the city and knowing she had exciting options even if she was never going to do any of them. Joni hadn't messaged her since right after she'd gotten to Spring Fork. She was sure they were all forgetting about her.

Even worse, it was days before Lucy could sneak into the yellow house again. She'd been waiting at the edge of the property since not long after her shift ended. She had the next two days off from work and she wanted to make the most of them. Joel and Sydney finally left the house and headed for town. She was able to use her key and go back to her hideaway under the topmost rafters.

The next morning Lucy was in dire straits. It was an emergency that couldn't be contained in the bucket she had to use as a toilet when Joel was home. She could hear the couple moving around in the kitchen, so she cautiously made her way to the second floor bathroom. Of course, flushing was out of the question. They'd no doubt hear it and come to investigate.

When her business was finished, she crept in the direction of the attic door. A creak on the floorboards below signaled someone was coming. And then footsteps on the stairs. She quickly ducked into the guest bedroom on her left. She stood motionless behind the door until she heard the footsteps coming closer. She thought there was no reason for either of them to enter the guest bedroom until she spotted Sydney's suitcases on the other side of the room. They must have been put there to keep them out of the way. Lucy's worry turned to panic when she realized she was about to be caught. She tip-toed quickly to the empty closet and crouched inside, leaving the door ajar about a half inch. She buried her head between her knees and prayed silently that whoever was in that room wouldn't find her.

The antique hinges squealed when the bedroom door was opened. The light footsteps on the carpet sounded like they probably belonged to Sydney. She pulled up the handle on her rolling case until it clicked. Then, for some reason, she walked toward the closet door. Lucy turned toward the door. The gap under the door was wide and she could see Sydney's bare feet just inches from it. Her toenails were flawlessly manicured. And her second toe on her right foot was disproportionately longer than all of her other toes. Lucy made a mental note of this and filed it in her brain under Sydney's Flaws. Yet she was still fully aware she was in grave danger of being caught in Joel Ruskin's guest closet by his meddling girlfriend with freakish feet.

Suddenly Sydney's hand was on the closet door and she pushed it closed. The quick and loud movement startled Lucy who had been painfully anticipating the door going to other way. She covered her mouth when she let out a surprised screech. Luckily, Sydney didn't hear it and instead left the room with her suitcases in tow. Lucy heard the door latch when Sydney closed it behind her. Sydney crossed the hall to the master bedroom and then descended the stairs to rejoin Joel downstairs.

On shaky hands and knees, she crawled out of the closet and sprawled out on the carpet. She couldn't believe how close she'd come to disaster. While lying

264

there she heard voices through the large vent in the corner of the guest room. She pressed her ear to it and listened. She heard Sydney and Joel discussing their plans but couldn't hear them well. From what she could hear between them, she only knew Joel would stay in Spring Fork to work on the house while Sydney filmed on the West Coast. Lucy would have him all to herself.

She finally made her way back to the attic. Shortly after she did, Sydney returned to the master bedroom to pack her suitcase. A few hours later, a car came to drive Sydney to the nearest tiny airport which would take her to Denver where she could fly first class to wherever she was going. She listened at the attic door while Joel and Sydney exchanged parting words. Their goodbyes weren't as heartfelt and passionate as they'd been in the past. It was as if they were getting a little bit tired of each other. Perhaps that was why Joel had decided to stay behind.

When Sydney was gone, Joel seemed to move around the house like a truly free man. Music echoed through the first floor, floating up the stairs to where Lucy was still hanging out in the attic doorway. She crept out into the hallway to see if she could make out what he was doing down there. She stood at the top of the main stairs and listened. It was a risky thing to do, but she couldn't help herself. After all, luck had already been on her side once that day.

Suddenly Joel appeared in the entryway at the bottom of the staircase. He stopped, a bowl of macaroni and cheese in his hand, danced to the upbeat tune for a minute, and shoveled a huge bite of the pasta into his mouth. She stood frozen. How had he not seen her? He only needed to glance up and he would see her there. Her breath became loud inside her body. The more she tried to be still the louder it got. She was afraid if she moved she would draw his attention. Instead she stayed there like a statue watching his lower half dance while his upper half ate. Finally, after probably a full minute, he kicked a foot backward, did a smooth spin, and then proceeded to the living room. She breathed a sigh of relief. She put her hand on her rapidly beating heart and slinked back to her attic hideaway.

There wasn't anything she could do up there but wait. She didn't mind being trapped inside the house with him. She only wished she had been invited.

After an hour or so she heard water running. She stepped quietly down the stairs to the door which she nudged open a little bit. The shower was running. Joel must have plans to go somewhere.

Sure enough, not long after the water had been turned off, Joel whistled his way down the stairs and was out the door. She listened for his tires on the driveway. When she couldn't hear them anymore she emerged from her attic hideaway.

The bathroom where he'd showered was still bathed in steam. It smelled of his shower products. It smelled amazing. The old tub shower had a slow drain. A little bit of water still sat at the bottom, waiting its turn to go down. She plugged the drain with the rubber stopper, essentially trapping Joel's essence in the tub. She turned on the faucet and began to fill it. Somehow there needed to be more of him in there. She picked his discarded boxers and t-shirt up from the floor and tossed them into the water. She tossed her own clothes outside the bathroom door.

When the tub was half full she climbed in and submerged her body in Joel's old bath water. She let the faucet run as she reveled in the warmth of his watery touch. Who else could say they were as intimate with Joel Ruskin as she was? No one.

Eventually the water began to rise too high. It was now cascading slightly over the sides of the tub. She pulled herself from it, sloshing water onto the hardwood floor. Her wet, naked body dripped everywhere as she stepped out and reached for a towel. Then she fished out Joel's clothes and dropped them onto the floor where they had been. Finally she turned off the water and pulled out the plug.

"Joel, what the hell?" she shouted.

There were pools of water everywhere. She didn't know much about wood floors or what affect the water would have, but she knew Joel wasn't going to be happy when he discovered this possible plumbing issue.

"What?" He appeared behind her and looked over her shoulder at the mess.

"What happened in here?" She folded her arms in front of her. She'd never known Joel to be a messy person, but she also hadn't known him for long. Maybe they'd gotten to the point in their relationship when his true colors were coming out.

"You think I did this?" He stepped past her and surveyed the damage. Then he peered into the tub and shook his head. *"It's not draining. It wasn't like that when I got out of the shower."* He stuck his head closer to the

faucet. *"It must have a leak."*

"How could it leak that much that fast? And what about the floor?"

Joel stood and looked at her pointedly. *"I don't know, Lucy. I'll get one of the contractors to look at it. We'll use the other one for now."*

She smiled. Poor Joel. They were finally starting to sound like a real married couple. She shook her head as he left the room in a huff. Then she headed back up the stairs to the attic to wait for him to come home.

CHAPTER FIFTY ONE

It **was** obvious Joel was enjoying his time alone. He stayed up late into the night with the music still blaring through the old farmhouse. He seemed to be much happier with his girlfriend away. Lucy waited until well after she'd heard him turn in for the night. When he was finally in his bed, she still sat in the attic with only the light from her phone, listening to the silence and the occasional creaks of the old house settling. She listened to her own breath for what must have been an eternity. She thought of Joel laying under her, breathing in and out, sleeping and dreaming of what only he could know. Her breathing grew louder and she listened to it until she was convinced it was his she was hearing. He had to be asleep now.

She crept down the stairs, opened the heavy door, and headed through the dark to Joel's bedroom. The door was open. Now she really could hear him breathing in his bed. Snoring, ever so lightly. She had no plan. She wanted to be near him.

She approached the bed where she could see his outline in the digital light of his alarm clock. He was laying on his back with his head resting to the side. He was facing away from her. She stood over him. She watched the comforter rise and fall with his breathing. She reached out her hand to touch his face, but stopped short of contact. She didn't want to wake him up. She wanted to feel the heat from his skin and the breath as it escaped his beautiful mouth.

Joel's phone buzzed suddenly on the bedside table. Lucy jumped. The screen was glowing, casting a blue halo on the ceiling above their heads. It cast her shadow in giant form on the wall and the ceiling. When Joel didn't stir, she picked up the phone. The text message icon was centered on the screen. She swiped it.

Sydney: *Hey, Baby. Got here safely.*

Lucy cringed. A knot balled in her stomach. It was bad enough seeing them together. Catching these intimacies was even worse. She looked at Joel who hadn't moved at all and then typed a reply to his girlfriend.

Joel: *Glad to hear it.*

Sydney: *Sorry so late. Hope I didn't wake you.*

Joel: *Just got into bed.*

Sydney: *Ooo. Wish I was there with you.*

Joel: *Me too. The things I'd do to you.*

Sydney: *Hm Like what?*

Joel: *Tie you up.*

Sydney: *I'd like that.*

Joel: *Slap your fat ass.*

Sydney: *My what??? Joel WTF?*

Joel: *Maybe lay off the carbs this week, babe. You're gettin chunky.*

Sydney: *Screw you.*

Joel: *Lol. Whatever. Go to sleep.*

Sydney: *We'll talk tomorrow.*

She smiled in the glow of the cell phone. She knew the princess wouldn't let him live this down. She was nowhere near overweight, but all actresses worried about gaining even a single pound. Sydney was shallow enough to let it get to her.

"Dumb slut," Lucy whispered as she typed her own number into his phone and hit send. "You're not the only girl in Joel's phone." She ended the call after two rings. It was sufficient.

She held the phone over the bed and snapped a photo of the sleeping man. Then she texted it to Sydney.

Joel: *Already asleep.*

There was no reply. She waited for ten minutes with the phone in her hand, but Sydney didn't answer. She was mad. Lucy was elated. She set the phone back onto the table and leaned over Joel.

"Joel," she whispered. He muttered unintelligibly but stayed asleep. She could tell he was dreaming and she wanted to insert herself into his dream. "I love you, Joel. You belong with me. With Lucy."

Then she crept back up the stairs to the attic where she retrieved her silenced phone and added him to her contacts. The bed she'd made was right above him. She smiled when she thought of how exciting the next day would be.

CHAPTER FIFTY TWO

"I have no idea, Sydney."

Lucy could hear Joel in the kitchen early the next morning. He was on his phone talking to his girlfriend. She was hiding in the upstairs bathroom and could hear him through the vent. The smile on her face was actually starting to hurt her cheeks.

"I didn't send those texts and I didn't take that picture. How could I have? Look at the angle."

There was a long pause. Joel stomped his foot and then pulled a kitchen chair across the tile floor.

"There was no one here last night. At least, if there was, they weren't here by my invitation. I have to check this out because I assure you I had nothing to do with any of that."

Another long pause.

"I don't care if you believe me. Obviously I have bigger things to worry about."

Pause.

"That's not what I meant." His voice was softer now. Lucy had to strain to hear him. "Of course I care about you, but I'm telling you I didn't have a girl here last night."

Pause.

"It's not ghosts, Sydney."

Lucy covered her mouth with her hands to stifle a

chuckle. Ghosts. Sydney wasn't only shallow and disgusting, she was irrational.

"I get it," Joel continued. "Old house. Whatever. I have to go. I need to make some phone calls."

The front door opened and Joel stepped out onto the porch. She took the opportunity to scramble up the stairs to the attic. Joel would be calling the sheriff and the sheriff would be checking the house. She quickly moved her bedding and all her belongings into the darkest corner of the attic, pushed a huge, sealed moving box in front of it, and huddled there behind it, flashlight in hand.

The sudden vibration of her cell phone on the wood floor scared her half to death. She quickly swiped the screen to ignore the call. It was Moon. A minute later a message indicator appeared on the screen. She didn't need to hear the message to know why she was calling, but she listened anyway.

"Hi, Lucy. It's Moon." There was that friendly-but-annoyed tone again. "I'm wondering where you are. Maybe your body didn't feel like getting up again today, but I need you here. Call me back. Or just come in. Okay, bye."

Oops. She hadn't even thought about work. Moon was a nice lady and Lucy was sorry for putting her out, but she had more important things going on. Plus, Joel hadn't even left the house since Sydney had gone, so it's not like there was anything she could do about it.

An hour later, the sheriff arrived. The squeaky front door hadn't opened since Joel's phone call, so she assumed he'd waited for him outside. He was scared to be alone in his house with the photo-snapping intruder. Or

273

the ghost. Whichever.

"Don't be afraid of me, Joel," she whispered.

The sheriff clomped around the house in his big, black boots. He was a loud man and his voice carried all through the old halls. He trudged up the stairs to the second floor, asking Joel questions all the way. But they weren't personal safety questions. They were Hollywood questions. How did he get into show-biz? Was he working on anything new? Does he know Kevin Bacon?

Finally, the sheriff climbed the narrowest stairs and groaned his way into the attic. He un-belted his silver flashlight and shined it around the empty room. She sat still and imagined she could be invisible. She held her breath in her chest as long as she could and tried to slow her racing heartbeat. It must have worked because, after thirty seconds of checking, the sheriff declared the house clear and wobbled his way back down to the second floor.

"I suggest you get a security system, Mr. Ruskin," the sheriff boomed. "Clint down at the fire station can hook you up, no problem. There's a company that comes up from Denver. Some of our vacation home types use them to keep their homes safe during the off-season. Afraid of squatters and looters, I guess. Although, we don't get much of that kind of stuff in this town. Not a lot of crime around here. The usual meth-heads of course, but I've got my eye on all the ones I know of. I guess you being a celebrity..." He trailed off as his boots crossed the entryway floor.

Lucy stood up in the dark attic. She imagined herself on the porch standing next to Joel.

"Thank you for coming, Sheriff," She said to no one. She extended her hand and shook an imaginary hand. The ghost of the Sheriff gave her a professional smile.

"No problem, Mrs. Ruskin. Hopefully you won't have any more trouble. We sure enjoy having you two in our little town. Wouldn't want anything to scare you off."

The front door squeaked open again as Joel came back inside. She pictured herself in the breezeway waiting for him.

He rolled his eyes as if she'd given him her I-told-you-so face. But she hadn't. He was freaked out by the unusual things going on in the house and she understood that. Celebrities had all kinds of things to worry about that regular people didn't. If he truly believed a crazed fan was stalking him then she would do everything she could to help him feel safer in their home. She opened her laptop and searched for the nearest home security company.

CHAPTER FIFTY THREE

The next morning Joel was gone before Lucy woke up. She knew this because she heard the front door squeak and then slam. Joel's car crackled down the driveway.

When she ventured downstairs, she found the newspaper on the kitchen table. It was still in the plastic bag that was supposed to protect it from the rain but never really did. Thank goodness this was a dry day. She scanned the entertainment page to see if anything interesting would catch her eye. It did.

Has Sydney Been Unfaithful to Joel?
Photos surfaced this week of Headlining *star Sydney Panting on a secret rendezvous with co-star Preston Childers. The pair were spotted holding hands and embracing in a secluded park near the set of their upcoming film.*

She couldn't read anymore. Her ears burned with anger. This wasn't the information she'd wanted to find, but it was useful nonetheless. It was so bad it gave her pleasure to be enraged. Here was the woman who had stolen her man, who didn't deserve him, tramping around with someone new. Joel would no-doubt be hurting. She would be there for him. He could have her shoulder to cry on.

His number was in her phone. She picked it up and called, wondering what she would say if he picked up. The adrenaline coursing through her wouldn't let her stop. He didn't answer. There wasn't even a personalized message on his voicemail, just the standard robot voice greeting. She called again. Still no answer.

This was unacceptable. Hadn't she warned him about people like Sydney? She headed straight for Joel's office. She found a pen and pulled a sheet of paper from the printer.

Dear Miss Sydney Panting,

I'm writing to you with concern for my dear friend Joel Ruskin. I understand that as of late you've been keeping close company with the likes of Preston Childers. It makes me sad to think you wouldn't see the value in protecting a relationship with a dear soul like Joel. He loves you. He trusted you. And you turned out to be nothing but a dirty skank. He didn't see this coming, but I did, and I told him so.

Since you've taken what's mine and crushed his world, I'm going to return the favor. First, I'm going to shave off that auburn hair of yours that Joel loves so much. Then I'm going to take a very sharp knife and carve up that cute, fake nose that your whore money bought you. Then Joel will finally see you're as ugly on the outside as you are on the inside.

Joel Ruskin is mine. I will love him until I die.

Sincerely,

Your Nightmare

Lucy got into her car and cranked the angriest music she had on hand. She stopped at a gas station on her way out of town. She bought a bag full of snacks and drinks which she stuffed into a cooler she'd taken from Joel's house. Denver was a long drive. She hated the drive down the mountain even more than the drive up. But she had to do it. She had to do it for Joel. She had to drive to Denver and deposit her letter in a mailbox there so Sydney wouldn't be able to trace it back to Spring Fork.

She grinned as she left the tiny mountain town. She grinned because she was smart enough to think of it. She grinned because she pictured Sydney's face when she read the letter. She was sure Sydney would never return to the little town and would leave her boyfriend in her superficial dust.

At a gas station on the way, she pulled over to make a phone call.

"I'm sorry, Moon," she told her boss. "A friend of mine was in a bad skiing accident and I had to come to Denver."

"Oh, honey. That's terrible." The woman's concern was genuine. She might even have felt bad for considering firing her. "I hope your friend's alright."

"She'll recover. I don't feel good leaving her right now. She doesn't have any family in Colorado."

"Of course. You do what you need to do. Cory and I will work it out. Goddess bless you, Lucy."

She grinned again. Everything was going to be fine.

CHAPTER FIFTY FOUR

Lucy was exhausted when she got back to Spring Fork the next day. The trip had taken longer than she'd expected due to the heavy Denver traffic. When the sun set she was too afraid to drive back up into the mountains, so she'd slept in her car.

Normally she would wait at the edge of Joel's property to make sure there were no signs of life before she went on to the yellow house. Her head was throbbing and she couldn't think straight. She wanted to get back to the attic. So, seeing no car in the driveway, she parked her own vehicle and circled around to the back of the house.

There was no movement in the kitchen. She searched her bag for her keys which she had just had in her hand. She scolded herself silently for dropping them in there when she knew she would need them. Plenty of small-town people left their doors unlocked. It was sad that Joel felt he couldn't do that, too. It was obviously a habit leftover from city life.

While she fumbled in her bag she didn't hear the footsteps coming around the house.

"Who are you?" said a male voice. She looked up sharply and was stunned. It was Joel. He was standing in front of her in ratty jeans and a gray t-shirt. His chin and jaw line were dark from a few days of growth.

"What are you doing?" He didn't sound happy. He didn't look thrilled, either.

Her mouth opened but no sound came out. What should she say? She hadn't at any time in these past months thought of a legitimate-sounding excuse for why she would be on this man's property uninvited. Because in her mind she was his wife. This was their house that they shared together. She had every right to it. The stark reality of Joel's question reminded her that none of that was true.

So, she ran. She turned quickly, dodging Joel's hand as he tried to grab her arm, and she ran all the way to the trees at the back of his land. There she crouched down in the tall weeds and watched him pacing behind the yellow house. She couldn't see him well, but she assumed by his silhouette he was on the phone with the sheriff.

Then she mentally kicked herself. She could have made something up. She could have pretended she was lost or whatever. Her only instinct had been to run. Joel had been right there in front of her and she'd squandered her opportunity because of some stupid fight-or-flight instinct.

She made her way quickly and stealthily to her car. Obviously she needed to get out of there if the sheriff was coming. But she'd seen him in action and knew she had a little bit of time before he got there.

Sure enough, on the highway back to town her car passed the sheriff's going the opposite direction. He didn't even glance her way. She breathed a sigh of relief and prayed silently that Joel hadn't recognized her from the gift shop.

Or maybe he had. Maybe she had been on his mind this whole time. He obviously couldn't say anything in front of his girlfriend, but maybe he'd remembered her from when they met in Omaha and had been happy to see her. Now when he saw her standing at his back door he might have felt a little disbelief. Because he'd thought about her and wished to see her again and now here she was in the flesh. But she'd acted like an idiot and ran away. Tomorrow he would come to the gift shop and tell her how he felt. She smiled. She couldn't wait for tomorrow.

CHAPTER FIFTY FIVE

Six hours working at the gift shop dragged on like twenty. Lucy's mood was sour because Joel hadn't come by. Which meant he hadn't recognized her and he wasn't going to ask her to move into the yellow house with him.

She was also annoyed with Moon who had asked her way too many questions about her imaginary injured friend in Denver. How did it happen? Where was she skiing? Did they take her in a helicopter? What hospital did she go to? Luckily she'd had the whole trip to figure out her answers.

When Cody showed up for his shift he had a suspicious grin on his face. He walked slowly from the front door to where she stood by the counter. His eyes were on her the whole time. She furrowed her brow and stared right back at him. She could tell he had something to say to her.

"Someone called for you yesterday," he said in a weird, sing-song tone.

"Who?"

"She didn't tell me her name. Just said she was a friend of yours from Omaha. Said you worked together."

She began to perspire but she didn't know why. She knew something was off. Her only female friend in Omaha was Joni. Why would she call her at the store? Why wouldn't she call her cell phone? Or text her?

Maybe she had some awful news. But Cory wouldn't be teasing her if that were the case. He stood there waiting for her to ask him the details. She felt more like strangling the information out of him.

"What did she want?"

"She asked if you still worked here. She asked about your boyfriend." He said "boyfriend" the way a third grader would when trying to make someone uncomfortable.

"And what did you say?" She was sweating now. She avoided Cody's amused glare because she knew whatever information he had it wasn't good.

"I told her I didn't know you had a boyfriend. She said you live with him and you're fixing up a house together and that you told her he comes into the store all the time." He paused for a minute to gage her reaction, but she said nothing. She couldn't think of anything to say. "I told her you live in the boarding house and I've never seen you with a guy since you've been here. So, what's the deal, Lucy? Are you living a secret double life or something?"

"I have to go." She grabbed her bag and hurried toward the door. Her cheeks were flaming red. She was humiliated. Her lie had been exposed. And worst of all, it had been spread to her annoying, jerky coworker. She didn't ever want to see Cody's face again.

"Why in such a hurry?" he shouted after her. "Got a date with your imaginary boyfriend?"

Damn. She should have known Spring Fork was too small to keep secrets. She hadn't even told Joni where she worked, just that it was a tourist shop. She had obviously

283

tracked her down. Maybe she'd called every shop in town. And why? Because she didn't believe she could meet a man and live happily ever after? Some friend she was.

Once inside her car she tapped out an angry text to Joni.

Did you call my work?

The reply didn't come until she had started the car and was ready to pull off.

Why did you lie to me?

Cody's an idiot, Lucy replied. *He doesn't know anything about my life.*

Stop making shit up.

Stop stalking me. She yelled it out loud as she typed it. *Why are you obsessed with me?*

There was a long pause before Joni's answer. She listened to the birds chirp incessantly and to the angry storm brewing inside her head.

You're a loser, was Joni's reply. Lucy pounded her phone onto the passenger seat and then left it there. She threw the car into drive and pulled onto the nearly empty main street.

And with that, she and Joni were no longer friends. Which meant she and Leron were no longer friends because there was no way Joni wasn't relaying all of this to him. Which meant Lucy had no friends. Her quest for Joel's love was even more desperate now. She needed to find a better way to get him to notice her.

There was nothing she could do about it in that moment. She returned to her room and lay down in a fetal position on top of her bedspread. There she quietly cried herself to sleep, thinking of the mess she'd made of everything.

Lucy couldn't ever face Cody again. The next morning, she went into the store and told Moon she needed to take a few weeks off to reset her energy. She began to cry real tears when she told her there was too much going on in her life right now. It was the truth. Everything was caving in on her. Nothing was going as planned. With a sympathetic tilt of her head, the shop owner sent her on her way with a handful of crystals to aid in the process. The rocks ended up rolling around on the floor of Lucy's car.

When she finally got to the farmhouse, Joel's car and three trucks were in the driveway. She parked in her usual spot and made her way through the grass. This time she would be more careful. She crouched in the shadow of the garage and waited for hours until the other men got in their trucks and drove away.

Joel was alone now, but she couldn't go in. She knew he'd be on high alert after finding a stranger at his back door. Not a stranger, though. His wife.

The sun set. The farmhouse windows were lit. Carefully, she approached a side window directly above a newly-installed air conditioning unit. When she stood on the unit she could see through the sheer curtains into the living room. Joel was sitting on the couch scrolling through his phone.

It was so intimate seeing his profile, an angle rarely shown in interviews and photos. She had a candid view. It was as if they were spending a quiet evening at home together. So much love swelled in her heart as she gazed at her husband. How had she gotten so lucky?

As she stared through the curtains, Joel suddenly looked up from his phone. He scanned the room as if realizing he was being watched. Lucy backed up as far as the air conditioning unit would allow. Could he see her out there in the dark?

Still gripping his phone, he stood from the couch and looked around the room. Lucy's heart raced. A strange energy surged through her. His suspicion of being watched was proof that he could feel her presence. They were meant to be. How else would he know that she was so near to him?

Still, she couldn't reveal herself. Not like this. As he came toward the window, she hopped down to the ground and squatted by next to the house. She was now mere feet from him once again, separated only by concrete and wood. And she knew that he knew that his destiny was right outside that window.

After a few minutes the living room light went out. Lucy figured the coast was clear. The weird feeling surely wouldn't give him enough reason to investigate further. She ran back to her car like a scared child running from the dark.

Eventually Joel would leave and she wanted to be around when he did. So, she settled in to sleep in her car.

When she woke up in the morning, neck sore and cramping, Joel's car was heading down the long driveway. She ducked in case he drove past her. Although, why would he? The only place he would be going was town. It was finally her chance to get inside..

CHAPTER FIFTY SIX
Denver, Colorado – Present

Elijah watched Lucy fidget in her seat. Her hair was in a tight ponytail. Her jail-issued top was looser than at their last interview. Maybe it was a different size. Maybe she was losing weight.

She swiped some stray hairs from the left side of her forehead. Then she swiped the right side in the same way. She grimaced and swiped the left again and then the right. She appeared uneasy. He would be uneasy, too, if he were locked in here.

The notebook Elijah had given her was between them once again. This time, its outer corners were bent. There were scribbles on the cover. The pages didn't lie as neatly as they had when it was brand new. He could tell without opening it that she'd filled the whole book.

"I appreciate the work you put into this, Lucy."

She smiled briefly. Then she nodded.

"You can tell my story now?"

"Absolutely. I'm going to look this over and I'll come back and see you in a few days." He slid the notebook from the table and put it in his bag. "Can I ask you a few questions before I go?"

"Everything's in there." She chewed on her lip. Then she wiped her brow. The other side, again.

"And I can't wait to read it. But tell me, how did you

get into Joel Ruskin's home?"

She scowled at him like he'd asked her the stupidest question.

"I have a key. Well, I had a key, but it burned up in the fire."

"You had a key? How did you get a key?"

Lucy stopped biting her lip. Her face softened and her shoulders relaxed. She sighed, tilted her head, and smiled.

"Joel gave me a key."

"He gave you a key to his house?"

"Our house." She laughed. "Why wouldn't he give me a key to our house? I'm his wife."

Elijah had read the transcripts of her hearing. He knew she had claimed to be Joel Ruskin's wife. It had also been mentioned in every news story about her. But she'd been lying, right? Lying to save her ass?

"How long have you been married?"

"We got married last Valentine's Day." She looked down at her hands and rubbed the ring finger on her left hand where a wedding band would be. There was no visible mark there that he could see.

"Lucy, last Valentine's Day you were here." He glanced around the visiting room at the other inmates and their families. How many of them were still emphatically professing their innocence?

She looked at him and shook her head as if to say, "You silly man." When she spoke again her tone was slow and steady and she seemed to believe every word. "Last Valentine's Day, I was in Las Vegas. Joel and I were married at the Bellagio. Our parents were there. It

288

was beautiful."

A sinking feeling spread through Elijah's middle. He began to realize the notebook in his bag might be of no use at all. His book would have none of her personal touch.

CHAPTER FIFTY SEVEN
Spring Fork - 2016

Things were busy around the house for the next few weeks. There were workers in and out during the day. Joel busied himself with small projects when they were gone. Then he would watch Netflix until he fell asleep on the couch or in his bed.

She hadn't heard him talking to anyone on the phone other than his agent. There was no gossip online about his breakup with Sydney, but she knew they weren't together anymore. She'd heard his pathetic Skype conversation with a friend late one night. Joel was upset, but it sounded like his friend was trying to convince him it was all a big misunderstanding. Joel wasn't buying it. He said was done with her. This made Lucy happy. She wanted him to be strong. She wanted him to see that girls like Sydney would never be good for him. He needed someone who cared more for him than for herself. He needed Lucy.

When Joel was in town, she stayed hidden away in the attic, trying not to make any noise. Whenever the house was empty, she would go down to the pantry and take what she needed. When he was around, she had to pee in a bucket she kept in the corner of the attic. She wasn't proud of it, but she had no other choice. Now that he was getting over Sydney, maybe she could finally make her presence known and be part of his life without sneaking around. Maybe she could stop being the ghost in his attic.

Then one day Joel packed his suitcase and left. After she heard the door slam, she headed down to his bedroom where she found his luggage missing. She checked her phone, but he left no clue on his Twitter account about where he was going. In fact, since his breakup with Sydney, his Tweets had been scarce and boring. He didn't seem to be in the mood to communicate with the outside world.

She pulled up his contact in her phone and called. He didn't pick up. She called again. Voicemail on the first ring. He was avoiding her. Why? She only wanted to help.

For two more weeks, Joel stayed out of Spring Fork. She was so bored she could cry. Sure, she had free reign of his house. The work was finished on the inside and the landscapers only worked during the first half of the day. In the afternoons she would go into town and wander. She considered leaving Spring Fork for good. Maybe she should go to New York and find Joel's apartment. What good would that do? She wouldn't even make it past the doorman, if he had one.

A change of scenery would help her think. She decided to go into town. When she got to the back door of the yellow house she remembered she'd left her key up in the attic. She sighed heavily and slumped her shoulders. Being too lazy to climb two sets of stairs again, she opted to leave the back door unlocked so she could get back in. No one else would be visiting the house, anyway.

She hopped in her car and drove to Boney Mahoney's where she ordered lunch. She stared at the empty seat across from her and tried to think of a plan.

Maybe she would give up and go home. She could go back to her same old boring life in Omaha and forget about Joel. After all, his flighty nature was starting to piss her off. He had let Sydney walk all over him and now he was moaning and groaning because he missed her. It was pathetic. Was he even working now? Or was he laying around his apartment, growing out his beard and feeling sorry for himself?

Lucy's blood boiled. She was sitting in the same diner where she'd once fed him crushed glass. He hadn't even been man enough to do anything about that incident. He didn't post about it. There was no story in the gossip news. If something like that had happened to her, she would have sued Boney Mahoney's and had it shut down.

The heat of anger rising through her body made her decision final. She was done with Joel. She was going to the yellow house to get her things from the attic and then she was leaving Spring Fork forever.

First she needed to stop by the boarding house and tell the landlord she was moving out. He didn't give her much more than a shrug. In fact, it seemed nobody there had even wondered where she'd been. It was just as well. Maybe if she hadn't been focused on Joel she could have made some friends there. It was too late now. She was done with this tiny mountain town. She packed her only bag and tossed it into the trunk of her car.

On the short stretch of highway before Joel's house,

she vented her anger by screaming obscenities at the steering wheel. Her tiny car sputtered along. She was barely paying attention to the road or the car that passed her and took the turn to the yellow house. She could only see Joel's face in her mind's eye and the sheepish look he wore.

It wasn't until she got to her usual hidden parking spot in the trees that she recognized the car that had passed her. It was his. Now it was parked in front of the screened porch. Joel was taking bags out of the back. A figure emerged from the passenger side. A woman. That woman. That Sydney!

Lucy was fuming. How could he let that cheating bitch back into his life? And why was she back in Spring Fork? She hated the little town. She hated the farmhouse.

She sat in her car wondering what she should do. Even though she'd left the back door unlocked, she couldn't go back into the house with those two in there. She could wait until she thought they were asleep, but how would she know? They could be up late doing unspeakable things. Lucy pictured the two of them in the act. She shuddered. How could Joel do those things with Sydney after she'd been with someone else?

Finally, after an hour, Joel and Sydney exited the front door. He held the car door for her like a gentleman. Lucy made fake gagging gestures to no one. The two were dressed nicely and it was nearly six o'clock, so she figured they were going to dinner.

Maybe she could stop them. She could talk Joel out of dinner with Sydney. Remind him of what a terrible person she was. She took out her phone and called Joel's phone. She watched him stop while getting into the car. He retrieved his phone from his back pocket and looked at it. Lucy listened to it ringing, connected to him now with a mutual experience.

"Answer," Lucy growled.

But he simply looked at it and shoved it back into his pocket. Lucy's phone connected to his voicemail. She disconnected and threw the phone onto the seat next to her. Joel climbed into the driver's seat and closed the door.

When Joel's car was finally out of sight, she left her car and approached the house. She hoped they hadn't noticed the unlocked back door. To her relief, it was still the way she had left it. She stepped inside and headed for the kitchen. In one of the drawers she found a large pair of shears which she took with her.

Upstairs in the bedroom, three rolling suitcases were standing neatly at the foot of the bed. She could smell Sydney's expensive perfume still lingering there.

"Jeez, does she bathe in it?" she questioned out loud.

It was easy to pick out the two bags that were Sydney's. Hers were brown Louis Vuitton that looked like they'd taken their first flight. Joel's suitcase was plain black.

She hoisted the heavier of the two brown suitcases onto the bed. She unzipped it and threw it open like a book. The bag was neatly packed. She wondered if lazy Sydney had packed it herself or if she had people to do that for her. Either way, it was about to be unpacked.

Not knowing when the couple would return, she worked quickly. She took out each piece of overpriced designer clothing and cut the fabric haphazardly. One blouse she held in her hand for a minute before she destroyed it. She rubbed the silk over her forearm. It really did feel expensive. It's too bad she had to murder it.

One inside pocket of the suitcase was packed with Sydney's folded underwear. It was all frilly and nice—the kind you would only wear for someone else to see. This made her even more furious. She cut the crotches out of every pair.

"I assume you like easy access, Sydney," she spat out loud. "You whore."

When she was finished she put everything back inside the suitcase and placed it back exactly where she found it. The kitchen shears went up into the attic with her. There she waited for the happy couple to come home from their misguided date.

Lucy had fallen asleep on her makeshift bed in the attic. She was woken by footsteps in the second floor hallway. Then Sydney's hideous laughter broke through her sleepy haze. She lay still to listen to their conversation.

"He couldn't have been serious," Joel was saying.

"They're all serious," Sydney replied with a superior tone. "These fans think I owe them something. They're all delusional."

Lucy fumed again. What an ungrateful bitch. How dare she talk that way about the people who made her famous? These were the people who made it possible for her to live in her shallow, sheltered world.

"Like, I got this letter the other day," Sydney continued. "Some lady—I mean, I think it was a lady—

threatened me for dating you. She said she'd cut my hair or something stupid like that."

"Because she doesn't want you dating?"

"She doesn't want me dating you. She claimed she's the only one for you."

"Ah," Joel boasted, "so she's not really your obsessed fan. She's mine."

"Yes, Joel," she joked. "Do you want to keep score?"

Then he mumbled something. They got quiet which could only mean something gross was about to happen. She didn't even want to listen. She turned onto her back and pulled the pillow over her ears.

Sydney hadn't even taken her letter seriously. She was actually amused by it. Why hadn't she reported it to the police or something? Was she that stupid? Did she not believe Lucy would do what she said she would do? She was a bigger idiot than she had thought. What a waste of her time. She was going to have to step up her game to scare this princess.

CHAPTER FIFTY EIGHT

When morning came, Lucy was disoriented. She didn't remember falling asleep, but apparently she had. Now she could hear yelling through the vent. It was Sydney's voice, and the pauses indicated she was on the phone. She quickly opened her laptop to hear the conversation more clearly.

"Call them again, Jim," she was shouting. "This is not acceptable. No one else handled my luggage but the driver in L.A. and the airline. Do you really think the driver could get into my bags and cut up my shit while I'm sitting right there in the car? That airline is going to pay. There were at least twenty-thousand dollars' worth of clothes in that bag. And my underwear," she shrieked. "I have to go buy all new underwear in this podunk town. Where the hell am I supposed to get that? The fricking general store?"

There was a long pause. Lucy had both hands covering her mouth, lest she lose control and laugh out loud.

"Have my assistant, um, what'-her-name, the new one, overnight them. I'm not walking around in polyester granny panties, Jim."

There was a loud thump and all was quiet. Then Sydney let out a short but furious scream. The house was quiet again. Joel was obviously not there. Lucy could barely hear her muttering to herself. She considered trying to scare Sydney in that moment. She could bang on the walls and send her running out the door. Or maybe she would even hurt her. Anything to scare her away again.

Lucy descended the attic stairs as noiselessly as possible. She checked the hole in the door to make sure the coast was clear. Before she emerged, however, Sydney walked out the front door, slamming it behind her.

She pushed the attic door open so forcefully it banged on the wall with an echoing crash. If she couldn't get to Sydney, she would reach out to Joel. This had to be putting a strain on Sydney and Joel's relationship, or whatever it was. Clearly it was time for Lucy to step in. There would be no better time.

The bed in the master bedroom was unmade. She sat on Joel's side and began composing a text message to him.

You don't know me, although you do know me. Deep inside we are connected. A cosmic energy has bound us together, has reached through the screen and brought my heart to yours. Why? Perhaps we were lovers in a past life. Perhaps we were once atoms in the same bright star that died and sent us out into the universe. Now here we are living in the same world. When I saw you I felt that particle of life inside of me awaken from a decades-long slumber. It told me to find you and to piece back together what once made up that great celestial body. If we can talk face to face I know I can make you understand.

When she finished typing, she hit send and smiled. It was done. It was real. Joel was reading her text right now and realizing that someone loved him more than Sydney ever could.

She hugged the phone to her chest and waited in the silence of the yellow house. Minutes went by. She checked the phone. He hadn't answered. She touched the text message icon. Nothing new. Why wasn't he answering? He should be asking who was texting him, at least. He should want to know.

"Damn it, Joel." She rose from the bed and went to the door. "Damn it," she yelled into the hallway.

A row of framed pictures hung in the hallway between the bedroom doors. She took one down, stepped toward the banister, and threw it down the stairs. It crashed at the bottom, glass flying. She gazed down at what she had done, picturing him finding the mess and wondering what had happened. How could a picture have fallen off that wall and landed in that spot? Maybe it was Sydney's ghosts again. She laughed out loud. Then she retreated back to her hideaway in the attic.

CHAPTER FIFTY NINE

Life in Spring Fork was quiet and mostly calm. It was a slower life than we had in New York. Joel wanted to be in the little town any time he wasn't working. I wasn't as enthusiastic, but I stuck it out for him.

One afternoon I was cleaning the kitchen after lunch while Joel took a shower upstairs. His phone sat on the corner of the table. When it chimed and the screen lit up, I glanced over. I didn't mean to snoop, but I couldn't help myself. He'd gotten a text and the name caught my eye: Sydney Panting. We'd run into her the last time we were in Hollywood. I'd felt then like she was flirting with Joel, which was ridiculous because she had to have known we were dating then. She was clearly the Hollywood type who had no fear of being called a home wrecker.

I picked up Joel's phone. Even though the screen was locked I could still see his most recent alerts. I could read the text Sydney had sent. *Call me when you're in LA. Found a hot new club for drinks.*

My heart seemed to shrink inside my chest. I became sick to my stomach. Joel and I were just getting started. We'd gotten married. We'd bought this house. And now it seemed it was all crumbling to pieces. Was my new husband already having an affair? How long had it been going on? Suddenly I couldn't breathe.

When Joel came down the stairs I was sitting on a

stool trying to catch my breath. He saw his phone in my hand and immediately looked concerned.

"What's wrong, Lucy? What happened?"

I stared at him for a moment. This could be our final moment together. Had we come to the inevitable crossroad where he would be ripped away from me? He could, in the next second, tell me he was seeing Sydney Panting and we were over. A tear escaped to my cheek and I held the phone out to him.

"You have a text from Sydney Panting." My voice was shaking. The words I spoke now made me feel more angry than sad. I expected him to react defensively, but he didn't. He looked confused and took his phone.

"What does she want?" His tone was casual and unapologetic. He read the text and then looked at me again.

"She wants you to come back to L.A., apparently. How long have you been seeing her, Joel?"

"I'm not seeing her."

"Then why is she texting you like you are?"

"She said she found a new club. That doesn't mean I've ever been anywhere with her."

"Why would she invite you out if she knows you're married?"

"I don't know."

"Maybe because you gave her the impression it was okay?" I was shouting now. The windows were open and I was aware my voice would carry outside. It didn't matter anyway. There were no neighbors close enough to hear the noisy end of our marriage. "Maybe you've discussed it before? Maybe you're already sleeping with her behind my back, Joel."

"Lucy, calm down." He sounded annoyed which only made my blood boil hotter. He had no right to talk down to me in that moment. "I didn't do anything with her. I barely even know her. She's an actress and actresses like to stir up drama. That's exactly what she's doing. She's seeking attention."

"Then text her back and tell her to go screw herself."

Joel shook his head and rolled his eyes. The phone clicked as he typed in his reply. Then he handed me the phone so I could read it. *My wife and I will keep that in mind.*

I tried to scroll up but there were no previous messages before hers. Either it was the first text she'd ever sent him or he'd deleted them all. Then a thought crossed my mind.

"Why does she have your number if you barely know her?"

"I don't know. Maybe her agent got it for her. Maybe she got it from a friend. You have no reason not to trust me. I bought this house to get away from drama like this."

I was still holding the phone when it chimed. Sydney had replied, *You should leave the wifey at home.* Then a winky face.

What Joel was saying made sense. So far I'd had no reason not to trust him. He was wanted by women everywhere and he chose to stay in this quiet mountain town with me. But I'd had enough of this tramp. I thrust the phone at Joel's chest and went up the stairs to our bedroom. I needed time to cool down.

CHAPTER SIXTY

Joel and Sydney returned to the yellow house late that night. Lucy had been lounging comfortably in Joel's bed, replaying Sydney's angry conversation in her head. She wasn't sure if she should be angry that Sydney again wasn't giving her credit for what she had done. Either way, it had ruined Sydney's day, and Lucy was definitely glad about that.

When the front door creaked open, she scurried back up to her attic hiding spot. She listened as the couple stumbled up the stairs and to the bedroom. They must have both been drunk. Fortunately for her, they were too intoxicated to want to do anything other than sleep. Within a half hour the house was dead quiet once again.

When she believed them both to be out cold, she crept down the stairs and into the bedroom with her flashlight. She tripped over some discarded clothes on the floor but caught herself before she got to the bed where the two were sleeping. She hovered over them, staring with her flashlight aimed at their passed-out faces. She could probably do anything to them without waking them up. To test her theory, she pulled back the comforter and ran her hand over Joel's bare chest. A chill went through her whole body and lingered between her thighs. It was hard to believe she was actually touching him like this. Would she dare lean over and kiss him? Before she could he rolled onto his side and flung his arm over his girlfriend. Lucy scowled. He had ruined the moment. He had ruined it for that drunk bitch.

Lucy's face was red hot. She swung her arm back in anger, hitting the nightstand and knocking Joel's cell phone onto the floor. She picked it up and opened the camera while mumbling to herself that he should start locking his phone. Then she snapped a picture of the sleeping couple and texted it to Sydney. Across the bed on the other table, Sydney's phone flashed and then reduced to a blinking blue light. It lit up the ceiling with intermittent color.

The closet door was standing wide open. Sydney had finally gotten around to hanging up her designer garments. Lucy ran her hand over a dozen pieces, feeling the fabric. She stroked one cotton top and then pulled it from the hanger. It didn't feel any different than her own shirts from Target. There was no doubt Sydney paid ten times more for this one. She threw it on the ground. She proceeded to pull every other top and dress off of their hangers and let them fall to the closet floor. She spent a few more minutes disrupting various objects in the room before retreating again to her attic perch.

CHAPTER SIXTY ONE
Spring Fork – Present

It was 2:30 in the afternoon, which meant Boney Mahoney's was well past the lunch rush. Elijah was the only guest in the restaurant. He had a sandwich in front of him. His laptop was open.

On his screen was an old magazine article from right after the incident. It featured, in bold print, a quote from Miss Sydney Panting herself: *"I never liked that town. Joel said it was safe and quiet and I'd be able to go outside without getting mobbed. Turns out it wasn't going outside that was the problem. The danger was inside that house the whole time."*

An email alert popped up in the corner. Elijah opened it. He clapped his hands together one time and silently thanked the universe.

There was a link in the email to a video he'd waited weeks for. It was Joel Ruskin's statement to police. If the B-list celebrity wasn't willing to talk to him, he'd use what he he'd said to someone else.

This video wasn't the crappy kind they show on TV. It wasn't from a discreet camera in the corner of a cold room. Joel was sitting in a high-back chair, probably in a hotel somewhere. The video was in color and was of good quality.

He skipped through the formalities at the beginning.

When he pushed play again the officer was talking off-camera.

"Did you have any suspicion someone had been in there? Was anything out of place?"

"Well, at first things would go missing. Like, Sydney had a bracelet I'd given her and within a few days she lost it. I thought she didn't like it and didn't want to tell me."

Joel scrunched his brow and stared for a few seconds as if deep in thought.

"You know what?" he continued. *"There was a thing that happened that didn't make sense. One of the bathrooms flooded, but I never figured out where the water came from. There was at least half an inch of water on the floor and out in the hallway. But I didn't find any leaks."*

"Miss Panting mentioned some weird messages on her phone."

"That's right!" His face lit up with the excitement of remembering. *"She was mad at me because of some messages she said I sent her. I didn't send those texts. She even screen shotted them to me, but I swear they didn't come from me. I even checked my phone. And there was a picture of me sleeping. I found that in my photos after she told me about it. It was the creepiest thing. That happened twice, actually. Do you think that was this lady? Was she in my room when I was sleeping?"* He shuddered.

"We assume so. We also have the Sherriff's reports. One says you found a woman on your property."

"Yes. I'm almost sure it was her. Now looking back, I

have no doubt."

"But you'd never seen her before"

"I don't know. I could have. I see a lot of people. All the faces start to blend together, you know?"

Joel leaned forward and reached his arm down. When he sat back there was a glass in his hand. He took a sip.

"What was she doing when you found her on your property?"

"She was standing by my back door."

"Did she say anything to you?"

He looked over his shoulder. Then he shifted in his seat as if he was tired of answering questions.

"No. I think I said something, like asked her what she wanted. But she ran away. She literally ran across my yard and through the trees."

"Miss Panting had an issue with her bags, correct?"

"That's right. She came to Colorado and when she opened her suitcase her clothes were all cut up." Another lightbulb seemed to go off in his head. It appeared he was realizing all of these things could have been Lucy's doing.

"So you had a security system installed?"

"Yes."

"Were there cameras?"

"No." He put the glass down, then rubbed his hand through his hair. *"Just sensors on the doors and windows. The company I used didn't have cameras. They only respond to break-ins. I was planning on ordering those cameras you can link to your cell phone. I never got around to it."*

307

"And the sensors were never tripped?"

"Not once." He threw his hand in the air. *"That's what I don't understand. How could she have gotten into the house that night without setting off the alarm?"*

"Joel, we think she was already in the house. We think she never left."

CHAPTER SIXTY TWO
Spring Fork - 2016

Joel and Sydney's verbal exchange the next morning was music to Lucy's ears. Sydney was freaking out and Joel was trying to calm her down.

"My stuff was moved, Joel," she shouted. "Did you move my diamond studs? I put them on the dresser and I found them behind the door. I didn't do that."

"We were both pretty hammered last night, Syd. Maybe you took them off and dropped them."

"I didn't wear them last night. I took them off and put them here so I could put on my gold hoops. I put the gold hoops on the nightstand." There was shuffling as Sydney went to check beside the bed.

"They're not here," she squealed.

Lucy stroked the gold hoops between her fingers. They had been a gift to her from Joel, although Joel wasn't aware of it.

"And what about the clothes? Do clothes fall off of hangers on their own? Was it the wind?"

"Okay, calm down." Joel sounded tired. Maybe tired of Sydney in general.

There was silence for a while and the bed squeaked when one of them sat on it. Finally Sydney was recognizing Lucy's handiwork which made her proud. She thought about how much more she could do.

"Holy shit." Sydney's voice sounded deliciously frightened. "Joel, look at this."

"Who took this?"

They had finally found the picture she had taken in the middle of the night. She almost squealed with delight, but caught herself.

"It's like the one you texted me." Sydney was starting to panic now. Her voice was shaking. "Joel, what's going on? It's this house. There's something in this house."

"Okay," he said calmly. She could hear Sydney sobbing. Joel promised her he would do something. What could he do? There was no way to get rid of Lucy now. Sydney was the one who had to go.

Two days later the security company arrived. Lucy huddled in the attic. As the man downstairs affixed sensors to all the outside doors and windows, she felt the bare walls closing in around her. She couldn't leave now. If she did, she couldn't come back. Not that she ever wanted to leave Joel. But she might like to get outside and walk around every now and then. And what if Joel left town again? What if he left for a long time? She'd starve to death.

When everyone had left the house, Lucy stomped around the attic like an angry toddler. How could Joel let that woman manipulate him into installing a security system? It was to keep her out. She knew it. Sydney was threatened by her. She couldn't handle Joel's attentions on another woman. Well, she wouldn't be a pushover. Joel didn't want her gone, that was a sure thing.

"She's jealous." She spoke to no one. "She thinks she

310

should be the most important thing in his life. That shows how self-centered she is. And Joel deserves better than that. I can give him better than that, and he knows it."

The line between reality and her fantasy was blurred now. It was more than blurred, it was nearly non-existent. Had she broken into this old, yellow farmhouse? Or had she been living here with Joel this whole time? Had they been together in his bed, showered together, promised their lives to each other? And how did Sydney get her manicured claws into him? How did she tear him from the woman he'd vowed to love?

"She won't be rid of me so easily. Joel loves me. She's tricked him. She's a demon." She gasped. Her pacing stopped. That was it. That was the answer. Sydney was a demon. She was a succubus sent to steal Lucy's man away. And how does one get rid of a demon? She knew there was only one way.

CHAPTER SIXTY THREE

Several days passed before Lucy got the chance
to execute her plan to rid Joel's home of the succubus that
had planted herself there. Circumstances needed to be
perfect for it to work. Finally, after four days of waiting,
she saw her opportunity.

Sydney had gone to bed in the master suite. She was
poised on her satin pillow with her arms straight down
over the comforter like a Barbie doll placed carefully into
a toy bed. Lucy was able to look in on her while Joel was
still downstairs. She could hear him unloading the
dishwasher in the kitchen. His girlfriend was fast asleep
already, oblivious to such a thing as housework.

Lucy entered the master bathroom, switched on the
light, and closed the door. In the antique medicine cabinet
she found a few orange bottles. She took one out. Zoloft
prescribed to Joel Ruskin. She opened her phone's
camera and flipped it to the front camera. Then she hit
record.

"Hi, Belinda," she whispered to her own image on
the screen. "I'm recording this from the bathroom
because Joel is asleep and I don't want to wake him up.
He doesn't want me talking to you because he thinks
you're a psycho. He's never liked you. You're not
friends."

She smiled and then scanned the bathroom with the

camera's lens. She held the Zoloft bottle in front of it, making sure it was in focus.

"See?" She faced the camera again. "Do you need more proof than that? You don't know me, Belinda. You don't know anything. Things are going to happen. Joel is ready to make our relationship public. And you're going to feel so stupid." She growled the last words. Her hand clutched the phone so hard it nearly flew from her hand.

She tapped the red button to stop recording. How satisfying it would be when everything came to light. Sydney would be gone tomorrow and Lucy would be Joel's savior. He would be eternally grateful. They would no longer have to love in secret.

She turned off the bathroom light. The door squealed when she pulled it open. Sydney stirred only a little but remained deep in sleep. Lucy crept cautiously to the dark hallway and through the attic door. She sat on a step where she could watch the hall through the hole she'd made.

While she waited for Joel to turn in, she emailed the video she'd made to Belinda. Hopefully she was sleeping and wouldn't get the message until morning. Perfect timing.

After a while Joel finally came upstairs and settled into the newly remodeled guest bedroom to watch a movie. She knew this would be his destination because he and Sydney had had a blaring argument about it only two hours ago. Sydney needed her beauty sleep and didn't like Joel turning on the TV in the master bedroom while she was trying to sleep. He wanted to finish a movie he'd started that she'd made him turn off for some reason unknown to Lucy. So, he'd agreed to finish it in the guest room after he cleaned up the kitchen. That was hours ago.

Finally the flicker of the moving pictures was gone and she could see from the end of the hall that the TV had defaulted back to the Netflix menu. That meant Joel was asleep and she was free to rid him of the manipulative demon and take back their love forever.

Moving quietly, she headed for the master bedroom. In one hand she carried a length of rope. There'd been plenty of time after Joel had left the other night for her to sneak downstairs and find it in the pile of tools left by the workers. It was a lucky thing the rope had been there or she would have been forced to be more innovative.

Now she inched toward the bedroom with only the light of the candle in her other hand to guide her. She wrapped one end of the rope around the old glass-ended doorknob and tied it securely. She'd already practiced this part, so she was sure her knot would hold and the grooves of the knob would secure the rope. She let the other end of it fall to the hallway floor.

She entered the master bedroom quietly. She could hear Sydney's drawn-out breaths and knew she was fast asleep. When she reached the windows on the other side, she set the candle on the dresser beside them. The drapes Sydney had picked out were conveniently long and of high-end material. The lighter fluid soaked easily into the fabric. She tossed the half-empty bottle to the side and reached for the candle. She set it on the ground against one of the curtains and then backed away.

When the fabric caught fire, she was already at the door. A satisfied grin crossed her face. What a sight it would be to see the bitch burn. Unfortunately, she wouldn't get to. She had more work to do. She had to save Joel from his burning home. She needed to be his hero.

The flames rose quickly, and she saw them licking the ceiling as she closed the bedroom door. She stretched the rope across the hall and tied the other end to the banister. Smoked seeped out from under the door. From inside the bedroom. she heard a startled cry. Sydney ran for the door and was met with resistance.

The rope had a little more stretch to it than Lucy had anticipated. At first the door opened only half an inch and then snapped back. On her second attempt, Sydney pulled it hard and peered through the crack at the smiling arsonist. Her face was panicked which made Lucy's insides flutter with excitement. Finally she would be rid of this woman.

"Help me," Sydney cried.

Lucy was perturbed. It wasn't a desperate cry for help, but a command from someone who'd become accustomed to bossing people around and getting her way. She thought right then that even if she hadn't set the fire herself, there's no way she would help this entitled celebrity with that kind of tone in her voice. She needed to be humble. She needed to beg Lucy to save her. And even then, she would definitely rather watch the demon go up in flames.

Sydney's manicured hand reached through the gap and groped for the anything within reach. Lucy swatted at it, quickly losing her patience. She finally grabbed Sydney's ring and middle fingers and pulled them back sharply against the doorframe. Sydney let out an angry and terrified yelp. Lucy saw her eyes widen as she pulled the door shut and tied the slack of the rope to the length to tighten it more. Sydney tried to pull it open again but was unsuccessful. She pounded on the door with both fists as thicker smoke billowed out from underneath it.

Lucy wasted no more time. She rushed down the hall to the guest bedroom where Joel was still sleeping, unfazed by the screaming and the smoke that was now creeping toward him. For a moment, she gazed on this sleeping man. In any other scenario she would kiss his cheek and lay down with him, but right now his life was in danger. His house was on fire. And she was here to save him.

"Joel," she shouted, shaking him gently at first, and then more aggressively. She was touching him. She was actually here in this room with him. Her dream was becoming reality.

Joel's eyes were crazy when he woke up. It took a few seconds for his face to register understanding of what was happening. He sat up quickly and stared at her. Then his face changed as he seemed to recognize her. Yes. Finally he knew her.

"How did you get in here?" he demanded. She thought it was a stupid question. His house was on fire. She was saving his life. What did it matter?

"You have to get out. The house is on fire."

"What?" He looked around in a panic. Why wasn't he wasn't doing anything. The room was filling quickly with smoke.

Fully awake, Joel reacted to Sydney's screams for the

first time. He shouted her name, put his hands on Lucy's arm, and pushed her to the side. He ran past her in a panic toward his bedroom.

Lucy was furious. He'd again chosen Sydney over her.

"Joel, come back here," she screamed. She ran after him and grabbed him with both arms around his waist. He was trying to get to the bedroom door to release that witch, but she wasn't going to let him.

"It's too late for her." She wavered between sobbing and screaming in anger. How dare he miss his chance to be free of Sydney? She was doing this for him. "We have to get out of here, Joel."

Wrestling her arms from his midsection, Joel turned and pushed her to the ground.

"Are you crazy?" he shouted.

Crazy? Crazy for wanting to save the love of her life from a tragic house fire? Crazy for wanting him to adore her over everything else? No. He would not get away with calling her crazy.

"Come back here," she screamed again from the hallway floor. All self-control had left her body. There was only anger and desperation. She was so close to having him. They were together in this frantic moment. They could be together forever, sharing whatever life threw at them.

"We can't be apart, Joel. We can't be. I love you. Why can't you see it? Forget Sydney." She pounded on the wood floor. Her throat was becoming raw from the smoke. She screamed through the pain, "What about us, Joel? What about us?"

Joel was now coughing forcefully. He tried to untie the knot that Lucy had done. The darkness and the smoke hindered his efforts. He ducked under the rope and then heaved his whole body against the bedroom door. It was solid and wouldn't budge.

On the third attempt he looked exhausted and ready to give up. Good. He was coming around. But when his body hit the door again, the antique banister gave way and crashed to the floor, allowing him to push open the door enough to rescue his girlfriend from the flame-engulfed room.

He helped Sydney get to the top of the stairs. She was already weak from the smoke and heat and looked like she might not make it. Lucy watched his heroic act with deepening respect for him. He was such a kind and generous person, willing to risk his life to save even the vilest person. Still, her anger was not gone. She wouldn't let them have their happy ending. She pulled herself onto all fours. Then she lunged forward and with a maniacal scream threw herself against Joel's legs. He and Sydney went tumbling down the old staircase to the entryway below.

CHAPTER SIXTY FOUR

I woke up in the hospital to learn that our beloved yellow farmhouse had burned to the ground. Somehow I'd made it down the stairs and to the front lawn, but had passed out from the smoke before the volunteer firefighters were able to get to us. They must not have had much fight against the big, wooden structure. Tears rolled down my cheeks as I thought about the house that Joel had loved; burned to nothing now.

When he was well enough, Joel came to visit me in my room. He carried a bouquet of roses. His other arm sported a cast. We'd both been through so much. He laid back on the bed with me and put his arms around my shoulders. I wiped the tears from face, not wanting him to know I'd been crying. I wanted to be strong for him.

"I thought I'd lost you, Lucy." There were tears in his eyes and one slipped onto his cheek. "I couldn't go on if that had happened."

"Neither could I. Please tell me we won't ever be apart."

"You go where I go," he whispered. Then he kissed me gently on the end of my nose. "After all, you saved my life. I need you around as my bodyguard."

I chuckled through my tears. There was sadness for what we'd been through and what we'd lost. But I was happy and grateful for this man I had and whom I would never let go. Nothing could destroy that.

SPRING FORK, CO—Joel Ruskin's rustic castle came tumbling down this week. A fire caused complete loss of the Colorado farmhouse. Ruskin and his girlfriend Sydney Panting were flown by helicopter to a Denver hospital where they are both in stable condition. A woman, identified as 27 year old Lucy Bonneville of Omaha, Nebraska, was found on the lawn of the home suffering from smoke inhalation. According to police, Ruskin claims Bonneville broke into his home and started the blaze. She is also in stable condition at an undisclosed medical center and is in police custody.

A uniformed officer was posted outside Lucy's room. She assumed he was there to keep the press away. He was really there to guard the prisoner. She didn't see it that way. Somehow the daydreaming side of her brain had taken over while she was unconscious. She couldn't remember sneaking into the yellow house or even her own crappy apartment back home. The memories that kept her company in the lonely hospital room were of her beautiful life with Joel. She remembered the dates. She remembered the parties. She remembered their beautiful private wedding and every emotion she'd experienced that day.

Two nurses entered the room. One wordlessly removed the food tray from the cart beside the bed. The other greeted her and handed her a cup of pills.

"How's Joel today?" Lucy asked her. The nurses looked at each other strangely but didn't exchange words.

"Joel Ruskin? I haven't heard. He's not on my rounds." She took the empty pill cup from her and tossed it in the trash.

"He must not be doing well," she fretted. "He hasn't been able to come see me yet."

"I'm sure he's fine." She straightened the blanket on the bed.

"Will you make sure he visits me? Don't turn him away."

"Okay, Lucy." As she turned to go she whispered something to the other nurse who looked back at Lucy with an angry glare. She must have been jealous. Lots of women were jealous of her relationship with Joel. After all, she'd stolen him away from them for good. She'd have to get used to those reactions.

CHAPTER SIXTY FIVE
Elijah - Denver – Present

Elijah checked in at the prison and proceeded to the visitation room. He told himself it would be the last time. Unless he could get her to tell him the truth of what happened, her account was useless to him.

It didn't make any sense that she would lie to him. Did she get a kick out of making him look like a fool? If she didn't want him to write the book, she could have said so in the beginning and saved him all the time and money.

But he was writing it anyway. He didn't need her permission. The things he had learned were enough, even if he had to fill in the gaps with speculation. A lonely woman had fallen so hard in lust with a celebrity that she'd made up stories, moved to a new town, and had even lived in his attic for months undetected. Then when she had burned his house to the ground. But why? It was the only part of the puzzle he still needed from her.

He looked at the clock on the wall as the room filled with women in prison garb. Lucy was one of the last inmates to arrive. She sat down across from him and smiled as if she was happy to see him.

"Hello, Elijah."

He tried to ignore her cheerful demeanor. This was business, and he couldn't allow himself to feel sorry for her. He needed to try to get the truth and then get out of there. The book would come together somehow. It wasn't likely to be a best seller without her point of view, but he wasn't going to give up.

"I can't use this." He dropped the notebook on the table top, making a sharp noise that echoed off of the gray walls. Heads turned. The guards all put their hands on their belts and glared at him with wide eyes. Elijah put his hands up in apology and then rested them on the table in front of him.

"Why not?" Her pleasantness went away.

"It's not real. This is a made-up story. You were going to write about what actually happened with Joel Ruskin. Instead you're giving me this fan-fiction."

"This is real." She jabbed her finger onto the notebook. "This is how I met Joel. This is my life with Joel. That's what you wanted."

"What life with Joel? The public wants to hear your story about why you stalked Joel, how you broke into his house, why you burned his house down. They don't want to read fiction about how you wanted it to be. They want the truth."

Her eyes closed. She took a deep breath and let it out slowly. He could tell she was trying to tamp down her frustration. The prison guards scanned the room absentmindedly. If she shouted or even stood up from her chair one of them would escort her back to her pod.

She opened her eyes and stared at him for a few seconds before responding.

"I didn't burn the house down," she said calmly through clenched teeth. "It burned down. It was an old house."

"Too bad you couldn't convince the judge of that."

Her eyes squinted, giving him a chill. Yes, they were safely locked in this prison, but he knew what she was capable of. He had to tread lightly. What if when she got out she came after him?

"It's the truth. Joel is my husband. We're very happy together."

Elijah sat back and folded his arms. "Fine. You're Mrs. Joel Ruskin. You lived in an old house in Colorado and it mysteriously burned down. So, how did you end up in prison?"

"Misunderstanding. I go to court next month and we're going to straighten this all out. Joel will be there. He'll tell everybody what happened."

He sat up straight again. His scalp tingled like he could actually feel his hair graying from frustration. It took all his self-control to keep his voice down.

"You've been to court already, Lucy. You were sentenced. You're here for a long time for attempted murder, arson, breaking and entering, and whatever else."

She closed her eyes and shook her head again. Elijah looked at the inmate for a silent minute. She wasn't backing down. Her face showed no sign this was all a ridiculous joke designed to make him look stupid or to waste his time. He could see now that Lucy Bonneville truly believed the story she'd written on paper. There would be no sensational memoir straight from the stalker's pen. She had officially gone off the deep end.

CHAPTER SIXTY SIX
Lucy- Denver- Present

Visiting hours were over. Elijah took the notebook Lucy had filled for him. She was proud of what she had written. People would read it and they would know the truth. They would see her side of it.

She was escorted to the hall to line up with the other inmates. A female guard stared silently at the group. Her face was expressionless. Lucy didn't like her judging eyes. The guard could think what she wanted about the other women. They were criminals and crazies. Lucy was a victim of circumstance. She didn't belong here.

Elijah's book would set her free. She smiled as she considered the impact it would have. Maybe Oprah would lead a women's march on the prison and demand her release. She could finally go back to New York. She and Joel could forget the whole thing.

"Yo." A thin, hard-looking inmate nodded her way. "What you smiling about, Crazy Laura?"

"Shut it," said the guard.

Lucy mumbled under her breath, "My name's not Laura."

"What, Laura?" The woman stepped out of line. Other inmates laughed and began to taunt her as well. Lucy looked to the guard to stop the harassment, but she only smirked and watched it happen.

"Crazy Laura," Another woman raised her hands in mock surrender. "Don't burn my house down" Everyone laughed, even the inmates not taking part. Lucy hung her head. It was like high school again. And elementary school. Basically every place where she was forced to be with people who didn't understand her.

Her eyes burned. She began to shake. Where was Joel? When would he take her out of this place?

The guard watched on. The inmates continued to mock her.

"Crazy Laura," they chanted. "Crazy Laura."

The swelling rage escaped her mouth. "My name's not Laura," she screamed, rushing at a cluster of them. "I'm not crazy." She swung her fists, hitting air, hitting flesh. "Fuck all of you!"

Finally, the guard took action. She slapped her palm on the concrete wall and shouted, "Enough."

The inmates stepped back in line, smiles still glued to their faces. The guard retrieved her cuffs from her belt, pushed Lucy face-first to the wall, and clamped the metal around her wrists.

"Let's go." She led Lucy down the hall, away from the murmurs of the others.

Panic washed over her. What if she was going to solitary? She'd never been, but she'd heard stories. She pulled frantically at the handcuffs and turned to the guard.

"Please. I'm sorry."

The guard nudged her shoulder to turn around and walk again.

"Relax." Her tone was sympathetic. "I'm just taking

you back to the pod."

Lucy sighed when she saw the familiar door held open by another officer. She was ushered through and to cell 409. When they were inside the guard removed the cuffs and returned them to her belt.

"Try to stay out of trouble, Bonneville," the guard said. She shook her head, stepped backward, and closed the heavy door between them. There was a click and a loud buzz. Lucy was locked in. The others were locked out. Away from her.

She turned to the empty room. Her spirits immediately lifted. Sitting on her bunk at the other end of the cell was Joel. He stood and put his arms out to greet her.

"I've missed you," she whispered when she was in his embrace. "Where have you been?"

"You know where." He stroked her hair, then kissed her forehead. *"I've been making arrangements. I want everything to be perfect when you come home. Perfect for all of us."*

His hand rested on her belly. She covered his and beamed. Inside she thought she felt movement for the first time. Alone in her shared cell, she stood smiling and dreaming of their future.

ACKNOWLEGEMENTS

Thank you to my family for their love and support.

Thank you to my husband for helping me find time to write.

Thank you to all the people who helped bring *The Crazy One* to print: Felicia Grossman, Allison Bitz, Aaron Wheeler, Kellye Garrett, Cindy Calzone, Julie Webb, Sarah Lifford, and Melanie T. and any others I may have missed.

For updates and other works by Rebecca Markus, visit rjmarkus.com.

18428384R00181

Printed in Great Britain
by Amazon